Dear Adam,

My deepest gratitude to you for your time, experience, and wisdom this week. May D.O. Black continue to ascend the heights!

Godspeed,
Rick

Limited Edition

Praise For Jake Fortina

"Urgent and compelling, from a spectacular art heist to a ruthless Russian mercenary leader hell-bent on replacing the Kremlin's current occupant; from weapons of mass destruction to rogue military officers brokering arms deals out of a US Embassy, with *The Roman Conspiracy*—the latest entry in the *Major Jake Fortina* series—Rick Steinke once again runs at the head of the military thriller pack delivering that hair-raising feeling you've charged past the "ripped from tomorrow's headlines" plotting of most books into real-world "kept out of the headlines" events, events that we sleep better at night for not knowing.

As with his first novel, *Major Jake Fortina and the Tier One Threat*, right from the very first page you understand you're in the hands of an author who knows his stuff because he's lived this stuff and you're darn glad he's here to write about it. As the action spirals out from the military attaché offices in the US Embassy, Steinke's care for local detail and history enhances time and place realism. His deep knowledge of the innerworkings and chain of command protocols of the US Army, State Department, the Intelligence Community all the way to the Resolute Desk in the Oval Office tightens the spring of his ticking clock the hands of which are all too human.

And while all of this would be enough for any fan of the genre, with Steinke, you get flesh and bone characters who come alive; because they feel, they *make* you feel—their hearts and their hopes, their honor, and their faith. *Jake Fortina and the Roman Conspiracy* is a must-read thriller by an author at the top of his game."

> **—Michael Frost Beckner**, author of the *Spy Game* novels (motion picture of the same name, 2001), Hollywood screenwriter, and executive producer.

"Do not pick up this book unless you have a few hours to spare, as once you start you are unlikely to put it down! This is a well-researched barn burner of a story, literally torn from today's headlines about the Wagner Group, revolt, and instability in Russia. Steinke picks up the Jake Fortina saga a few years after Jake and Sara's first adventure in *Jake Fortina and The Tier One Threat*. The author's detailed knowledge of both the US and Italian governments' military, law enforcement, interagency, and international cooperation processes are clear as he leads us through the labyrinth of coordination that success would require. *Roman Conspiracy* includes a wonderfully volatile mix of right-wing extremists on two continents, Russian oligarchs bent on replacing the Russian President, and a rainbow of international Special Forces – some good, some bad, some both. It also details several US and Italian law enforcement, intelligence, and diplomatic officials. I would be remiss not to mention weapons of mass destruction directed against the United States, Italy, and NATO Alliance countries, crafted into the story for good measure. Enjoy this exhilarating read!"

> **—James Q. Roberts**, Senior Executive (Ret), Office of the US Secretary of Defense

"This is a gripping story, ripe with reality, reflecting today's environment of hybrid warfare, and world leaders who demonstrate a complete disregard for the rule of law and the rules of war, placing humanity at risk. *Roman Conspiracy* imagines a step further with the deployment of weapons of mass destruction against civilians outside the theater of war. Steinke deftly weaves this with a parallel plot focused on an extremist network in the United States. Roman Conspiracy also provides hope—hope that has its parallel in the real world—a testament to the importance of strong relationships among U.S. government agencies and their international counterparts."

—**Lauren Anderson**, Former FBI executive and Women's Global Advocate

"*Jake Fortina and the Roman Conspiracy* is ripped from today's headlines about violent war in Ukraine, international art theft and potential nuclear war in Europe. Author Ralph Steinke does not spare the tension and the reader is likely to find his blood pressure starting to rise from the first chapter to the last in this classic thriller. The graphic descriptions of Rome and eastern Europe and the ornate delineation of the security world of NATO and other organizations inform as well as entertain. An excellent read by an expert who well understands the covert twilight that exists all around us."

—**John J. Le Beau**, CIA Operations Officer, (Ret.) and Author, *Collision of Centuries*

"Colonel (Ret) Rick Steinke continues the engrossing story of Jake Fortina, now stationed in Italy, and his adventures to keep America and its allies safe in a complex, dangerous world. Drawing on current global events and contemporary domestic issues, Rick boldly takes on and weaves a fictious story that easily darts in and out of a chilling and realistic tale. Rick further draws on his vast experience as a military Foreign Area Officer and professional educator to portray the events and characters in a believable narrative only he can accurately illustrate! This story continues further to fill a gap in depicting what our US military and federal government interagency heroes are doing in the shadows daily around the world. Do not be fooled by its fictional heading!"

—**Colonel (US Army, Ret) John E. Chere Jr.**, Assistant Professor of Security Cooperation at Defense Security Cooperation University, Adjunct Prof. at Joint Special Operations University, and former Defense Attaché and Senior Defense Official to Morocco, Algiers, Tunis, and Israel

"Rick Steinke's stories continue to skyrocket through the in-depth geopolitical, military, and diplomatic expertise of the author. Linking the theft of three Italian masterpiece works of art to an emerging global threat, Steinke has again produced an extremely realistic, compelling, and spectacular techno-thriller! I highly recommended it for Italian, US, and international readers alike."

—**Major General (Italian Carabinieri, Ret) Sebastiano Comitini**, former Commander, Carabinieri Special Intervention Group (GIS) and Commander, 2d Carabinieri Mobile Brigade

"Enthralling from the very first lines to the end of the fast-paced story, *Roman Conspiracy* is a true page-turner. Combining a gripping plot, expert knowledge, and elaborate storytelling, this thriller is a timely and fascinating read. Rick Steinke artfully uses his military and diplomatic expert knowledge as the foundation for a fast-paced and engrossing story. First-hand experience and a talent for story-telling blend to make the perfect recipe for an absorbing thriller!"

—**Daniel H. Heinke**, Director General for Public Safety, Bremen, Germany

"Rick Steinke has done it again! Bringing his own unique military background, experiences, and voice to his equally unique character, US Army officer Jake Fortina. Be ready when you pick this book up! Steinke's ability to blend historical fact and his prescient view of current and developing geopolitical events keeps Jake on his toes and the reader continually engaged and looking for the next installment. Highly recommend this captivating sequel to *Major Jake Fortina and the Tier One Threat!*"

—**Captain (US Navy, Ret) Dirk Deverill**, Former Director, Defense Plans, US Mission to NATO; and Foreign Policy Advisor, US Air Force Global Strike Command

Jake Fortina and the Roman Conspiracy

by Ralph R. "Rick" Steinke

© Copyright 2023 Ralph R. "Rick" Steinke

ISBN

Paperback:

ISBN: 978-1-962243-05-6

Hardcover:

ISBN: 978-1-960116-92-5

All rights reserved. No part of this publication may be reproduced, stored in a retrieval system, or transmitted in any form or by any means— electronic, mechanical, photocopy, recording, or any other— except for brief quotations in printed reviews, without the prior written permission of the author.

Published by: Urban Book Publishers

JAKE FORTINA

AND THE

ROMAN CONSPIRACY

Ralph R. "Rick" Steinke

Author's Note

THE VIEWS EXPRESSED in this publication are those of the author and do not necessarily reflect the official policy or position of the US Department of Defense or the US government.

While this book references historical facts, events, and names, this is a work of *fiction*. Except for those individuals obviously referenced in history, all the characters—even though some names may be the same as or approximate living individuals—are completely fictitious, as are some commercial businesses.

DEDICATION

To Sofia, Isabela, Elena, and Gonzalo...forever.

"The strength of the pack is the wolf, and the strength of the wolf is the pack."
-Rudyard Kipling

"People generally see what they look for and hear what they listen for."

-Harper Lee, in *To Kill a Mockingbird*

CHAPTER 1

THE THEFT, PART I

THE FORMER SERBIAN ARMY SPECIAL FORCES SERGEANT and his two accomplices intermittently shuffled and stepped across the church's marble floor. Felt soles used by fly-fishermen to safely wade on slick rocks silently cushioned each former commando's steps. The requirement for stealth rivaled the nighttime raids the trio's members had individually executed in Afghanistan, Chechnya, Iraq, Syria, Ukraine, and other places of conflict.

The three men approached their target from behind, wearing black skull caps, shaded swimming goggles, and black Covid face masks. The masks were intended to further disguise the wearer, not stop the virus. Strapped around their skull caps were headlamps typically used by hikers and campers. Switched to the red-light mode, the lamps served the dual purpose of seeing through the church's darkened spaces while eliminating the dilating effect of white light on the operators' pupils. Black overalls, boots, and surgeon's gloves—for masking fingerprints and minimizing stray DNA evidence—rounded out the trio's fashionable ensemble.

The trio's Serbian leader eyed the church's slumbering security guard. The guard was where he was expected: seated in an old oak chair, hunched over, chin on his chest, eyes closed, breathing heavily. It was almost 3 a.m. The guard still had four hours to go on his 10-hour shift.

Except for inside the Vatican, on-site physical security was rare for Roman churches. Instead, a few churches with highly valued paintings, statues, and artifacts depended on closed-circuit security cameras connected to nearby Carabinieri or city police stations. Other than locking their ancient and often massive doors, many Roman churches had no security measures at all. After all, what kind of lowlife would steal from a church?

This *San Luigi dei Francesi* (Saint Louis of the French) church, administered by the French Catholic church in Rome, held some extraordinary treasures valued at hundreds of millions of dollars. The church's French leadership believed that a physically present night guard inside the church at night was warranted, even if the church's monsignor considered it "overly cautious."

Crouching in the nearby shadows of the church, a good forty feet from their three colleagues, a former special operator from Kazakhstan and two former security agents from Hungary and Kyrgyzstan awaited their signal to join the trio once they completed their business with the church's night guard.

The Serb slowly approached the snoring guard from behind. The Serb crouched down, positioning himself a foot behind the guard. His two wingmen, one from Russia and the other from Belorussia, moved around to opposite sides of the chair. A second later, in one swift action rehearsed multiple times, the Serb–a six feet, two inches tall, 220-pound bull of an athlete–clamped the guard's mouth shut with his powerful left hand. A millisecond later, his two teammates each pressed down on one leg and arm of the seated guard, rendering him completely immobilized.

The physical force exerted by the Russian and Belorussian prohibited the guard from even squirming. With his right hand, the Serb near-simultaneously injected the guard in the neck with the magic sleep elixir, propofol.

A teammate had recommended the drug for sedating the guard. The teammate's German doctor had used it on him for minor outpatient rectal surgery. The German surgeon had called it the "Michael Jackson drug." Allegedly, overusing the deep sleep inducer ended the global pop star's life.

"Propofol's beauty is that it works fast, and its duration, if effectively dosed, can be managed and accurately predicted, with minimal hangover effect," explained the surgeon.

The exhausted guard, a corpulent 40-something Neapolitan working two jobs to feed his family of five, didn't budge. Between the Serb's vice grip on the guard's face and head and the immobilizing pressure on his arms and legs, the guard couldn't discern if he was locked in a nightmare or a frightening reality. Several seconds after the injection, the guard's eyes, arms, and legs felt heavy. Within another ten seconds, he was helpless, floating to a dreamscape of an unknown destination. Within a few more seconds, he was completely out.

The three men carefully removed and laid him on his back to ensure the guard didn't fall out of his chair and hit his head on the marble floor. The guard was expected to be out for roughly eighty minutes.

The Serb nodded to the Kazakh, standing next to one of the church's massive pillars with the other two members of the entire six-man team in the church. The former special forces soldier replied with a nod. He instantly complied with the nod's meaning, sending a simple "go" message with his burner phone to Alexei, "the Cyberkid," who was with Conners at the Operations Center outside of Rome.

Within seconds, the church's emergency exit lights were remotely deactivated by one of the most talented cyber criminals ever to speak Russian as his mother tongue. Then he quickly froze the outdated, marginally effective black-and-white video feed to the nearby Carabinieri police station.

Alexei, in his early thirties, had been an All-Star in the vanguard of Russian government cyber criminals who flooded multiple US social media platforms with pro-Republican and anti-Democrat messages leading up to the United States' 2016 presidential election. In February 2018, a US Federal Grand Jury indicted thirteen Russians for "federal crimes while seeking to interfere in the United States political system, including the 2016 Presidential election." Alexei, perhaps because he was not among the criminal group's leadership, evaded discovery, and indictment.

Outside the church, a former Russian GRU Spetsnaz (military special forces) operator stood watch. His task was to observe the long, wide street in front of the church. The Russian special forces veteran had been hired by the Wolf's American Chief of Operations, retired US Army Special Forces Sergeant First Class Blake Conners, to join the Wolf's internationally forged special operations team. That the team be called the "Wolfpack" was almost a foregone conclusion. Eventually, "the Pack" moniker stuck. Conners was forced to hire the former GRU operator against Conners' negative judgment of the Russian, who had been accused of torturing civilians while serving with the Warner Group in Syria. The Warner Group was a paramilitary group widely considered the "private army" of Vasily Puchta.

Conners, on the other hand, had ended his Army career as an embittered soldier who was at the US Capitol on January 6, 2020.

Conners' Spidey sense tingled before he'd done anything to incriminate himself at the Capitol. *Leave the grounds*, it told him. *There are too many whack-jobs videotaping everything. This won't end well*, he thought. *The crowd is increasingly riotous.*

From the Pack's operations center, located in an old farm warehouse about 14 miles east by southeast of Rome, Blake Conners monitored–through chest-mounted video cameras carried by each operator–the Pack's operation. Thus far, Conners was pleased with the Pack's Phase I execution of the operation. Not a single word had been spoken by any Pack member. All actions–communicated through simple, silent gestures and signs–had been based on exhaustive and high-level training standards.

Conners required his teammates to be strong, disciplined, and, above all, competent operators, and he had forged them as a team accordingly. No extraneous "amateur bullshit" would be countenanced by Connors. Besides, for this mission, the orders had come from the top man himself, the Russian oligarch Anatoly Roman Volkov, aka *the Wolf*: "no collateral deaths to guards or anyone else. It's not good for business."

In classic Wolf style, it was all about business. In cases of self-defense or operational necessity, sure, deadly force was authorized for this mission.

The Pack was made up of former professionals, albeit with varying degrees of experience and expertise. They were primarily former international military special forces operators or security agents, with a few former intelligence agents sprinkled in. Exceptional at doing their jobs, they didn't hesitate to kill when required. But the way the Wolf saw it, killing had to have an objective. Objectives included eliminating anybody who got in the way of the Wolf's twin goals of accumulating extraordinary wealth and political power. The Wolf learned this lesson well from Vasily Puchta: kill to win.

CHAPTER 2

NEXT MISSION, NINE MONTHS BEFORE THE THEFT

US ARMY LIEUTENANT COLONEL JAKE FORTINA and his bride of 18 months, the *olivastra*-complected Florentine beauty and Italian Carabinieri officer Sara Simonetti-Fortina, couldn't believe their good fortune. It had been nine months since Jake had informed Sara of his—actually, their—next assignment: the US Embassy, Rome.

When a US Army personnel (human resources) officer first mentioned the Rome assignment as a possibility, Jake was not sure it would happen. Being married to a non-US citizen could sometimes negatively affect a soldier's ability to retain the high-level security clearance required for positions like the Rome Embassy job. But in the end, Jake was grateful to whomever in the Department of Defense bureaucracy performed the background check on Simonetti. Someone had deemed her a trustworthy married partner to a senior US Army officer involved in military-diplomatic affairs; said another way, she posed no threat to US national security.

Sara had shined a bright and loving light on Jake's life, and Sara had felt the same way about Jake.

Sara had served with the Carabinieri for over fifteen years. However, Sara had struggled with whether to remain in the Carabinieri Corps since marrying Jake. The Carabinieri, Italy's highly esteemed police force with military status (or armed military force in permanent police service), served domestically as Italy's premier national law enforcement organization and as a military police force when deployed with Italy's other armed forces abroad.

Sara increasingly thought about starting a family. She had gone back and forth about staying in the Carabinieri. That her leadership ensured Sara was assigned to Rome with Jake and she could take "plenty of maternity leave" if they had a child, sealed the deal for her to continue her service with the Carabinieri forces.

As they entered Rome's city limits from due north, heading southbound on the *via Cassia*, a north-south running road and one of Rome's seven original roads into the city, a giddy-feeling Simonetti-Fortina couldn't help but ask a burning question. Jake had told her the basics about their new assignment in Rome some seven months prior, but she still had questions.

"So, Jake, tell me again how you—we—happened to get this Rome assignment?"

Jake glanced at Sara and smiled before looking back at the road.

"Like most assignments in my life, Sara, it was part good fortune, part personal desire, and part Divine intervention. I can't explain it any other way." He chuckled. "It was good fortune to have met you at the Marshall Center when I did. It was a great fortune to be your partner in stopping the Iranian threat."

Sara laughed. "Good start," she teased. "We did make a pretty good team."

Just over two years ago, they had teamed up to apprehend an Iranian international security threat directed at the United States, Israel, and Jewish people around the world. The case had thrown them into each other's paths once more. Interest had blossomed into love.

"It was harrowing there, in the end," she stared off into space for a moment, remembering the bullet she had taken for him.

"Yes, *cara mia*, it was," Jake squeezed her hand. "We made an excellent team."

"And the personal desire part?" asked Sara, shaking off the memory and squeezing his hand in return. "Why Italy, besides the fact your beautiful wife is from here?"

Sara winked at him. Despite the increasingly busy Roman road, Jake squeezed her hand once more in response.

"I wanted to be assigned to Rome because I know Italy better than most American soldiers and speak pretty OK Italian...." Jake said, "Don't I?"

"Jake, your Italian is, well..." Sara hesitated.

"Let me think about that for a minute," she taunted. She watched, silently enjoying Jake practically squirming in the driver's seat. Deciding he'd been teased long enough, she continued, "Your Italian is better than 'pretty OK,' Jake. It's excellent!"

"Whew, you had me there for a sec," he laughingly replied.

Jake had worked hard on his Italian, and eighteen months of marriage to Sara had tremendously honed his speaking and listening skills. Pillow talk and love do that to someone learning a foreign language. His improved Italian language skills, much like his French speaking skills when he served in Paris, would allow Jake to be exceptionally effective in his duties, many of which revolved around serving as a liaison from the US Army to the Italian Army and representing the US Army and the United States to the Italian government and people.

Sara also helped Jake eliminate sounds and mannerisms in Jake's speech that reflected an American accent. With time, Sara's coaching, and Jake's talented ear, Jake eliminated those sounds. He knew his Italian speaking ability would be critical in his new position as the Assistant Army Attaché at the US Embassy in Rome.

Unlike their NATO military partners from north of the Alps, few Italian officers spoke fluent English. And while the US embassy had a full colonel serving as the US Army Attaché to Italy, this was the first time since before the wars in Afghanistan and Iraq began that the Army had assigned an Assistant Army Attaché to Rome. So, it was important for Jake to get off on the right foot.

Continuing, Jake said, "Overall, Sara, I think I'll be a pretty good fit here because previously, I served with the 173d Airborne Brigade in Vicenza as a lieutenant. Then there was our little escapade in Italy together two years ago. Those experiences improved my knowledge of

Italy, the Italian Armed Forces, and Italian culture. Besides, I didn't think you'd mind coming to Rome."

Sara smiled broadly. "Not at all, Jake, not at all. This Florence-born girl will do just fine in Rome!" She settled back against the seat, content in a way she had not been before Jake had roared back into her life. Sara listened as he continued.

"Obviously, as a European history buff, it doesn't get much better than Rome, with over three millennia of history, with some of it fortunately still evident above ground, haha," added Jake, alluding to the subterranean layers of civilization below the Eternal City.

"And how about the Divine part?" she asked.

"That's harder to explain," he answered. "Sometimes, fortunately, God works in mysterious and wonderful ways."

Fortina was grateful he could say that. He had lost his wife, Faith, and two children, Kimberly and Jake, Jr., in a horrific car accident eight years prior. For a while after the accident, Jake was not even sure there was a God, let alone a loving one. But Jake knew his faith alone kept him from falling into a deep and depressive crevasse after his devastating loss. It is what had allowed him to get to this point, where his soul felt joy, and his path was his again.

Jake glanced at Sara, silently thanking God. They encountered increasingly heavy Roman traffic as they got closer to the city center. The buildings, from one to six hundred years old and older, got denser. Pedestrian traffic swelled. And Jake again said a quiet prayer of gratitude.

How fortunate I was to marry my laughing, teasing, beautiful Sara, thought Jake. *She saved my life in more ways than one.*

CHAPTER 3

THE THEFT, PART 2

OUTSIDE THE CHURCH, Nikolai, the Russian GRU (Russian Military Intelligence Directorate) veteran, had a simple job: keep an eye on the street in front of the church and ensure the street remained clear for the arrival of the electric Mercedes Benz eSprinter van. Blake Conners didn't want the former GRU official to perform a job that might put him in touch with anybody other than his teammates. Nikolai had a reputation for having tortured people–civilians and military–in Syria.

Conners did not want to hire Nikolai. But Boris Stepanov, the Wolf's chief of staff and confidant, insisted that Conners do so. That decided the matter.

The van's purpose was to haul away the Pack's team members and the priceless cargo that had hung inside the church since 1602. The timing of the van's arrival, loading, and departure had been planned, trained for, and rehearsed multiple times. This operation would be much like the military special operations that every Pack member had conducted in their own countries and abroad.

The van's exposed position on the street, even on a street that rarely saw traffic at 3 a.m., had to be minimized. Every move, particularly from when the van arrived at the church's front door, had to be practiced down to the second. The team's goal was for the van to stop in front of the church entrance for no more than 40 seconds.

The Mercedes van was perfect for the task. Its electric power allowed it to travel quietly along the Roman streets. Its cargo area had high ceilings. And it had plenty of space to carry away the stolen cargo and the 6-man international team that would soon bring the cargo out of the church and into the van.

Once the van's driver was assured no vehicles were to their front or rear, he would switch to blackout drive, with no lights on, including parking lights. In the event of an unsuspected passing vehicle, the team did not want to give the passing vehicle's driver or occupants reason to think that the van was out of place in front of or near the church. Tourist vans pulled up late at night to vacant curbs in Rome all the time just to get a few hours of rest. For any nosy driver or pedestrian passing by, the image—and ruse—that the team was trying to project was "some tourists just getting some sleep."

Rome is not like Los Angeles, New York, or Las Vegas, cities that never sleep. In Rome, while one will find (mostly) illegal street vendors, many of whom came to Rome with the massive European migrant crisis of 2015, Roman streets and sidewalks contain relatively few homeless people.

The Pack performed reconnaissance of the streets surrounding the church over a two-week period. They discovered that between the hours of midnight and 5 a.m. on Sunday night—or rather, very early Monday morning—provided the best window to pull off their operation. The "sweet spot" for the heist was between 2 a.m. and 4 a.m. on Monday morning. That was when traffic was almost nonexistent because most Romans, who had to work on Monday, had an earlier Sunday night bedtime.

During their reconnaissance, they identified the Carabinieri guard posts for the *Palazzo Giustiniani* as an obstacle to successfully pulling off the heist. These two guard posts, each about the size of a highway tollbooth in the US, enclosed with tinted, bullet-proof glass, gave their occupants a 360-degree view outside their posts. The *Palazzo Giustiniani*, the former palace of the wealthy Giustiniani family of the 16th and 17th centuries, was their primary security concern.

The Giustiniani palace served as the modern-day residence of the President of the Italian Senate. It also provided a few offices for retired senators. Securing that palace—not the church—was the guards' major security concern. However, the palace was across the intersection on the corner opposite the church, providing one guard with a clear view of the front of the church. So, he—and his colleague one block down the street—had to be temporarily immobilized before pulling off the heist.

After receiving the "go" message, while the interior Pack members incapacitated the church guard, two Pack operators, located in separate—

and legally parked—cars, each opened their doors. They leaned slowly to the left, dropped down to the cobblestone street, silently closed the driver's door, and momentarily laid flat on the damp cobblestones. The operators removed the dome lights and disabled the alarm systems of the cars beforehand to ensure there would be no chance of being observed by the guards.

One of the men low crawled about 40 yards across the cobblestones to reach his intended target. The operator targeting the guard between the palace and the church had to approach the guard post from behind. He walked along the darkened *via Giustiniani* for about fifty yards before dropping to the sidewalk. He low crawled for the last 30 yards to reach the Carabinieri security guard inside the post.

Once the Pack's two operators reached their assigned guard posts, their mission was straightforward: spray the contents of the aerosol containers they carried into the intake fans of the air conditioning-heating unit attached to each guard post. The aerosol quickly entered the enclosed, tight spaces, rapidly sedating their occupants. It took less than a minute for the aerosol to do its job. The guards would not wake up for at least ninety minutes.

The aerosol was much improved since its first crude employment against Chechen terrorists in a Moscow theater some 22 years prior by Russia's FSB (Russia's principal security agency, a rough approximation of the FBI). The terrorists had held almost 800 international citizens hostage. On the third day of the siege, the Russians forced the aerosol into the theater. The Chechen hostage-takers became disoriented and physically disabled. However, during the ensuing assault by the Russians, while all forty Chechen terrorists died, so did over 120 civilians. Many civilians were later confirmed to have died from the aerosol.

With the two guards immobilized, the Cyberkid received the awaited text message: "Drop." The cyber whiz remotely and instantly lowered the street-embedded hydraulic barriers, normally controlled by the guards, now unconscious in their observation posts. With street access no longer blocked, accessing the church's front door with the Mercedes eSprinter van would be a piece of cake.

The Pack's planning team conducted a half-dozen reconnaissance missions to determine how to eliminate the need for bringing large and potentially noisy ladders. That is why the six men inside the church knew where the equipment and maintenance closet was and that it contained two twenty feet long aluminum ladders. They were for cleaning the church's upper reaches but would serve the Pack beautifully in stealing the three paintings.

With the security officer deeply slumbering on the floor and the electrical power for the alarm and exit light systems cut off, the entire six-man team, broken down into three two-men "fire teams" (old military monikers were hard to dispense with), headed for the church's *Contarelli* chapel. It is typical for churches and cathedrals in Italy to contain several small side chapels. The Contarelli chapel is directly to the left of the church's main altar.

Given their mission's logistical and time challenges, Conners knew they needed to cut the roughly ten feet by ten feet paintings from their marble frames. They had honed their Exacto razor blade technique on countless similar materials, approximating the over four-hundred-year-old canvases.

The Wolf secured the monetary deal– "without frames"–for the paintings before their theft. The Wolf was informed that the extraordinary works of art, painted by one of Italy's great masters, could fetch as much as 250 to 300 million dollars each. Leonardo da Vinci's *Salvator Mundi* (circa 1500) sold for 450.3 million dollars, a fact the Wolf deftly used to his advantage in selling the three paintings.

The Wolf made private, "win-win" deals for 200 million dollars per painting. He had already received three 20-million-dollar, pre-delivery down payments. The way the Wolf saw it, 600 million dollars was fair payback for the Italian government having "unjustly" seized his luxury yacht, valued at over 500 million dollars. Furthermore, the 600 million dollars would help finance the Wolf's return to Russia.

To the Wolf, the heist from this church was perfect because this Catholic church was France's Catholic representational structure in Rome, including an accompanying French ambassador. Once the theft was known, there would be back-biting between the French and Italian governments and the Vatican to cast fault for the three most magnificent Italian Baroque paintings in existence going missing. That fighting was exactly what the Wolf wanted.

Inside the darkened Contarelli chapel, the two-man teams went to either side of the first painting. One man held the ladder while another scurried up to cut down his half of the canvas, working toward the middle to meet his partner cutting from the other side. They repeated this three times. They had allotted six minutes to get each canvas safely cut from its frame, carried down the ladders, and laid out on the floor.

A third two-man team stood by to help secure the canvases as they were brought down the ladders. They then enveloped the canvases with specially measured and fitted anti-abrasive silk sheets. Next, they rolled up each silk-covered canvas like a carpet. As they worked, the two-man teams who cut the canvases from their frames returned the ladders to the maintenance closet. Finally, the three teams carried the three canvases to the Mercedes van.

The entire canvas removal and preparation for transporting the three paintings, accomplished without a single spoken word among the six team members, took no more than 25 minutes to accomplish. In all, including the time to gain entry through the back door and approach and subdue the guard, the team had spent no more than 36 minutes in the building.

With the three teams lined up inside the church's exit door with the three paintings, the Serb texted Nikolai: "Ready." Meanwhile, the Serb unlocked the church's front door from the inside.

Nikolai, the lookout stationed one block north of the church, turned on his cellphone's flashlight of his cell phone. He flashed the Mercedes van parked two blocks down the street. The van's driver, anticipating the signal, put the electric vehicle into gear and drove for 14 seconds, stopping to pick up Nikolai, who jumped in the shotgun seat. In ten more seconds, the van pulled up to the chapel's main entrance door. Nikolai jumped out to open the van's back doors.

Six seconds later, the first team arrived at the back of the van with their multi-million-dollar cargo. Six seconds after that, the second duo came out with their canvas, followed by the third duo and the final canvas, another six seconds later. All three canvasses were carefully laid, in succession, into their pre-made, floor-mounted crates. Nikolai shut the van's back door, jumped back in the shotgun seat, and the entire team was rolling down the via della Dogana Vecchia.

As it pulled away, the van's co-driver texted another message to the Cyberkid: "On." Within seconds, the church's lights and alarm systems were set to the same configuration as before the heist. The hydraulic street barriers were also reset to their original blocking positions.

Back at the Ops Center with the kid, Conners thought it was ironic that the Roman street that the van was now traveling on–*via della Dogana Vecchia*–was called "the old customs road." He wondered what the "customs" charges would be in 2024 for the three paintings, painted from 1599-1602 by one of Italy's most famous artists and worth at least 600 million.

CHAPTER 4

AWAKE

THE NIGHT GUARD OPENED HIS EYES. He tried to focus on the vast, heavenly ceiling over 100 feet above him. He curiously observed the colorful and vivid Baroque and gold-adorned fresco with the "Apotheosis of Saint Louis" at its center. In the many nights he'd spent working the graveyard hours in the church, many of them asleep in the 100-year-old oak chair, the guard had neglected to appreciate the extraordinary scene depicted on the ceiling above him.

Am I still in a dream? he asked himself.

It took him several seconds to comprehend that he was lying on his back and staring at the colorful images. The cold marble floor at his back quickly convinced him he was not in a dream.

In bits and pieces, more clues came: the smell of urine from the accidental discharge that happened during the initial terror he'd felt; his inability to breathe through his mouth as this strange being—*a creature*, he thought—with some type of strange goggles over his eyes and a black mask covering his nose and mouth, and whose face was only inches from his own—stared at him from his right side. Little did the guard know that another "creature" was on his left side, too, doing the same thing, pressing down hard on the guard's left leg and arm. Or that a beast of a man was behind him, locking his head in a vice grip and sealing his mouth from screaming out.

The guard had barely felt the needle go in. As to the liquid substance entering his bloodstream, he hadn't felt it at all. Increasingly alert now, his arms felt sore. He had a slight itch—an almost mosquito bite feeling—coming from a tiny spot on the right side of his neck. He felt refreshingly rested ... but how did he end up lying flat on his back on the floor?

He sat up. For several seconds, he looked around. All seemed as it had been. He got himself to a standing position, not easily done for an overworked almost forty pounds past his healthiest weight.

The church's few emergency exit lights were just as they were when he'd fallen asleep in the chair. But something felt different. The guard thought he needed to relieve himself. He turned to head toward the bathroom. But after taking several steps, he paused. Embarrassed, he realized that had already happened.

Deciding to continue, he finally reached the small individual bathroom in a remote corner of the church. The guard tore off a paper towel, dipped it under the running faucet, and vigorously tried to wipe the urine stain and smell out of his pants. His efforts had minimal effect.

He washed his hands and face in the bathroom's small porcelain sink and returned to the church's cavernous nave. The main altar, almost 120 feet away, was at the far end of the church.

He walked about three-quarters of the distance to the altar and stopped. To his left, he could see the Contarelli chapel. It was a side chapel in the massive cathedral. He turned to examine it. Peering through the chapel's semi-darkness, he tried to focus. He raised his eyes to the chapel's center wall–directly behind the chapel's altar–where a painting should have been hanging.

The guard prayed his eyes were playing tricks on him. He stepped toward the chapel's outer railing. The guard could feel his heart rate pick up. He wanted desperately to believe he wasn't seeing correctly through the semi-dark haze.

As panic began to creep in, the guard did something hundreds of tourists did every day. Due to the chapel's limited artificial and natural light and the church's administrators' desires to defray expenses, there was a metal box, about chest high, to the right of the chapel's entrance. With the insertion of a one-euro coin (a bit more than one dollar), the box would turn a bright spotlight on the chapel. The spotlight vividly illuminated all three Christian Apostle and Saint Mathew paintings. As the bright light struck the more than 400-year-old canvases, the chatter among the international onlookers would promptly begin.

The guard reached into his pocket and pulled out a one-euro coin. The coin was one of two he reserved each day for an espresso at a nearby coffee shop immediately after he got off his all-night shift. He put the coin in the metal box's slot. The machine made a whirring noise as it began to light up the chapel for the standard two minutes of viewing.

There it was. It was unmistakable: an empty space on the wall, with the large frame still intact, where the Inspiration of Saint Matthew *should* be hanging.

The painting must be there! He thought. *This must be a bad dream! Please, please, dear God, let this be a dream!*

With his back to the church's spacious nave, he advanced up to the waist-high railing at the edge of the chapel proper, where several hundred–and some days thousands–of international tourists stood every day. They came from all over the world to admire, absorb and analyze the three extraordinary works of art. Each had been stroked by the divinely talented hands of *Michelangelo Merisi da Caravaggio*, known the world over as simply Caravaggio.

Caravaggio had completed the paintings–each depicting the life of Saint Mathew–from 1599-1602. An endowment left by Cardinal Matthieu Cointerel (in Italian, *Matteo Contarelli*, hence the chapel's name) funded Caravaggio's efforts. With pilgrims coming from around the world to Rome in 1600, a Catholic jubilee year, and the immediate years thereafter, the paintings elevated Caravaggio's notoriety–as well as his chiaroscuro (light-dark) painting technique–in Italy and around the world.

With a pit in his stomach, the guard forebodingly turned his head to the left.

The Calling of Saint Mathew painting is gone, too!

The only thing marking its former presence was a large, empty marble frame. The frame had not been altered or replaced in over 400 years. With extreme dread shrouding his soul, the guard did not want to look to his right. But he knew he must. Slowly turning his head, what he observed completed a trifecta of cosmic and crushing body blows to his soul and spirit: the Martyrdom of Saint Matthew painting, which should have been hanging high on the wall to his right…was also…*gone*!

The guard dropped to his knees. He hung his head and began sobbing. His entire torso began to quake.

A loud cry of "Dear Mother of God!" echoed throughout the vast cathedral. He desperately and slowly cried out loud, "No…no…no," as the panic grew.

Mental screams of *It's my fault! It's my fault! How could I have fallen so deeply asleep?* -cascaded over him.

The excruciating pains in his chest came almost immediately. They caused him to move from kneeling on his knees, hunched forward in a kneeling praying position, to laying on his right side and, eventually, on his back. The guard felt like someone was standing on his chest. The pain was becoming otherworldly.

On the hard stone floor in front of the Contarelli chapel in Rome's St. Louis of the French church, the guard gasped for his life through the agonizing and incessant pain. He managed to bring his hands up to clutch his chest. It was a natural reaction to somehow make the pain stop. But the pain did not stop. Unable to bear the horror of it all, the Neapolitan guard's heart stopped beating. He was pain-free.

CHAPTER 5

GRAZIE, SIGNORE

OUTSIDE THE CHURCH, the 23-year-old carabinieri guard raised his head off the security booth's narrow desktop. It took him a moment to understand where he was. It was dark outside his guard post, and with its dark tinted windows, darker still inside. Only a nearby streetlight cast a faint light on the damp cobblestone street outside his post.

The guard realized he had fallen asleep at his place of duty. He was simultaneously disappointed and surprised at himself.

I have never, never fallen asleep on duty, he thought.

Indeed, the Carabinieri police guard had never completely fallen asleep at his post. Sure, he'd begun to doze off for a few seconds in the dead of night more than once in his ten months of service at the guard post. But he had always caught himself, never allowing himself to completely turn off his mental lights and his awareness of his surroundings.

The guard looked at his watch. It was 4:12 a.m.

How long have I been asleep? I knew I was tired when I began work tonight, but I didn't think I was that tired!

The Carabiniere *scelto* (pronounced "shelto"; about the rank of a US military E-3 or private first class in the US Army), who was approaching his two-year mark of Carabinieri service and a possible promotion, went from being disappointed in himself to being angry with himself. He glanced at the Senate building behind him. He did a 360-degree check of the immediate urban surroundings around his guard post. The street's hydraulicly operated, 6-inch diameter and two feet high columns, which could be raised or lowered from the cobblestone street to block or allow vehicles to pass, were raised. They were exactly where they were supposed to be. There was no one around. Everything was exactly as it had been before he'd fallen asleep.

The Carabinieri guard was relieved that nobody had discovered him asleep at his place of duty. It also appeared that nothing had happened to the nearby Senate building that he was responsible for guarding.

"*Grazie, Signore,*" he mumbled out loud, thanking God that his indiscipline had not resulted in a breach of security at the Senate building or, as far as he could see, any other building around him, including the church across the street.

CHAPTER 6

LOOSE NUKES: 32 YEARS BEFORE THE THEFT

"LOOSE NUKES." IT WAS A TERM allegedly coined in the early 1990s by Harvard professor and future US Defense Secretary Ash Carter. Those two pedestrian words came to signify a major national security concern by the United States, Canada, and European and NATO allies: the loss of accountability for Soviet nuclear weapons. Two major political events—the fall of the Berlin Wall on November 9, 1989, and the breakup of the Soviet Union on December 26, 1991—exacerbated this concern.

From 1992 and beyond, the question of unaccounted-for nuclear weapons kept Western intelligence, diplomatic, law enforcement, and military professionals up at night. Across the recently imploded Soviet Union and the newly free and independent 15 states that resulted, how safe were the 27,000 nuclear weapons which some of the states possessed? In 1992, Western intelligence agencies also assessed that there was enough weapons-grade nuclear material in the Soviet Union to produce an additional *three times* that number of 27,000 weapons. How *safe* was *that* material? At any given moment, who possessed it? Who was responsible for controlling it?

International measures, led by the United States, were eventually established to account for the security of Russia's strategic nuclear arms. The accounting effort was under the auspices of the Cooperative Threat Reduction Program. Nonetheless, US, Canadian, and European concerns remained over the security of the Russian tactical nuclear weapons arsenal. An international debate ensued over the status of what was known as "suitcase nuclear weapons." They were relatively small Soviet-era nuclear devices. The term *suitcase nuke* was and is generally used to describe any type of small, human-portable nuclear device. Among NATO's ranks, similar-sized and yielding weapons were often called "atomic demolition munitions."

Soviet suitcase nukes were small enough to be portable by a single human. During the Cold War, military special forces from both sides were trained in their employment to blow up key enemy enablers, like high-speed roads for tanks, artillery, and troops. Their detection was far more challenging than finding missile-launched nuclear weapons. Satellites or high-altitude overhead flight reconnaissance could discover those big missiles and their launchers.

Such a discovery occurred during the Cuban Missile Crisis of October 1962, when the United States took black and white photos of nuclear launchers and their deadly missile cargoes in Cuba. The discovery of the deadly missiles, which had ranges capable of covering most of the continental United States, brought the United States and Russia to the brink of World War III.

Suitcase nukes, however, could evade overhead imagery from satellites and aerial reconnaissance. They could also be *hand-carried*, by a single individual, thereby avoiding detection not only by searching eyes in the skies but also by security forces on the ground. The small nukes immediately threatened population centers or major political centers of influence (e.g., capitol or parliament buildings). Once detonated, they could potentially decapitate a country's political leadership or major institutions, not to mention kill thousands of people.

By most accounts, the kiloton yields of such weapons were in the single digits, with some estimated to be less than five kilotons. By way of comparison, the bomb dropped on Hiroshima in August of 1945 was 22 kilotons. Targeted to maximize human casualties-e.g., sports stadiums, dense urban centers, automobile racetracks, and shopping malls, one terrorist-ignited bomb could kill tens of thousands, perhaps more. By some accounts, the Soviet Union had built hundreds of these devices, of which several dozen reportedly went missing during the 1990s.

In May 1997, Russian General Alexander Lebed admitted to an American congressional delegation that Russia had lost dozens of atomic demolition units. In a subsequent interview with the American television program 60 Minutes, General Lebed modified that estimate, stating that they had lost over 100 units, an assertion that the Russian government later denied.

To thirty-something Muscovite Vladislav Popov, an early 1990s expert in developing, maintaining, and employing those menacing weapons, their "loose" accountability during the tumultuous days of the Soviet Union's breakup represented an enormous economic opportunity.

CHAPTER 7
A ROLLED-UP CARPET

LUCA ROMANO PIETROSANTI entered the church's nave from a side door adjacent to the main altar. It was 9:00 a.m., the time it always was five days per week, when he began preparing the church for opening to the public at 9:30 a.m. On the other two days, his Filipino colleague, representative of the large Filipino community in Rome, took care of business.

After turning a corner in the church's grey light and moving toward the church's main doors to turn on the lights, he unexpectedly stubbed his right toe on a large, lumpy object on the floor. Fortunately, as he fell forward, the former standout Italian soccer player managed to break his fall with his arms and keep his head–and front teeth–from hitting the marble floor.

What was that? A rolled-up carpet, he thought.

Pietrosanti quickly realized *the only place there was a carpet was right in front of the main cathedral altar*.

As he rolled to his side, he saw the shape of what had tripped him up. But his brain didn't–or couldn't–process what he was seeing. He reached through the semi-darkness to feel the object. Touching the dead guard's shirt from the back, just above the guard's belt, Pietrosanti realized it was a shirt, and the shirt's wearer was either deeply sleeping, unconscious, or dead.

The thirty-something Roman sat up and scooched on his buttocks to the front of the body. He checked it for a pulse. There was none. The man's wrist and neck felt cold. Pietrosanti trembled as he reached into his pants pocket for his cell phone. He dialed 112, the number for emergency services throughout Italy and the European Union. Pietrosanti was unaware that the Contarelli chapel, just off to the side where the body was lying, was devoid of the three Caravaggio paintings which had graced the chapel's interior walls since 1602.

CHAPTER 8

A LONG-TERM INVESTMENT: 30 YEARS BEFORE THE THEFT

IT WAS A MODEST *DACHA* (country house). But Vladislav Popov loved his small home and the verdant fields and forests surrounding it. Located about 3 miles northeast of his Russian hometown of Tosno (roughly 30,000 inhabitants in 1994) and about 30 miles southeast of the much larger city of St. Petersburg, the winters could get rough here.

But they are nowhere near as brutal as in Siberia, Popov often reminded himself.

Vladislav Popov loved the privacy that his 2-bedroom, 1000-square-foot dacha afforded him. It was a far cry from the packed apartment buildings found in most of the Soviet Union's large cities, to which Popov had tried–but failed–to grow accustomed. All Popov ever dreamed of was a place in the country.

A two-track dirt road enabled access to the dacha from the nearest paved road. It was just over a half-mile–almost a kilometer–through the forested mix of ash, birch, fir, and oak trees to get to the dacha. If one wasn't looking for the dirt road, a road concealed by adjacent high grass in the summertime, it was easily missed. Passersby had no idea his home was back there.

In the winter, the road was barely passable. That mattered little to Popov. When he was short of food or vodka, he was more than happy to put on snowshoes, throw on a backpack and hike the 3 miles to town to get supplies.

However, the real treasure on his property was his little garden house. It was located about 70 yards from his dacha. It stood near a small meadow, just inside a tree line. The wonderful thing about the entire arrangement was that as a former Russian nuclear weapons design, manufacture, and employment expert, Popov had made a substantial down payment on the dacha and plot of land. He'd built the garden house by hand. It was not much bigger than an American backyard storage shed.

Under the garden house, in a converted seven-foot-tall lead safe, which had formerly contained hunting rifles, was a store of incalculable value. Each of the five devices stored in the safe could cause enormous physical damage. Popov knew that if such a device were to be detonated–God forbid–in his nearby hometown of Tosno, the destructive blast force would likely kill roughly one-fourth of the 30,000 inhabitants. Many others would subsequently become sick from nuclear radiation exposure. Some would eventually die from that exposure. He knew many in the West's political leadership had lost sleep from worrying about where destructive weapons like these had ended up after the fall of the Soviet Union.

It fell apart in 1991. Some two and half years later, Popov found himself laid off. In a crumbling former Soviet economy in 1994, he had no prospect of near-term employment. At 36 years old, he'd already had a few 40-something-aged friends who had died from the over-consumption of cheap vodka and sheer boredom. Popov swore it would never happen to him.

Some day–in five years, ten years, or thirty years–those devices will be worth a fortune to the right buyer, thought Popov.

Before the nuclear weapons plants in Ukraine were completely shut down and abandoned, Popov had seen the handwriting on the wall. Near the end of the Cold War, Ukraine was briefly the third-largest nuclear weapons power in the world. In the months leading up to December 1991, when the Soviet Union collapsed, the Ukrainian government began hinting that it wanted to rid itself of those weapons.

Based on an international agreement called the Budapest Memorandum, the Ukrainians did precisely that: they gave up all their nuclear weapons in exchange for the promise of security provided by the new Russian Federation, the United Kingdom, and the United States. But not before the anxious Popov made a nerve-wracking but otherwise uneventful drive back to his Russian hometown of Tosno. The drive was completed during the chaos, lawlessness, and uncertainty, and in many former Soviet countries, sheer joy that resulted from the Soviet Union's collapse.

Popov's fateful drive occurred on New Year's Eve, December 31, 1991. It stretched into the early morning hours of January 1, 1992. By 10 p.m. on New Year's Eve, about the halfway mark of Popov's drive from the Ukrainian nuclear plant to Popov's home near Tonso, some three-quarters of Russian and Ukrainian adults–and many younger–citizens were thoroughly intoxicated from consuming pretty much anything that had alcohol in it.

Sure, in 1994 Russia, Russians were "free," but the economy in Popov's area was severely depressed. Today's summer day meeting with an old school friend, Igor Kozlov, was just what Popov sought.

As Popov stood on the stoop of his dacha, he observed Kozlov driving up the two-track dirt road in his late-1980s Volkswagen Golf. Popov smiled and shook his head approvingly.

That's just like Igor, thought Popov. *Igor's not only driving a West European car, but it's a German one. Everyone else around here, if, if they can afford it, is driving a fifteen-year-old Lada. What a resourceful son-of-a-bitch Igor is, just like always.*

Popov and Kozlov, also 36, had been friends since childhood. They were as thick as thieves. Kozlov *was* a thief and a very good one. A former FSB officer who had served tours in Kazakhstan and Uzbekistan, as well as a previous combat tour in Afghanistan, his official FSB days were over. But Kozlov was easily making more than three times his FSB salary working as a criminal for the Lubyanka crime organization.

The Lubyanka criminal group was made up in large measure of either retired or, because of the reduction in need after the dissolution of the Soviet Union, out-of-work and disgruntled FSB officers. Some *active* FSB officers were also colluding with the Lubyanka group. The Group was doing a banner business in running drugs from Afghanistan and Turkey to Russia and, when needed, even blowing stuff up for aspiring oligarchs.

Among the FSB power players who were emerging, the name "Puchta" was a name that Kozlov had heard. Rumor had it that anybody who trifled with the old Cold War KGB agent was known to have fallen off a balcony, gotten mysteriously ill, or simply disappeared. More recently, in 2021 and 2022, Russian business tycoons who crossed Puchta mysteriously "fell" down flights of stairs, "hit their heads," and died.

As Kozlov exited the VW, the two men greeted each other warmly.

And then Popov said exactly what Kozlov was waiting to hear.

"Let's have a drink."

You did not ask another Russian if he *wanted* a drink. That was bad form. You assumed a drink was going to happen, like breathing. And the drink would be vodka. The Germans had their beer, the French had their champagne, and the Italians and Spaniards had their wine. But in Russia, by God, it was vodka, typically distilled from wheat, rye, potato, or sometimes, whatever you could get your hands on.

Entering the dacha's kitchen, Popov filled two shot glasses. The two old friends raised them. Clinking them together, they looked each other in the eyes and near simultaneously said, "To your health!"

Now, they could get down to business.

CHAPTER 9

A BODY

CARABINIERI *MARESCIALLO* (WARRANT OFFICER, a technical rank between a senior sergeant and lieutenant) Giuseppe Benini and his fellow criminal investigator departed for the church. Nine minutes earlier, a caller had dialed 112, Italy's emergency services phone number. The call was from a nearby church. The caller had identified himself as Luca Romano Pietrosanti. He said he was "the archivist and daytime administrator of the nearby San Luigi dei Francesi church" in Rome. Pietrosanti had reported the discovery of a body in the church.

The Carabinieri station desk officer had just received a similar–but cranky–phone call the previous day. Pietrosanti was not prepared for the response.

"How do I know you're not bluffing, that this is not some sort of prank?" asked the officer. "We get one of these calls about every second week or so."

"You don't *know* if it's a prank," replied Pietrosanti. "But if I don't convince you to send someone now, the next phone call will be from the French Ambassador to the city police chief and then the mayor's office, not to you."

Pietrosanti was surprised at his rather cheeky response. But Luca Pietrosanti was in no mood to trifle. He did not know what his next move would be, but he did know that he wanted a police officer–Carabinieri or city police or whoever–to get to the church as soon as possible.

After a couple more questions to confirm the caller's identity, the Carabinieri receptionist responded.

"My apologies. We will get someone there quickly," was the response.

"How quickly?" responded Pietrosanti.

"Within 10, 15 minutes maximum," replied the officer.

"Thank you," responded Pietrosanti. "I will be waiting."

"There is one more thing," added the Carabinieri sergeant, "please keep the church closed until further notice."

"Will do," replied Pietrosanti.

After ending the call, Pietrosanti realized he could have run across the street to alert the Carabinieri guard at the nearby Senate building's guard post. But help was on the way, so that would no longer be necessary.

As he had not yet switched on the church's main lights, and the partly cloudy weather outside was temporarily hiding the sun, thus reducing the natural light streaming into the greyish church, Pietrosanti was still unaware that the three Caravaggio paintings were gone from the nearby Contarelli chapel.

CHAPTER 10

THE ELECTION: 24 YEARS BEFORE THE THEFT

IT HAD BEEN A TUMULTUOUS ELECTION CAMPAIGN. The Russian election in 2000 saw more turbulence than most former-Soviet-bloc eastern European countries. On the line was the choice between democracy, capitalism, and the rule of law over communism. But this was Russia, and, in the end, the former KGB agent, Vasily Puchta, was declared the winner. In some Western media corners, the election of the former Russian intelligence operative was reported as "one step forward, two steps back" for democratic values.

The First Chechen War in 1995 was a disaster for Russia leading up to the election because it concluded with the Russian military's nose being seriously bloodied by Chechen forces. Under the command of Shamil Basaev, the Chechen military intervention in Dagestan freed "the Dagestani from Russian imperialism."

In 1996 Boris Yeltsin sent Alexander Lebed to negotiate a settlement and bring the war to a conclusion. The fact that a Russian leader chose to negotiate with, rather than vanquish, Russia's opponent caused a severe blow to Yeltsin's political standing and Russia's political and military reputation. In the eyes of the Russian people, Yeltsin was a weak leader. Historically, that almost always signaled political death for a Russian leader.

In the summer of 1999, several apartment buildings in Russia were bombed. Some of the bombings resulted in the deaths of many children. The bombings were reported to have been done by Chechen terrorists. (However, at the cost of his life, Alexander Litvinenko, a former Russian FSB officer, later reported that the Russian secret services committed the bombings.) These bombings encouraged Russian President Boris Yeltsin to respond to the ensuing public outrage through his Prime Minister, Vasily Puchta.

The outcome Puchta orchestrated for Russia and the Chechens was far different from the one in 1996. Under a relentless bombing campaign, the city of Grozny, a Chechen enclave, was reduced to a hellish moonscape of rubble. Russian news outlets enthusiastically reported the brutal result as a great Russian military victory. Puchta took full credit.

Puchta's Chief of Staff Anatoly Roman Volkov wisely took no credit. Every rising national leader needs a Mr. Fix It, and Volkov was that person for Puchta. Volkov did whatever Puchta required of him ... but Volkov never took any of the credit. If Puchta wanted the local Russian forces in and around Grozny to carpet-bomb civilian neighborhoods, Volkov directed it. If Puchta wanted the Russian military to be authorized to torture Chechen soldiers, Volkov communicated that to the commanders on the ground. If Puchta wanted a deadly hit performed on an "excessively bold" Russian journalist, Volkov ensured that the FSB organized and executed the journalist's assassination.

With Volkov always handling the dirty work, Puchta managed to keep a degree of separation between himself and the crime. It was Volkov whose name was always on the dotted line. But Puchta got all the credit for tamping down the Chechen terrorism and other political successes.

Their talk two days after Puchta won the election in 2000 launched the ruthless Volkov on his path to business success and the accrual, by hook or crook, of massive wealth. As Puchta's Chief of Staff, Volkov had already been growing his commercial interests in industrial chemicals, fertilizer, and gas production. As a rapidly emerging multi-million-dollar oligarch, Volkov earned the gratitude and, more importantly, the trust of Puchta. Puchta had literally gotten away with murder, and Volkov knew it. So had Volkov, and Puchta knew that, too. It became like a blood pact between the two former FSB operators. Except that Puchta, as newly elected President, had the upper hand. He now held all the levers of power in the Russian state: its intelligence services, military forces, nuclear arsenal, ... everything.

Their conversation was straightforward.

"To you, my friend, Russia is open for business," said Puchta to the Wolf. "Of course, if you make sure I *always* get my fair share, you will become very wealthy and live to be an old man."

CHAPTER 11

GONE!

MARESCIALLO GIUSEPPE BENINI and his assistant arrived within minutes of being notified of the body in the *San Luigi dei Francesi* church. As the two Carabinieri officers approached the church's front door, Benini reached in his pocket for his cell phone. He called the church's daytime attendant, Luca Pietrosanti.

The Roman, whose last name was in honor of Saint Peter, approached the front door to open it from the inside. Before opening the door, he switched on the church's lights. The lights were positioned mainly in the nave (the central and main open space of the church) and ceiling, leaving the church's several side chapels unilluminated, except for the natural light provided by each chapel's window, located high on the chapels' walls. To take maximum advantage of natural sunlight, all the church's windows were in the upper reaches of each chapel and the nave itself.

"*Buongiorno*," said Pietrosanti to the two officers after he pulled the door open.

"Good morning," Benini replied for both officers as they flashed their badges at the ashen-faced Pietrosanti. "I am Maresciallo Benini. Are you Luca Pietrosanti, the one who called the station?"

"Yes, that was me," replied Pietrosanti as he led the two Carabinieri officers up the left side of the nave toward the church's main altar. The trio passed a series of small side chapels on their left as they advanced to the body lying in front of the Contarelli chapel. It was the last one on the left and the closest of the chapels to the church's main altar. Endowed by a wealthy French cardinal, Matthieu Cointerel (Contarelli in Italian), upon his death in 1585, the chapel was to be decorated with scenes honoring the life of his name-saint, Saint Mathew.

"Is this how you found him?" Benini asked as they approached the body lying five feet from the chapel's entrance railing.

"Yes. Well, I didn't exactly *find* him. I tripped over him," replied Pietrosanti. "In walking this way," he indicated his path from the church's back door, opposite from the public's main entrance, to where they stood, "I literally stumbled upon him in the semi-darkness. I always come this way each morning. When I do, our poor guard has always left the church by then. As I recall, he's typically gone from his guard shift by 7 a.m."

Officer Benini's junior partner checked the body's pulse just to be sure. The dead guard's skin was cold. There was no sign of life.

Benini's cursory examination of the corpse did not suggest foul play. There were no apparent wounds, bruises, or blood stains on the guard's body. Benini asked Pietrosanti a follow-up question.

"Did you notice anything that might have seemed suspicious or out of place?"

Pietrosanti stared silently at the Contarelli chapel, a look of horror fixed on his features. Benini had seen that look before when he was serving with Italy's *Folgore* "Lightning" Infantry Airborne Brigade in Afghanistan before he joined the Carabinieri. It was a look of newly witnessed trauma, of eyes trying to come to grips with the terrible scene they were observing.

"What's wrong?" asked Benini.

"I...I...did not–*could not*–see that this morning!"

"See what?" asked Benini.

"The clouds were too heavy outside," he continued in a panicked voice. "The church was quite dark. The three magnificent paintings of Saint Mathew...by Caravaggio...are gone!" Pietrosanti wailed.

Benini turned his head toward the Contarelli chapel. High on the chapel's three walls, he saw three massive, empty frames. Benini had no idea what the three missing paintings were worth, but within a day, much of Europe and the free world would hear several estimates of their enormous value.

CHAPTER 12

THE ANGRY OLIGARCH: TWO YEARS BEFORE THE THEFT

AN ANNUAL STOCK-TAKING CHAT had become a tradition between Anatoly Roman "the Wolf" Volkov and his most trusted Mr. Fix It and confidant, Boris Stepanov. They had known each other since Volkov had first hitched his wagon to Vasily Puchta's fortunes in 1999. Since then, Puchta had given the first-in-class oligarch plenty of business room to maneuver inside and outside of the Russian Federation.

For his part, Stepanov had done everything required of him to help to make the Wolf successful. This ranged from having the Wolf's business competitors and political enemies killed to helping the Wolf find a luxury yacht to guiding him in selecting the best international lawyers and tax advisors–and military operators–money could buy. It had become a tradition each year, as December 31 approached, for the two to sit down and take stock of the previous year before discussing and projecting the Wolf's broad plans for the next year or two. When and where the stock-taking occurred was always up to the Wolf.

As they sat in the Wolf's luxury penthouse apartment–his second, occasionally-occupied, Italian home–not far from Rome's Spanish Steps, the Wolf decided it was time to bounce his thoughts off Stepanov.

"2022 was a terrible year," he said, sipping his favorite 150-dollar bottle of vintage 2015 Italian *Amarone* wine.

The disgruntled and increasingly anti-Puchta oligarch was still hair-on-fire angry at the Italian authorities for seizing his 540-million-dollar yacht.

"The bastard Italians seized my yacht," he said. "It still makes no sense. They didn't seize my home in the countryside; they didn't seize this apartment; they seized my prized possession."

In fact, his heavily secured hillside home in the Alban hills southeast of Rome, only 7 miles from the well-known wine town of Frascati, had been left unmolested by Italian government authorities. Perhaps it was left alone because it was too secure. Or, more likely, they hadn't touched it because the Wolf had spent millions on improving the large farm property, which offered many locals solid work for almost a full year. Many locals—and Italian politicians—thought highly of the Wolf and his extraordinary accumulation of wealth, while others considered his construction projects to be a blight on the Italian countryside.

The more he thought about it, the angrier Volkov became.

"Sure, I have known Puchta for over twenty years. And yes, I was present at the initial discussions about attacking Ukraine. But I was not the one who made the decision to attack Kyiv!"

The initial "discussions" Volkov referred to on the eve of Russia's February 24, 2022, attack on Ukraine were not really discussions. Anybody who read the room of the 37 Russian oligarchs, generals, and *relatively* trusted confidants of Puchta's inner circle who were present on that day knew that the autocrat, who had alternatively "served" as Prime Minister or President for Russia for 23 years, had already made up his mind: Russia was going to attack Ukraine.

"Russia needs to get the world's attention," said Puchta. "The world needs to know that since the collapse of the Soviet Union, Russia has not become some third-rate power."

At the February 24 meeting, Puchta described how Russia would demonstrate to the world that it was still a major player in European and world politics. And when it was eventually successful in taking all of Ukraine, Russia's military success in Ukraine would splinter NATO, and Russia would welcome back some of its former Warsaw Pact allies, now NATO members, into a regenerated alliance with Russia. Russia would then subdue those who refused to be allies. The prime candidates for subjugation were Finland, Sweden, and the Baltic states.

At least, that was the plan.

At the meeting, Puchta was not seeking any kind of open discussion or feedback per se. What Puchta was looking for, like most deeply insecure autocrats of his ilk whose primary mission is to cling to power, was enthusiastic cheerleading from the group. His fragile ego not only needed the group's approval, but it craved it. Blind obedience to support his crimes, publicly and privately, was what Vasily Puchta demanded.

Puchta also knew that the meeting would serve to smoke out those who were not wholly in support of his intent to conquer Ukraine. As to the handful of business moguls present at the meeting who expressed doubt or communicated, inadvertently or intentionally, that they weren't all-in, they would each pay for their lack of absolute loyalty.

On September 2, 2022, international news outlets reported that at least eight prominent Russian businessmen had "died by suicide or in as yet unexplained accidents since just before the war had begun, with six of them associated with Russia's two largest energy companies." Other sources reported the number, including one journalist who had been killed, was closer to thirteen.

Four of the businessmen were linked to the Russian state-owned energy giant Gazprom or one of its subsidiaries. Two others were associated with Lukoil, Russia's largest privately-owned oil and gas company. Those business leaders had the temerity to speak out early against Russia's savage war with Ukraine.

In the case of Lukoil's chairman, he died in a manner that for twenty years had been all too common by those who opposed Puchta: he "fell" out of his hospital window. For some reason, apartment balconies throughout Russia, but mainly in Moscow, had also gone through a structural weakening during the previous two decades. This resulted in many "unfortunate" and "coincidentally similar" falls, down staircases, off balconies, and other such "accidents."

The war had gone terribly for Puchta and his bumbling generals. Thinking his military forces were easily up to the task, Puchta believed the Ukrainians would drop their weapons and run at the mere sight of a Russian tank. He could not have been more mistaken. He severely underestimated the mettle of the Ukrainian people, their standup president, and the Ukrainian armed forces. From day one, the Ukrainians fought like lions.

Puchta and his generals completely disregarded what General Dwight D. Eisenhower, the former Supreme Allied Commander of the international forces who liberated Europe in 1944-1945, once said about warfare: "Morale is the greatest single factor in successful wars."

The Ukrainians, to virtually every man and woman who took up arms, were willing to defend their homeland to the death. On the other hand, most Russian soldiers, many of whom were conscripts, had no idea why they were risking their lives to invade Ukrainian territory, let alone fight their Slavic cousins.

The tactical battlefield proved this asymmetry in morale. Achieving battlefield successes against the Russians required significant support in equipment and training from Western allies, particularly the United States. But the sheer force of their elevated will propelled the Ukrainians to take back their criminally destroyed or temporarily occupied homeland.

The Wolf continued with Stepanov actively listening to his every word, only responding when it was obvious that the Wolf expected a reply.

"The war with Ukraine could not have gone worse for Puchta and our Motherland," continued Volkov.

Stepanov, the more cerebral of the two, thought briefly about how Russians referred to Russia as the Motherland and Nazi Germany thought of its country as the Fatherland. "I agree, Roman," replied Stepanov, picking up the thread of the conversation again.

Stepanov was one of a handful of people who were allowed to refer to Volkov by anything other than his last name. The only other people who could do so were Volkov's mistresses, one living in Italy and the other in Russia, and his mother.

If addressed informally, Volkov preferred his middle name, Roman, over his Russian first name. His grandmother had been Italian, creating in Volkov, who had spent part of his youth behind the Iron Curtain, an intense curiosity about Italy and all things Italian.

"It was a turn of events that I did not see coming, either," continued Stepanov.

"You didn't see them coming, my friend," replied Volkov, "because Puchta was simply *too weak*! He abandoned his original playbook from Grozny (referring to Russia's utter destruction of Chechnya's capital city in 2000). He should have razed entire Ukrainian villages and cities. He should have employed tactical nuclear weapons early in the war," Volkov said, referring to the smaller-yielding nuclear weapons which had far less destructive power than those employed at Hiroshima and Nagasaki. They had been prominent in Russia's nuclear arsenal during the Cold War.

Volkov's mention of nuclear weapons employment did not phase Stepanov. He knew that Puchta had been prevailed upon by conservative (*deranged*, thought Stepanov) oligarchs to employ nuclear weapons early in the conflict with Ukraine. But that was a Rubicon that Puchta had decided not to cross.

"The Americans and NATO would have been in a quandary as to how to respond if Russia had employed tactical nukes early," said Volkov. "I don't believe they would have been unified enough to respond at all. Hell, I don't think NATO got unified until the Russian military was on its heels, retreating to the Motherland. What an embarrassment for Russia this war has been to witness."

Volkov reached for his glass and took a sip of wine.

"Yes, it has," replied Stepanov. "Yes, it has."

Volkov paused and looked away from Stepanov. Volkov pensively stared out the window. And then Volkov turned back to Stepanov and confirmed what Stepanov knew the Wolf had been considering all along.

"I must go back to Russia when the time is right. And that time will be sooner than later, Boris. I must take leadership of Russia. The Russian people *need* me to lead them. They have always needed and respected strong—yes, *ironfisted*—leaders like me. Puchta has been too damn weak. Among his incompetent generals, there are perhaps three or four competent ones still around who want a stronger Russia and a strong leader to lead it. As to the rest, I will fire them and replace them with aggressive and competent colonels. I will not make the mistakes Puchta made. I will not be afraid to be bold. I will restore faith in our military. I will restore global respect for Russia. And I will not be afraid to use the decisive weapons Russia possesses. Boris, when we have our annual discussion in 2025, it will be a different conversation, it will be a different Russia, and it will be a different world!"

Thinking Volkov was finished with his privately expressed manifesto, Stepanov nodded affirmatively to the Wolf. But Volkov was not finished.

"And," the Wolf continued, "I will rally, from around the world, other like-minded and strong rulers like me who are sick of weak socialist and so-called democratic governments on our planet. Those who are *strong* rulers will be my allies!"

The Wolf thought of national leaders from Syria, Tajikistan, Turkmenistan, Chad, Myanmar, Laos, Mali, Saudi Arabia, and Venezuela, and autocratic-style leaders like the former President of Brazil, the Prime Minister of Hungary, and others.

These are rulers seeking to rule in the right way," thought Volkov, *with iron, autocratic strength, unencumbered by "legal" institutions or opposition parties or ever-changing "democratic" values.*

He thought of the Iranian regime. He thought of Assad of Syria and Madura of Venezuela. He thought of the military junta in Myanmar. He thought of the President of China and a former President of the United States.

"Eventually," said Puchta, "we will replace the United Nations with an autocratic alliance of leaders, protecting each other against the rise of socialism and overzealous democracy. There is an Alliance of Democracies, so why not an Alliance of Autocracies?"

The Wolf thought briefly about Germany's post-World War I experiment with a democratic, constitutional republican government, the Weimar Republic (1918-1933). The multi-party government experiment was considered a political disaster, even if it evolved from Germany having been "unfairly" damaged by World War I reparations and abysmal global economic conditions after the Crash of '29. The German Weimar

Republic ushered in exorbitant annual inflation and cost of living increases of more than 17-fold in six months, leaving a piece of bread costing hundreds and eventually thousands of German marks.

It was no wonder the Germans "elected" Adolf Hitler as Chancellor of the German Reich, thought Volkov. *And the Italians, who underwent similar political and economic problems, did the same as the Germans, producing Benito Mussolini as Prime Minister.*

Volkov forgot, perhaps expediently, about the enormous economic and political changes Germany and Italy made in the aftermath of World War II, with both republics becoming variations on republican, democratic, and federal states. Economically, like the rest of Europe, Canada, and the United States, they had also become variations on capitalist-socialist economies.

"Russians intuitively and rightly believe that democracy is a weak form of government," he told Stepanov. "What Russia—and the world—needs now is the strongest leader they've ever had. And that leader is me!"

Stepanov nodded.

"There is no doubt about it, Boris," concluded Volkov. "I must prepare to go back to Russia."

CHAPTER 13

US CONGRESSIONAL DELEGATION: 15 MONTHS BEFORE THE THEFT

SENATOR JAMES BROCK was taken aback. The Mississippi senator, who served on the US Senate Foreign Relations Committee, considered himself not only an expert on international affairs but a *doer*, a man *who got things done*. At least that's what he told anyone who would listen.

Johnson considered most of his Senate colleagues to be media-seeking glory hounds. He believed he was the best senator for leaning into and resolving problems. And what he–and the seven-person, bipartisan US congressional delegation (CODEL) he was with–had just heard from the Italian four-star general concerned him.

"Senator, the US Army used to have a liaison officer who was assigned to our National Armaments Directorate, which is within our Ministry of Defense," began General Giovanni Castiglione. "But that position has been vacant for two years. I understand we all go through periods when it's difficult to fill certain personnel positions. Italy has a similar position assigned to the US Army's Material Command, which we do our best to keep consistently manned. Our Ministry of Defense would very much appreciate it if the United States Army could again fill the position they have here in Rome."

Brock considered his response to the general. The senator understood that a lot was at stake for the United States in having US Army, Navy, Air Force, and Marine forces stationed in Italy. Stationed on Italian soil since the end of World War II, not only were the US bases in Italy important for US national security interests in Europe, but they were also important as strategic staging areas for US national security interests in Africa and the Middle East. Johnson was also fully aware that U.S. Army Southern European Task Force, Africa (or SETAF-Africa), an Army land component headquarters for any national security challenges and threats emanating from Africa, was in Vicenza, Italy.

Seeking to avoid a fraught moment, Senator Brock knew he needed to respond in a positive tone.

"General," began Brock, "I assure you that the United States Defense Department and Army will do its best to fill that position. We consider Italy to be a strong defense partner. We appreciate Italy hosting US Army forces in Vicenza, and other US military forces throughout Italy, including in Aviano, Gaeta, Naples, and Sigonella."

The Italian general nodded in response. The general was impressed at the senator's rattling off the US military installations located on Italian soil.

"Thank you, sir. We in the Italian Armed Forces appreciate your consideration."

The Italian general was fully aware of the modern equipment the United States had supplied to the Ukrainian armed forces in their tactical trouncing of the Russian army. Sure, he understood it was the courage, morale, and resilience of the Ukrainian soldiers that made a huge difference in that conflict. But the Ukrainians could not have repelled Russian forces without modern US weapons systems, such as the Javelin Advanced Anti-Tank Weapon, the Multiple Launch Rocket System (MLRS), the High Mobility Artillery Rocket System (HIMARS), and M1 Abrams Tank. In the hands of competent and courageous Ukrainian soldiers, these weapons systems wreaked havoc against Russian military forces.

As Senator Brock departed the conference room in Italy's Ministry of Defense headquarters, he whispered to his congressional aide:

"Don't let me forget this. When we get back, I have a plan for providing the officer they are asking for."

CHAPTER 14

AN ITALIAN LANGUAGE SPEAKER: 15 MONTHS BEFORE THE THEFT

"GENERAL RAYBURN," SAID MISSISSIPPI GOVERNOR Lewis Carlisle to his Adjutant General and National Guard Commander, "I just got a call from Senator Brock's office. I spoke to the man himself. Instead of Brock going around me and straight to you, I appreciate the courtesy of him contacting me first. Senator Brock was just in Italy with a congressional delegation, and he felt put upon by an Italian general. I think you might know we have several military bases in Italy, so we certainly don't want to piss off the Italians."

"The bottom line is that this Italian general asked Senator Brock about putting a US Army lieutenant colonel in a US Army liaison slot that has been vacant for over two years. It's a liaison position with an Italian logistics organization. I understand it's a combination of our US Army Material Command and Defense Security Cooperation Agency. Apparently, the Pentagon personnel people are either dragging their feet or just can't find the right officer to fill the slot. Johnson said one of his aides already did some checking with our National Guard people, and you apparently *do* have an officer in your ranks who speaks some Italian. He's a certain Lieutenant Colonel Beauregard Bragg."

Brock paused, expecting an answer. None came.

"Ever heard of him?"

"Yep, I have. An air defense officer, he's a solid guy. Not an all-star, but solid."

He's barely mediocre, thought the National Guard commander, recalling a racially-charged incident between Bragg and a couple of Black soldiers. It had happened three years before General Rayburn had taken command of the Mississippi National Guard, but he recalled the incident. Local law enforcement investigated the incident, and it was declared a simple disagreement. Fortunately, it hadn't become physical. The investigation was wrapped up with a nice ribbon on it, but the general–and many officers in the Guard–expected there was more to it than the official story. The general also did not want the governor to know Bragg was marginally effective and stood no chance of receiving another promotion within the Mississippi National Guard.

"Apparently, Bragg has some family lineage back to Braxton Bragg," added General Rayburn.

General Rayburn thought Carlisle knew who Braxton Bragg was, and he was correct.

"Braxton Bragg? As in Confederate General Braxton Bragg? Hell, I didn't know he was from Mississippi. I thought he was from North Carolina ... or Louisiana, maybe?" replied Carlisle.

"Right on both counts, Governor," replied Rayburn, who knew his Civil War history and many generals who participated in America's bloodiest war.

"Bragg was a North Carolina native but later owned a plantation in Louisiana. I don't know *how* he has lineage to Braxton Bragg, but Beauregard Bragg does," continued the general.

"With that name, I guess I should not be surprised."

Governor Carlisle chuckled.

"Listen, Donald," continued Carlisle. "We need to do everything we can to get Bragg federally activated for active Army duty and assigned to Italy. Should be a lot easier with Senator Brock's interest in this. I don't know if you are aware, but Brock is not only on the Senate Foreign Relations Committee, but he also serves on the Senate Armed Services Committee. I don't need to tell you what that might mean to our federal funding if we get this right. So, let's get movin' on this as soon as possible, OK?"

"Roger that, governor," replied Rayburn. "I'll make it happen."

CHAPTER 15

SETTLING IN: EIGHT MONTHS BEFORE THE THEFT

JAKE FORTINA PINCHED HIMSELF. He was in one of his favorite cities in the world. He was doing what he loved with the God-given gift of an amazing woman whom he loved and shared his most intimate moments with. Jake and Sara, 18 months into their blissful marriage, had lived for one week in their US embassy-approved apartment in Rome.

Located in the *Centro Rezidenziale Communale Avila*, the gated apartment complex had at one time hosted the former—and last—King of Afghanistan and his family. The King lived there from the mid-1970s to the 1990s after abdicating his crown in the face of a coup d'état in the early 1970s. The apartment complex was just off the *via Cassia* and north of the *Grande Raccordo Anulare*, Rome's main bypass and ring road.

Jake and Sara's 3-bedroom apartment was not, however, fit for a king. While its marbled floor rooms were spacious, the kitchen was bare-bones basic. Yet, to rent it privately, especially with gated security, cost more than what an average Roman could afford. The gated security was a primary reason the US embassy had allowed US embassy employees to live there. Overall, the apartment had met the embassy's other physical security requirements, including being reachable by the limit of any fully extended fire truck ladders in the city. What attracted Jake and Sara to the apartment was its beautiful view of the Roman countryside.

However, the apartment had no central air conditioning or heat. There were no wall-mounted air conditioners either, as was common in most of Rome's hotels. Before extended higher temperatures arrived in Rome in the 21st century, it was thought that a couple of open windows would be sufficient to cool things off. Not so now in Rome (nor in many other places in Europe).

Individual rooms had to be cooled with what Italians called a *pinguino*. The electrically run "penguin"—about the size and shape of a mobile industrial vacuum cleaner, or slightly smaller than the robot R2-D2 of the

Star Wars movie—rested on small wheels and stood about three feet high. To properly use the noisy air conditioner, one had to cut a hole—about six inches in diameter—in the glass of a nearby window and then hook a hot air exhaust tube running from the penguin to the hole. It was not exactly the most efficient piece of AC gear on the planet.

As Jake had quickly learned in doing his personal risk assessments, the traffic patterns in Rome were comparable to large American cities like Washington D.C., Boston, or LA. On a light traffic day, like Sunday, it took about 20-25 minutes to drive to the US Embassy. It was located near the heart of Rome on *Via Veneto*, a street made famous by movies such as *La Dolce Vita* and *Roman Holiday* of the 1950s.

During the workweek, however, local traffic conditions meant that if Jake exited the apartment complex and headed south on via Cassia by 7:10 a.m., he could make it to the Embassy by 7:35. However, if he left at 7:20, the difference in arrival time at the embassy did not correlate to an arrival time ten minutes later, but rather an additional 40 minutes of travel. But if he left at 7:30? Forget about it. That would make it a 2-hour trip, minimum. Such was the nature of driving in a dense urban area and on modern roads that had been built around—and on top of—the ruins of over 3000 years of Roman history.

From his introductory embassy security briefings—and from Sara, who had Carabinieri friends serving in Rome—Jake had learned that Rome, a city of 4.2 million people, was relatively safe from violent crime. Very late at night and in the wrong corner of town, sure, something bad could happen, especially if alone. But it was relatively rare. Thievery—to oneself, to one's car, and to one's home, on the other hand—was a threat one had to be vigilant about.

As in other large European cities, foreign counterintelligence agents were also a threat, particularly against US embassy personnel and certainly a US Army officer. Rome was not the hotbed of spies that Helsinki and Vienna once were, particularly during the Cold War days. But discretion and prudence were always necessary when, for example, dining out. Loose talk could inadvertently give away American national security or economic secrets. Chinese, Iranian, and Russian spies were active in the city.

Just as when he was assigned to Afghanistan, Kenya, Azerbaijan, or even Paris, Jake Fortina resolved never to let his guard down. He would thoroughly learn the "security lay of the land" in Rome: traffic patterns, driving habits, manner of dress, personal habits, and mannerisms of the locals, etc. Fortina knew he would need to vary his times going to and from the embassy, sometimes departing a 6 a.m., sometimes at 7:10 a.m., other times at 6:39 a.m., or whenever. No regular patterns of activity would be established. Fortina never forgot a principle of personal security: unpredictability is your friend, as well as a friend of your loved ones. Said another way, being predictable in your daily activities to an observing enemy puts you in danger.

CHAPTER 16

THE OATH: SIX MONTHS BEFORE THE THEFT

LIEUTENANT COLONEL JAKE FORTINA looked the US Army staff sergeant in the eyes. Fortina felt blessed and honored to be standing in the sergeant's presence. The sergeant felt the same about Fortina. They were about to perform a special ritual between American military warriors. It was a ritual in which Fortina had participated several times. He'd always felt fortunate to be asked to lead the ceremony for his Army teammates: enlisted soldiers, noncommissioned officers, warrant officers, and commissioned officers who had been selected for promotion to the next rank.

Administering the oath at the US Army base in Vicenza, Italy, the site of Fortina's first Army tour with the 173d Airborne Brigade, made the occasion more special.

"Raise your right hand and repeat after me," began Fortina, addressing the sergeant as Fortina also raised his right hand.

"I, state your full name," said Fortina, pausing for the Army noncommissioned officer (NCO) to fill in the blank with his name.

"I, Manuel Alvarez," responded the sergeant.

Fortina continued. After every few words, he would pause, so the sergeant could repeat the words of the sacred oath that Fortina was reciting. The El Paso, Texas, born and raised sergeant did not miss a beat in stating the entire oath with conviction:

"I, Manuel Alvarez, do solemnly swear that I will support and defend the Constitution of the United States against all enemies, foreign and domestic; that I will bear true faith and allegiance to the same; and that I will obey orders of the President of the United States and the orders of the officers appointed over me, according to regulations and the Uniform Code of Military Justice. So help me God."

With the oath complete, the two Army veterans shook hands. They wanted to hug each other. They had known—and highly respected—each other for more than a decade. But military decorum and self-discipline held the two professionals back.

After Alvarez's wife, Cristina, attached an epaulet reflecting the rank of an Army sergeant first class on one shoulder, Alvarez's father secured the other epaulet to the opposite shoulder.

In his remarks to the gathered crowd, including family and friends of Alvarez, Fortina made the point that US military service members don't serve at the behest of a single individual, like a king or a president or any potentate. Their north star of allegiance is represented by one document: the United States Constitution.

A lover of history, Fortina couldn't resist taking a moment to educate those in the crowd. In addition to being "a trainer of America's best," as Fortina considered it, being an educator was one of the things Fortina loved most about being an Army officer and leader of US Army soldiers.

"Our US Constitution is not the oldest living and working constitution in the world, as many people think," began Fortina. "The oldest one comes from right here in Italy. Does anybody here know what I'm talking about?"

An intrepid 20-something Army first lieutenant–and Alvarez's company executive officer–thought he might know the answer. But the junior officer was humble enough to realize he might be wrong. So, he offered an educated guess.

"Is it the Vatican's constitution?" asked the lieutenant.

"That's a darn good guess," replied Fortina. "But no, it isn't. The country I am referring to is not that far from us."

Fortina paused briefly for any responses from the crowd.

Alvarez's company first sergeant knew the answer but kept quiet. He had once visited the small principality with his family. Others thought the colonel's statement about a "not that far" country implied it was Switzerland.

"It's the very small—tiny, really—country of San Marino," said Fortina. "It's located about 80 miles south by southeast of here. Its constitution was ratified in October 1600."

A couple of people in the audience nodded their heads affirmatively, recognizing the name of the former Italian principality that eventually achieved national sovereignty.

"Ours is a tad newer than San Marino's constitution and is the second oldest in the world," added Fortina. "It was ratified in 1788."

After making a few more comments, Fortina turned to Sergeant First Class Alvarez for his remarks.

Gratefully wearing his new rank, the beaming Army sergeant first class addressed Lieutenant Colonel Jake Fortina, who would soon be his supervisor again.

"Thank you for taking the time to do this, sir. I really look forward to working with you again," said Alvarez, who had recently reenlisted to serve in the Defense Attaché System at the US embassy in Rome.

"The pleasure is all mine," said Fortina. "I look forward to doing great things with you in Rome as well."

Jake Fortina was absolutely delighted to be reuniting with the former Army Special Forces medic who had demonstrated exceptional courage and competence in the Korengal Valley, saving several men who had become wounded as all hell descended upon them in that God-forsaken Afghan valley.

There were three men whom Alvarez could not save during his two combat tours there. Those painful losses would stay with him for the rest of his life. But he knew deep in his soul that he had done everything humanly possible to save their lives.

In the intervening years after their service in Afghanistan, the two surviving soldiers, Alvarez and Fortina, had gone their separate ways but had remained in contact.

Fortina headed off to foreign language training in Monterey, California, to learn Farsi. After departing Monterey, Fortina went to the George C. Marshall European Center for Security Studies in Garmisch-Partenkirchen, Germany, to obtain a master's degree in international relations. That training and education were in preparation for becoming a U.S. Army foreign area officer (FAO), one who serves with foreign militaries, on the staffs of major US regional commands, in the Pentagon, or with US embassies abroad.

Along the way, Fortina had served at US embassies in Baku and Paris. But while in language training at the Monterey-based Defense Language Institute, an unspeakable tragedy happened to Fortina: he lost his wife Faith, daughter Kimberley and son Jake, Jr., in a heart-breaking car accident on a country road north of Houston. After that soul-jarring trauma, it had been a struggle for Jake to find his bearings again. But after almost six years of being a widower, Fortina considered himself blessed to have fallen in love with an Italian Carabinieri officer, Sara Simonetti. One year after meeting again in Italy, they were married.

Manuel Alvarez, on the other hand, had left behind his duties as an Army Special Forces medic at Fort Campbell, Kentucky, to reenlist for duty with the 173d Airborne Brigade in Vicenza. The prospect of serving with an elite, "high-speed" Army unit in Italy greatly appealed to his patriotism and sense of adventure. As it turned out for Alvarez, it was a life-changing assignment in more ways than one.

***

Walking into the Italian bakery in Vicenza, Italy, Manuel Alvarez noticed a beautiful, dark blonde, green-eyed Italian lady–probably in her late twenties, he guessed–standing behind the counter. Alvarez was instantly smitten. He had just turned 30. He had never settled down because he never really had the chance. Meeting and getting to know someone special–let alone settling down with them–was a hard thing to do, given that more than half of his Army time had been spent overseas, much of it in combat zones.

Seeking to make a good impression, Alvarez wanted to speak a little Italian to the lady he couldn't take his eyes off. Alvarez knew that the

Spanish language, Alvarez's second language (after English), handed down to him from his Mexico-born parents when he grew up in El Paso, Texas, had many loosely common words with Italian (both languages are Latin-based). So, he thought he would ask for a couple of pastries without using a word of English.

"Um, *quiero*...uhh *puedo*," he began in Spanish, pointing to a couple of croissants.

Alvarez hesitated, feeling momentarily frustrated. The beautiful woman behind the counter waited patiently.

The Italian word from his three-week Italian language orientation course he'd taken when he first arrived in Vicenza finally popped into Alvarez's head.

"*Vorrei* (I would like, in Italian) *estas* (these, in Spanish)," he mumbled, still pointing to the pastries under the glass counter.

There was another pause as the lady behind the counter, now with a big smile, stepped forward.

Like a third grader looking to his teacher for approval, Alvarez raised his eyes from the glass counter and smiled back at her.

"Wow, you are a *brave* man, Mr. Alvarez," responded Cristina Buongiorno in English upon reading Alvarez's nametag. "You get the top prize of the year for making a successful attempt at not speaking a word of English when ordering."

The Italian woman's bright eyes and beautiful, confident, and charming smile further melted Alvarez's quaking heart.

Buongiorno's parents owned three bakeries in the Vincenza area. At this bakery, about one out of six of its customers were US soldiers or their family members stationed at the nearby US military base, *Caserma Ederle*. Buongiorno had met a fair number of American soldiers over the years, as well as their wives and children, who had come into the bakery looking for delightful Italian baked goods.

Buongiorno had been dating an Italian man for seven years. For the previous six months, Buongiorno increasingly believed the man could never commit to marriage. Now, at 28 years of age, she was growing tired of the relationship. She was looking for a change. Her interactions with local Americans had complimented her high school English studies quite well, so her American-accented English had become pretty darn good.

After Alvarez paid for the pastries and was about to leave the store, he wanted to say something momentous, something memorable, maybe even humorous.

The best he could manage was, "Ciao. I'll be back."

Buongiorno played it cool but offered the heart-struck Army sergeant a dash of hope.

"And there is a chance I just might still be here when you do," she said, then giggled.

Alvarez returned to the bakery and pastry shop four more times over the next two weeks. On the fourth visit, Alvarez finally worked up the gumption to ask Buongiorno out on a date. When Buongiorno finally responded with "Si," Alvarez walked out of the bakery as high as a kite.

The rest was history ... *their* beautiful history.

CHAPTER 17

THE STICKER

LIEUTENANT COLONEL JAKE FORTINA walked into the weekly meeting of military leaders at US Embassy Rome. He was becoming increasingly comfortable in his new job as the Assistant Army Attaché to Italy. His immediate supervisor, the Army Attaché, Colonel Marion Seaton, happened to be a fellow Michigander. Seaton was a Michigan State University ROTC (Reserved Officers Training Corps) graduate. Fortina, although a staunch Army West Point football fan, had followed some Michigan college sports teams throughout his time in the Army. The Michigan State Spartans were his favorite Michigan team, but he also kept tabs on the Ferris State University Bulldogs, from his hometown of Big Rapids, as well as the University of Michigan Wolverines, especially when they were playing the Ohio State Buckeyes.

Both Army officers were also longsuffering—at least for the previous dozen years or so—fans of the Detroit Lions football and the Detroit Tigers baseball teams. Their familiarity with Michigan sports teams provided Fortina and Seaton with common ground and plenty of things to talk about socially.

The person in charge of all military personnel assigned to the US embassy in Rome, however, was the US Defense Attaché and Senior Defense Representative to Italy, Navy Captain Rebecca Cheman. The US defense attaché and senior US defense representative to the Italian Armed Forces was always a Navy captain. This was due mainly to the US Navy's significant 6th Fleet presence in Naples and nearby Gaeta, as well as Sigonella, located on the eastern coast of Sicily.

Cheman's father had been a US naval aviator and US Naval Academy graduate, but Cheman chose to attend Texas A&M University. The "Aggies" had one of the top-ranked Navy ROTC programs in the country, and Cheman had excelled in all aspects of her military training as well as academics there. Cheman had also commanded a Sixth Fleet destroyer and spoke good Italian before upgrading it to "excellent" by taking on an evening tutor in the Washington D.C. area.

Just before the meeting began, Army Lieutenant Colonel Beauregard "Bo" Bragg walked in and seated himself next to Jake. That put Bragg between Fortina and the US embassy military leaders just to his left, seated at the head of the large conference table. Bragg was representing the embassy's Chief of the Office of Defense Cooperation (ODC), an Army colonel.

The ODC's function was to work with the Italian government on issues such as US basing in Italy, as well as with the Italian Armed Forces for all military equipment purchases between the two militaries and the attendance of officers at each other's military education and training schools. For example, each year, the Italians sent an officer to the US National War College, and the Americans reciprocated, sending an officer to the Italian Armed Forces equivalent school for lieutenant colonels and colonels.

Captain Cheman made opening remarks for the meeting. Bragg opened his leather padfolio and jotted down a few notes. Bragg continued to face Cheman, who was speaking from the head of the table on his left. Fortina, seated to the right of Bragg but also having to look to the left toward the head of the table, noticed a sticker stuck to the inside of Bragg's padfolio.

At first, the sticker surprised Fortina. Then it perplexed him. Then it angered him. It was a sticker of a Confederate flag. It was about an inch and a half wide by an inch high. Nothing flashy or grandiose, just a simple sticker, like a teenager would stick to the outside of a laptop.

What the heck is that doing there? thought Fortina.

The divisive symbol distracted Fortina from the meeting and the conversation going on at the head of the table between Captain Cheman and Colonel Seaton, the Army attaché.

Other than the fact that Bragg had come to the embassy from the Mississippi National Guard, Fortina knew little about his fellow Army officer.

"Why would Bragg have that symbol of division inside his padfolio? Fortina asked himself. *Am I seeing it right? Is it maybe the old Mississippi state flag I'm*

57

looking at, with the old Confederate stars and bars? Or a Confederate flag sticker to help remind Bragg of the old Mississippi flag, which had been removed from the state's capitol within the past few years?

Fortina was not quite sure what he was seeing. He also did not want to be caught staring at Bragg's padfolio, so he averted his eyes.

Fortina continued to be distracted and deep in thought. His mind drifted away to what he knew about American history. During the US Civil War, the bloodiest in America's history, Confederate commanders had petitioned for a flag that was more distinguishable from the Union forces' stars and stripes, resulting in the Confederate stars and bars.

He decided to take another look at the sticker.

No doubt, it's the Confederate flag, he thought.

A voice from the head of the table brought Fortina back from his distraction.

"Lieutenant Colonel Fortina," came Colonel Seaton's question, louder than normal, from near the head of the table. "Captain Cheman just asked you a question: how did the event at the Spanish embassy go last week?"

Having been distracted and disturbed by the flag, Fortina was embarrassed that he had been so deep in thought that he had not heard the question and that his boss had to raise his voice to get Fortina's attention.

Thank God Colonel Seaton repeated Captain Cheman's question, thought Fortina.

All eyes in the room were on Fortina.

"My apologies Ma'am," replied Fortina to Cheman. "It was an excellent event with a good turnout. The Spanish Ambassador talked about Spain's commitment to NATO. Nothing out of the ordinary; just a recommitment to the US and NATO bases that Spain is hosting there and Spain's military commitment to the Alliance as a whole."

Colonel Seaton was content that his assistant had answered the Navy Captain's question. But he was concerned about what was going on with Fortina. Unlike this morning, Fortina was normally very focused and engaging.

CHAPTER 18

THE BLAME GAME

IT WAS THREE WEEKS since the Caravaggio masterpieces were stolen. The Cyberkid's tactics in implementing the Wolf's grand strategy were working perfectly. The squabbles between the three governments that had a stake in *Saint Luigi de Francesi* church and therefore shared responsibility for the loss of the three magnificent, highly valued paintings by the greatest painter of Italian Baroque were increasing. The visceral arguments between them had spilled out into the French, Italian, and European national news media outlets and were beginning to be heard and seen globally. Pundits and trolls were having a field day on social media.

It was in social media where the Kid excelled as a world-class cybercriminal and propagandist. He was a master at employing bots and devising conspiracies, accurately and persistently targeting the fears, hopes, confirmation biases, and prejudices of his audiences and individual targets.

Boris Stepanov, the Wolf's chief of staff and personal confidant, was thrilled with the Kid's work.

"Whatever you're doing, keep doing it," Stepanov told the Kid. "You have all three government entities angry at each other. There is daily sniping and the trading of barbs on the internet, television talk shows, and national news outlets. The governments of Italy and France are constantly blaming each other for the theft of those paintings. And the Vatican is also catching its fair share of hell from both governments. I find that beautifully ironic. The press is having a field day with this."

Stepanov chuckled.

"This is exactly the kind of Western international strife and chaos we want to portray," said Stepanov.

"Thank you, sir," replied the Kid. "I am thankful and surprised how well our campaign to discredit the French and Italian governments has gone so far."

"Indeed," replied Stepanov. "Of the three entities, I'm less concerned about the Vatican than I am about the Italian and French governments. I want them to be publicly at each other's throats. Let's continue to portray them as shining examples of weak socialist governments! The *San Luigi dei Francesi* church and our heist are the perfect means for this. The church is a very public symbol of France's representation of the Catholic church in Italy. It is administered by the French government, by French clerics and civilians, but it stands on Italian soil in the very *heart* of Italy. Over several decades—if not centuries—millions of people from around the world have been in that French church and seen or heard of those paintings. And if they haven't, they've certainly heard of them now! This is the perfect example for demonstrating how weak these Western European governments are in fighting crime."

The fact that the man the Kid was speaking to was also the man who orchestrated the great theft was not missed by the Kid. But that's why he loved Stepanov and the man who stood behind him, the Wolf. Once the Wolf decided to do something bold, the Kid knew the Wolf would be successful, and so would Stepanov in carrying out the Wolf's plans.

The Kid looked back with pride on the bots, fake posts, and outrageous lies he'd orchestrated on Facebook and Twitter during the 2016 US presidential election. Russia's efforts in influencing that election worked beautifully, with Stepanov pulling most of the levers in implementing the Wolf's and Puchta's visions. By doing so, the Wolf endeared himself even more than he already had to Vasily Puchta.

However, on November 7, 2022, the Wolf was very annoyed at Yevgeny Prigozhin.

"We have interfered, are interfering, and will continue to interfere (with US elections and politics) … carefully, precisely, surgically, and in our own way. During our pinpoint operations, we will remove both kidneys and the liver at once," said Prigozhin on Russian social media.

Media outlets made hay out of Prigozhin's statement across Europe and the world.

In employing cyber-attacks and cyber disinformation, the Wolf knew that it was always good to leave the cyber-targeted enemy with some degree of doubt as to the origins of a cyber campaign. This helped retain some degree of plausible deniability for the perpetrator.

"Prigozhin's statement was careless, stupid, and full of unnecessary–and quite damaging, actually–hubris. If I was in charge at the Kremlin, Prigozhin would be pushing up daisies in the Khovanskoye Cemetery," the Wolf told Boris Stepanov in referencing the large Moscow cemetery.

Stepanov nodded.

"He removed a lot of doubt about who did it," replied Stepanov, "and that was strategically stupid and completely unnecessary."

CHAPTER 19.

NOT DAVOS: THE CONFERENCE

"WE CANNOT HAVE a large group of the world's strong leaders gather in one place," said Boris Stepanov, Wolf's chief of staff and confidant.

Stepanov used the term "strong" leaders because that was the term the Wolf preferred. The Wolf didn't like the terms autocrat, dictator, or, God forbid–kleptocrat–even though those words described perfectly well the type of leader the Wolf was and was seeking to "partner" with.

"Why not?" replied the Wolf.

"It would raise too many eyebrows, especially in the West," replied Stepanov.

"Who cares?" replied the Wolf.

"You should care, Roman," replied Stepanov. "A conference like that would bring a thousand prying eyeballs on us and a thousand times a million on social media if it leaks out to the public. As to foreign intelligence operations, they would be all over us. Do you want to have to deal with that every day?"

The Wolf pondered the question. He took a swallow of his cappuccino.

"No, I certainly don't."

The Wolf paused.

"That would be a huge pain in the ass."

The Wolf appreciated Stepanov's consistent, matter-of-fact, practical style. That was precisely why the Wolf had kept Stepanov around for over twenty years.

"It certainly would," replied Stepanov.

"So, how do I get these leaders together?" asked the Wolf.

"You don't, at least not all at once," responded Stepanov. "I would not bring in the actual leaders. I would first gather their closest, most trusted advisors together in small groups. Let the leaders determine whom they want to send to represent them. Give the first meeting a banal cover name, like 'Energy Security Conference'."

"I will work with our mafia friends to hold the meeting in one of their most secure facilities," continued Stepanov. "And the Mafia will also think the topic is 'Energy Security' or whatever cover name we want to give the meetings."

"You mean like a Davos-type gathering?" asked the Wolf.

"Sort of, but only from the perspectives that they will be held in the mountains and that the meetings will be international. That's it. Our meetings will be smaller, shorter, and more discreet than Davos. Only ten to fifteen key participants at a time. Eyeball to eyeball. I recommend right here in Italy, in the Dolomite mountains. I will have an advance team ensure the meeting facilities are completely free of surveillance and bugs. Either you can meet with the participants face to face, or I'll do it on your behalf. Nobody understands your vision of a partnership of strong national leaders across the world like I do."

"If I want to reach out to the actual leaders from Africa, Europe, South America, the Middle East, etc. ... how do I do it?" asked the Wolf.

"Through video conference call," replied Stepanov.

"Is that sufficiently secure?" asked the Wolf.

"Yes, it will be if we connect through the right satellite. We will use the most secure means that money can buy. Elon Marski has his own satellite aloft. We will make sure you are transmitting through his satellite. And you will do so from one of the most obscure places, like our modest farm here in Italy," concluded Stepanov.

"I like it. Make it happen," directed the Wolf.

CHAPTER 20

A COMBINED EFFORT.

LIEUTENANT COLONEL SARA SIMONETTI-FORTINA appreciated her new role serving on the International Task Force. She and US Army officer Jake Fortina had been at the forefront of eliminating an Iran-based emerging national security threat directed against the United States, Israel, and Jewish people around the world. Simonetti had kept her cool, using her Carabinieri military and police experience and training when she needed them most. And in the aftermath, her humility about her success was an indicator of her true character.

"I was fortunate to have a very capable partner, and I credit all of the training I have received in serving with the Carabinieri," she told anyone familiar with the Iran operation.

Simonetti-Fortina's mentor, Italian (Carabinieri) Major General Sebastiano Comitini, had strongly recommended her to the four-star general who commanded Italy's Carabinieri Corps. Her new role was representing the Carabinieri in Italy's newly established International Crimes Task Force. The Task Force comprised representatives from Austria, Europol, France, Germany, Interpol, Malta, Slovenia, Switzerland, the United Kingdom, and the United States. Its overarching mission was to tackle major international crime affecting Italy.

The Italian Ministry of the Interior (a rough combination of the US Departments of Justice and Homeland Security) had considered forming such an organization for years. But the recent theft of three priceless Caravaggio paintings from the Saint Louis of the French church in Rome ultimately sparked the formation of the Task Force. Sara would serve as one of two Italian representatives, the other a Carabinieri brigadier general, to the new organization.

"She will be perfect for the job," stated General Comitini. "She attended the George C. Marshall Center in Germany, possesses serious law enforcement experience, speaks excellent English, and knows how our American friends operate. There is nobody who can match her in this role."

There was no resistance or subterfuge among the Carabinieri ranks nor within the Ministry of the Interior against Fortina-Simonetti's appointment.

On the US side, however, things were not so clear ... until the US Ambassador weighed in.

The US Ambassador to Italy, Ernest Dimaggio, decided who the two US representatives to the Crimes Task Force would be: Jean O'Connor, the Legal Attaché and the FBI's chief advisor to the Ambassador for law enforcement matters in Italy as well as the chief US representative to Italy for US-Italy law enforcement issues, and US Army Lieutenant Colonel Jake Fortina, the assistant Army Attaché to Italy.

The assignment of a husband and wife to the Task Force from different countries raised some diplomatic eyebrows. But the Ambassador, a non-State Department presidential appointee, made it clear where he stood on the matter. He used his characteristically undiplomatic language in addressing the negative voices.

"I don't give a rip what people think. Fortina is the right person for the job. He's proven himself in working with our international partners in high-stress, high-stakes US national security situations. I respect this Task Force and its mission to counter international crime. But I wouldn't care if Fortina was from the *Salvation* Army. He's got the experience and speaks three of the languages spoken by members of the Task Force, so he's got the job. And there is only one person who can overrule me on this."

While the Ambassador knew he had overstated his position, he also knew that the only people who could effectively overrule him were the Secretary of State and the President of the United States, the final decision maker. The Ambassador had driven home his point, and the issue about assigning Jake Fortina to the new force was never brought up again, neither in the US embassy nor beyond.

***

Jean O'Connor, the US Legal Attaché assigned to US Embassy Rome, listened actively to the Italian Carabinieri lieutenant colonel's situation briefing. A few weeks after the theft of the three Caravaggio paintings, valued at somewhere between 600 million and one billion dollars, Jean O'Connor realized there were precious few clues about the perpetrators.

"One thing is clear," concluded Fortina-Simonetti. "The thieves were top-flight professionals. We are still scouring the church for clues. The church—and the Contarelli chapel in particular—from where the three paintings were stolen is practically sterile. And that is saying a lot for a church that receives thousands of visitors a day."

A couple of the 21 international law enforcement professionals seated around the large conference table chuckled.

"What about the man who was found dead?" asked a representative from France's DGSI (Directorate General for Internal Security), a rough French equivalent of the FBI.

"Our autopsy showed that he had a heart attack. There was a trace of an anesthetic drug in his system, but we have yet to confirm its origin. However, there were no indications that it was a banned substance such as cocaine, which we were targeting in our original analysis. We are still stumped on that one but will continue to work it."

Jean O'Connor was about to ask a question, but then the high-ranking Italian government civilian overseeing the meeting selected another attendee who ended up asking the same question Connor was about to ask.

"Was there any indication this was an inside job?" asked a German representative from Germany's *Bundeskriminalamt* (Federal Criminal Police Office).

"There is certainly that possibility. That is a rock we will continue to look under. So far, we know that it was physically challenging to get high enough up the wall to cut those paintings down. Ladders were the likely means used. The church has them for cleaning, and we are following up with forensics concerning those ladders. There is no doubt that whoever did this had intimate knowledge of the inside of the church and the Contarelli Chapel in particular. Furthermore, to date, we have found no trace evidence. It seems they left none behind."

The questions continued. The answers were few and far between.

CHAPTER 21

THE RECEPTION

JAKE FORTINA WAS DELIGHTED to be attending the German Ambassador to Italy's reception. The reception was in honor of Germany's Unification Day. Each year, on October 3, the day is celebrated in Germany and in German embassies around the world. The day of celebration was established to remember the reunification of the states of East and West Germany in October 1990, after the Berlin Wall fell in November 1989, and with it, eventually, the Soviet Union.

Sara was delighted to be accompanying Jake. She felt blessed to have met and married the five feet, eleven-inch-tall physically fit man with perpetually tanned skin and dark eyes. Jake felt the same thing about the tallish, athletic Italian woman with brown olive-toned skin and auburn hair.

She could be part of my family, thought Jake when he'd first laid eyes on Sara at the George C. Marshall Center in Germany. They had both been students in the Center's Program in Terrorism and Security Studies.

With Jake in his medal-bedecked Army blues uniform and Sara in an elegant black gown, the pair made a striking couple. Although Sara was an Italian Carabinieri officer, she almost always wore civilian attire when attending international diplomatic functions in Rome with Jake. After all, Jake was the attaché and US Army representative to Italy. Besides serving on the law enforcement Task Force, Sara had no official representational role. However, on occasions when the Italian Ministry of Defense would host a reception with Sara as the main invitee, the couple, each in their resplendent formal military uniforms, looked spectacular together. It was not uncommon for their appearance to set crowds abuzz, although each would blush when they got unwanted attention.

With a mile to go through the streets of Rome before reaching the German Embassy, located in an impressive five-story, 18th-century palace on *Via San Martino della Battaglia*, Sara pondered how tonight's reception would go. She had fond memories of Germany and, more specifically, the Bavarian alpine town of Garmisch-Partenkirchen. It was about an hour's drive south of Munich, less than 25 minutes from the Austrian border, and about an hour from Italy's northern border. The George C. Marshall Center was located on the Garmisch side of Garmisch-Partenkirchen. Almost six years after their first meeting there, Jake and Sara were married.

"What are you looking forward to tonight, *caro mio*?" asked Sara as one of the US Defense Attaché's drivers took them to the reception.

"A cold beer and a warm bratwurst with spicy mustard, thank you very much," responded Jake with a smile.

"How about you, *cara mia*?" asked Jake. "What are you looking forward to?"

"I don't think I can top that one! Although I do prefer the sweet mustard over the spicy," Sara laughed.

Pulling up to the main door of the embassy, a German security official stepped up and opened Sara's right-side rear passenger door. Jake got out on his side by himself before another official could arrive to open it. Arriving at the embassy's main entrance, they showed their diplomatic identification and hand-written invitation cards to another German security official. Then they immediately passed through a metal detector. After clearing the metal detector, Jake and Sara entered the event's receiving line, which included the German Ambassador to Italy and his wife.

Departing the receiving line, they entered the large reception area with its impressive and brightly colored fresco ceilings. There were already about sixty guests at the event. Eventually, there would be over 140 guests from over 60 countries, each having a diplomatic presence in Italy.

Guests included some of Italy's more prominent government officials, including from Italy's Ministry of Foreign Affairs and International Cooperation, Ministry of Economic Development, and Ministry of Defense. Italy was a major trading partner of Germany and a highly valued tourist destination (second only to Spain) for German citizens. This reception was one for which the Germans liked—and needed—to roll out the red carpet.

Jake and Sara eyed the crowd. Sara spied an old Carabinieri colleague. She hadn't seen him since her early days of serving in Venice.

Jake and Sara had a standing agreement about separating when attending these receptions. If either wanted to break away from the other to converse with people, that was perfectly OK. Jake had diplomatic business to do. If Sara was constantly with him, it might prevent him from having necessary conversations. At other times it might make sense for the couple to stay together. It depended on where they were and the nature of the event. And sometimes, the choice was not theirs. For example, once inside a Saudi diplomat's residence or embassy, Saudi diplomatic officials were known to have separate social venues for men and women.

"I'm going to wander off and say hi to Dario, an old Carabinieri friend," said Sara.

"Enjoy," responded Jake.

"If I spot the bratwurst stand, I'll bring you one ... with spicy mustard," Sara said with a wink.

"Sounds like a plan," responded Jake. "*Grazie, amore mia.*"

No sooner had Sara departed than a 20-something German *Fräulein* approached Jake with a tray. She supported it from underneath with a toned right arm, adding additional balance with her left hand. The tray held chilled mugs of beer, each about 12 ounces in size.

The young woman was wearing a *dirndl*, the colorful Bavarian *trachten* dress with its décolleté and flattering shape. Her dirndl was blue and white, representing the official colors of Bavaria, Germany's largest and wealthiest state. The young blonde looked like she had just jumped out of a television advertisement for the original *Oktoberfest*.

Munich held the globally popular *Fest* each year from mid-September through early October. Octoberfest visitors consumed over 130,000 kegs of beer at the two-week event. In fact, the Munich Oktoberfest was happening at the very same time as this reception.

The mugs she is carrying are about half the size of a Maß (a one-liter beer stein) *at the real Oktoberfest,* thought Jake. *But I won't turn one down!*

"*Vielen Dank,*" said Jake, remembering some of his basic German as he took one of the mugs off the waitress' tray.

"*Bitte Sehr,*" she replied.

Jake examined the label on the heavy glass mug. He smiled broadly. The words *Augustiner-Bräu* jumped off the label.

Augustiner-Bräu was Munich's oldest independent brewery, producing what many Germans, at least those from Munich, thought was "the best of the best." Augustinian Monks who lived in a monastery outside Munich's city walls began producing the brew in 1328.

Dang, those monks knew what the hell they were doing, thought Fortina as he took some gulps of the chilled brew.

Fortina knew beer should not be drunk like wine or sipped like cognac. Big, robust gulps were the order of the day for a good beer, especially one from a Munich brewery.

Just as he finished taking his swigs of the Bavarian liquid gold and was about to go make some self-introductions, Jake felt a presence off to his side.

"Jake Fortina?" asked the voice.

Jake turned his head.

"Darn straight, my friend! Hennadiy, how the heck are you!"

"I'm great, Jake! And how are you, buddy?"

The two old classmates from the same counter-terrorism course at the Marshall Center warmly shook hands.

Almost simultaneously, they asked each other versions of the same question.

"So, what are you doing here?"

They both laughed out loud.

"You go first," said Jake, smiling.

"I'm the Ukrainian Defense Attaché to Italy," replied Colonel Hennadiy Kovalenko. "Can you imagine the good fortune? And you, Jake?"

Jake chuckled.

"I'm serving as the Assistant Army Attaché to Italy," he replied. "I'm here with my beautiful Italian bride, whom I met at the Marshall Center in our counter-terrorism course."

"You mean Sara Simonetti, the Carabinieri officer? She was in my seminar group in that course!" responded Kovalenko.

"We got married about 20 months ago," responded Fortina. "She's here tonight, and I will bring her over shortly. She'll be delighted to see you."

"You married well, my friend," responded the Ukrainian.

"Tell me about it!" replied Fortina.

As the evening went on, Fortina took the Ukrainian Air Force colonel over to meet Sara. It had been almost eight years since the two had been in the same seminar room at the Marshall Center. It was a fun reunion for all three international military officers.

Before the three old friends departed the reception for the evening, Kovalenko said something to Fortina that would make the evening's encounter even more momentous than it had already been.

"Jake, you and I need to get together soon for lunch, coffee, or a drink. You name it. I will follow up with you."

When he said it, Kovalenko gave Fortina a look that Fortina immediately understood. It was clear that their meeting was going to be about business. Most likely, international security business. They could have chatted all night long at the reception. But they knew there were prying eyes, always around, observing and gauging just how well these two military diplomats might be getting along.

CHAPTER 22

FOUR M

BEAUREGARD BRAGG LIKED THE NAME: Four M. It had a cool ring to it. It would represent the beginnings of something bigger, much bigger. Militia groups were springing up across the country. About half of all US states had one, and some had two or more. The militia groups hid out in America's less traveled, rural, and often remote places, meeting, or training in secret. They would put out what they *thought* were discrete markers on country roads, marking their territory, constructing firing ranges, and "training" to defend America *their* way when the need arose.

It didn't matter that all 50 states had versions of their own laws prohibiting private, unauthorized militias and para-military units from engaging in activities sanctioned for *legal* state militia organizations (read National Guard) or law enforcement. But if they did *not* cross the "*engaging* in activities" line, reserved for legally sanctioned government organizations, these militias could exist unfettered outside or in the law's grey areas.

Some of the more notorious—and largest—groups, like the Oath Keepers and 3 Percenters, who *did* cross that "engaging in activities" line, had some of their members prosecuted after participating in the storming of the US capitol on January 6, 2020. Their prosecutions, however, were not based on state laws. They were based on fundamental federal laws, like those prohibiting damage to federal property or assaults on federal law enforcement officers. In some cases, they were charged with sedition. As of January 2020, the United States government had no federal laws on the books explicitly addressing domestic terrorism.

The Oath Keepers and 3 Percenters, as well as a couple of other similar groups, were national in scale. But what Beauregard Bragg sought to achieve was different: to form a *coalition* of individual, extra-legal state militias, those physically located in and grounded in each state and existing in the grey area of the law.

The Four M coalition—Michigan, Mississippi, Missouri, and Montana—will be a great start, thought Bragg. *I will serve as the Four M's first overall commander, with each state's commander reporting to me. This is serious business, and the Four M coalition needs a serious leadership structure. If this works, we can expand our coalition into states like Idaho and Wyoming and further on from there.*

The Four M's goal was simple: to provide and sell each other weapons and equipment; to support each other with intelligence sharing, mainly targeted against local law enforcement and any FBI agents snooping around in their areas; to share training "best practices"; to advise and support each other with logistics and supplies; and to help each other with recruiting new members to their ranks.

And I will show them what that means, contemplated Bragg. *I will lead by example.*

CHAPTER 23

THE OPERATIONS OFFICER

RETIRED US ARMY SERGEANT FIRST CLASS Blake Conners started out as a superb soldier and then a non-commissioned officer, a sergeant. After an initial three-year enlistment with the US Army's 82d Airborne Division, Conners re-enlisted for the US Army Ranger School and the 75th Ranger Regiment. After six years with the Rangers, he became an Army Green Beret.

Conners' reputation was that he was cool under fire in the most intense combat situations. The army awarded him the Bronze Star with V, for valor, for operations in Afghanistan. But, later, choices in his personal life set him on an embittered path that eventually saw him leave the US military.

Conners desperately wanted to try out for the Army's Special Forces Task Force. The Task Force, like so many other military units, had nicknames. But nicknames or not, Conners knew in the depths of his soul that it was a military unit of which he wanted to be a part.

When he got the call for the arduous Task Force (or TF) selection process, which included an on-foot and timed land navigation course covering forty to fifty miles or more over extremely challenging and variable terrain, Conners was thrilled. However, as Conners was going through the uber-challenging TF selection process, two active TF Operators who served with Conners in previous assignments knew that Conners couldn't hold his liquor. More adversely for Conners, they made the TF recruitment and selection teams aware of Conners' drinking problem.

It also became known to the TF selection team that the Army Military Police were called to Conners' family quarters at Joint Base Lewis-McChord in Washington state some five years prior. A concerned neighbor overheard a domestic dispute between Conners and his wife and called the MPs. The at-times-violent argument occurred while Conners served with the 2d Battalion, 75th Ranger Regiment. The 2nd Battalion, 75th Ranger Regiment, could trace its lineage back to

Normandy and the battalion's heroic scaling of the cliffs at Pointe-du-Hoc.

Conners thought the dispute was a private affair that his "Second Batt"—as Rangers referred to it-- command team didn't need to know about. But unfortunately for Conners, they were notified.

Given the extremely high personal character, military proficiency, and reputational standards for selection into the elite Task Force, these two incidents, no matter how good Conners might have been when the heat of battle was on, severely stacked the odds against him. Ultimately, they derailed his chances of being a proud and highly respected member of the Task Force.

His dream shattered, Conners served his last two-year hitch in the army aimlessly. He did not serve a single day beyond the twenty years needed to retire.

Since the age of 18, the US Army was all Conners had known and all he lived for. When it turned its back on him, the now divorced and downtrodden Conners decided he would turn his back on the Army. He looked for military-centric organizations that would respect his martial talents.

That search led him to the Warner Group, referred to by many as Puchta's private army. A recruiter for the Warner Group made Conners a decent employment offer that Conners declined when he discovered many of his potential Warner teammates were released from a penal colony in exchange for joining the group.

That's not what affected his decision the most, however. The part that most disturbed him was that he had to swear that if he was about to be captured, he would kill himself with a hand grenade. That cut directly against Conners' mantra to always, always fight to the last breath.

Suicide in the face of the enemy is just plain jacked-up, Conners thought to himself.

But then the Wolf's Mr. Fix It, Boris Stepanov, learned that Conners had expressed some interest in the Warner Group. Stepanov, backed by the 17-billion-dollar fortune of the Wolf, knew he could offer Conners a much better deal than servitude with the Warner Group. He contacted Conners and offered him a salary and benefits package Conners could never dream of back home: a car, 150 thousand dollars a year, free health care, and bonuses up to 50 thousand dollars a year for pulling off "big" operations for the Wolf.

Sure, the offer was for the highly responsible, high-pressure position of the Pack's operations officer. A captain or major in most armies, including the US Army, normally filled that position. But the offer was just too good to turn down. It appealed to Conners' confidence and ego, confirming he was fully capable of performing the job's requirements. Conners enthusiastically accepted the offer, thinking he'd hit the jackpot with an organization that appreciated his exceptional military abilities and talents. The money was great, and the personal recognition was even better.

After the successful painting heist in the Contarelli chapel of Rome's *San Luigi dei Francesi* church, Stepanov delivered on his promise of a nice bonus for pulling off a "big" operation. To the phenomenally wealthy Wolf, the bonus barely amounted to chump change. But to Conners, it was proof positive that someone–unlike the Task Force–had recognized his superior military and tactical competence.

Conners was looking forward to celebrating with at least a portion of the $40,000 windfall he had received for his achievement in directing, planning, and executing the greatest art heist of the 21st century.

CHAPTER 24

DECIMATION

LIEUTENANT COLONEL BEAUREGARD BRAGG couldn't believe his good fortune. It had been three months since he had met the Italian Army brigadier general. The disgruntled Italian officer was passed over for promotion to his second star. He had been radically opposed to Italy's "weak" socialist governments, and he was happy when Italy, in 2022, demonstrated that it was lurching back toward a more conservative government.

For the Italian general, "it wasn't quite enough of a move back to fascism, but it's a start," he had told Beauregard Bragg.

The general was a cheerleader for Vasily Puchta, thinking that he was the kind of leader Italy needed: authoritarian, bold, ruthless.

The eccentric Italian officer with the handlebar mustache intrigued Bragg from their first meeting. Brigadier General Constantino Cadorna, assigned to a senior position in Italy's National Armaments Directorate, had mentioned to Bragg that he was very interested in the US Civil War and the Confederacy, specifically Confederate General Braxton Bragg. General Cadorna knew that General Bragg was controversial and judged by many as a brutal leader, at times shooting his own soldiers for indiscipline or cowardice.

"You know, Beau, I have great respect for your distant relative, General Bragg. He was not afraid to do what he had to, to maintain discipline in the ranks."

What surprised Beau Bragg, however, was what the Italian general said next.

"We had to shoot Italian soldiers in World War I for failing to fight. In fact, the very policy and act of decimation began with our Roman legions right here in Italy," said Brigadier General Cadorna.

Impressed by Cadorna's command of the English language, Bragg responded.

"I didn't know the word *decimation* comes from that form of … military punishment."

"Indeed, it does. And our Italian Army used it several times in the Great War. My great-grandfather, General Luigi Cadorna, was forced to resort to decimation more than once. Like your ancestor, my great-grandfather was unfairly judged by many Italians and Italian historians as having been excessively brutal. But in the end, he did what he had to do, to keep good order and discipline in the ranks. Later in his life, he became a highly respected Fascist under Benito Mussolini. Mussolini liked and respected my great-grandfather tremendously. Mussolini made my grandfather a field marshal, but unfortunately, my great-grandfather died too early, in 1928."

"It sounds like he still left quite a legacy," replied Bragg, pleasantly surprised at the general's implication that he was praising fascism.

"He did. I come from a long line of Italian military leaders dating back to the 1850s. More 'recently,' my grandfather Raffaele Cadorna was a partisan general who fought against Fascist forces in Italy in World War II. But it is my great-grandfather Luigi that I respect and admire the most. Had he lived longer, he would have made great contributions to the Fascist government under Mussolini. He is exactly the kind of leader my fellow Italian citizens need today."

There was a pause in the conversation. This was the third meeting between the two military officers. The senior ranking Cadorna had insisted to Bragg in a previous meeting to "call me Constantino." Calling a high-ranking officer by his first name was something rarely, if ever, done in the US military by a lower-ranking officer or soldier. But Bragg was beginning to feel comfortable around the Italian general. He certainly felt more comfortable around Cadorna than around the American military officers back at the embassy.

"So, where do you stand on Fascism, on authoritarian rulers?" asked Bragg.

"I don't shout this from the rooftops," replied Cadorna, chuckling, "but I greatly admire them. Authoritarian leaders are what Italy needs and, I believe, what the world needs. And I am not the only one in Italy who thinks this way. With the national election in 2022, when we voted into office someone the press called a 'far-right' prime minister and the 'most far-right government since World War II,' our country seems to be moving in that direction ... the *right* direction. But it is not moving there fast nor far enough for me."

Bragg shook his head affirmatively.

"I would say the same thing for my country," replied Bragg. "We need strong, very strong leadership. As far as I'm concerned, our US democracy is not working."

"So, Beau, you and I are kindred spirits! We see the political world the same way."

"Indeed, we do, Constantino. Indeed, we do."

CHAPTER 25

THE INVITATION

"HEY, JAKE, HOW ABOUT YOU AND I go for some drinks tonight?" asked Beauregard Bragg as he passed Jake Fortina in the US embassy's main lobby.

Fortina was surprised by the impromptu invitation. He and Lieutenant Colonel Bragg were not exactly best buddies. But they weren't adversaries, either. They worked in separate offices. Fortina worked in the Defense Attaché office, and Bragg worked in the Office of Defense Cooperation. Except for weekly meetings, they ran in different professional and social circles.

Fortina considered the invitation and figured *it couldn't hurt. Maybe I'll learn a thing or two about who Bragg is and what makes him tick.*

"When and where did you have in mind, Beau?" asked Fortina.

"Say, 1830 hours? At Fellini's … you know, that bar about two blocks from my apartment building, on the *via Cassia*?" replied Beau.

Jake was familiar with Fellini's Bar. The bar was named after Federico Fellini, the Italian film director and icon of movies from the 1950s to 1970s. Black and white posters of actors from Fellini movies blanketed the bar's walls.

Fellini's movies were different, but he did direct some good ones, thought Fortina.

Fortina's favorite was *La Dolce Vita* (1960; The Sweet Life). He loved the scene of then-Italian film superstar Marcello Mastroianni and his voluptuous Swedish actress counterpart, Anita Ekberg, standing in Rome's Trevi Fountain. It was perhaps one of the more famous scenes of any Fellini film.

The bar's black and white posters portrayed other Fellini film stars, including a very young Sophia Loren. One poster-sized photo was of the bar owner's smiling grandfather with Fellini, who had apparently made a spontaneous stop at the bar in the late-1950s. Before that stop, the joint was just called "Bar."

Gianluca, the owner, also served as the bar's main bartender. He was friendly to Americans. His sister had emigrated to the US some 25 years earlier.

"Gianni" always told customers that his sister was "doing pretty darn well, living in some swanky Italian neighborhood north of Chicago, on the western shore of Lake Michigan."

"That'll work," Fortina replied to Bragg. "I'll be there. See you at 1830."

Fortina was curious about the invitation. Since he had spotted the Confederate flag inside Bragg's padfolio, Fortina had been conflicted and felt uncomfortable. So, Fortina kept his distance from Bragg socially. But Fortina knew the US military community in Rome was a small one in which people should work and stick together.

How could a fellow soldier, let alone an officer, have or display such a symbol of hate and division? Is that even legal these days?

Fortina pondered the thought.

He knew that Confederate flags had been banned from all Veterans Administration cemeteries since 2016 and public displays on all US military installations since 2020.

But inside of a personal padfolio? Fortina asked himself. *Might make an interesting Supreme Court case. Or w*as *it a joke? A perverted sense of humor, maybe?*

It raised a lot of questions for Fortina.

The last time Fortina saw a Confederate flag belonging to a US Army officer was on the back window of a bright red, mid-sized truck, some ten years prior. Fortina was a captain, studying Farsi at the Defense Language Institute. The truck had cruised slowly by the Institute's main classroom building. The driver's uniform revealed he was a US Army captain.

84

Fortina's knee-jerk reaction to the sight of the big confederate sticker on the truck's back window was to mumble to himself a word of ... strong profanity. And then came the questions, flowing into his consciousness like a raging river, carrying a mix of anger and incredulity.

Why? Why? Why would a US Army leader have—dare to have, even—such a symbol of divisiveness on his personal vehicle? Jake asked himself. *Didn't the Civil War, the bloodiest war in American history that killed more soldiers than the United States lost in World Wars I and II combined, resolve the question of slavery and a divided America? Shouldn't that war have banished the Confederate flag?*

For Fortina, it was a rhetorical question. He believed that's what the war *should* have resolved. But Fortina also knew that the war's aftermath fell woefully short in doing so and that for well over a century, that flag had been—at least publicly—accepted in much of America.

Fortina wasn't a fan of the term "critical race theory" (CRT), mainly because of the word "theory." He thought the term was clumsily named and inadequately explained to the American public.

Fortina thought *the word "theory" implies that the entire concept is debatable, and it sweeps too many non-racist Americans under a racist rug.*

Jake's thoughts about race issues were clear, simple, and historically based.

Why don't we just teach US history? Call it what it is, for Pete's sake: American history! Four million humans were in chattel slavery at the beginning of the Civil War!

Jake shook his head.

Fortina knew his American history. Considering himself a lifelong learner, one of his passions—boring to many people—was to *study* American history. He knew that under President Lincoln's authority, General Grant could have applied a range of punishments to the Southern rebels the day the Civil War ended. However, Lincoln's priority was "to bind up the nation's wounds" and "reunite the country" as a functioning constitutional republic.

Fortina recalled the surrender of Confederate forces by General Robert E. Lee at the Appomattox Courthouse in Virginia in April of 1865. Union General US Grant's simple requirements for surrender placed on the rebellious and now militarily defeated soldiers of the Army of Northern Virginia were to surrender their arms, return home, and "agree not to take up arms against the Government of the United States." That was it. Grant also allowed Confederates who owned their horses to keep them so they could go home and tend to their farms and plant spring crops.

Grant's orders to his victorious Union forces after the bloodiest war in America's history were benevolent and straightforward: "The war is over; the rebels are our countrymen again; and the best sign of rejoicing after the victory will be to abstain from all demonstrations in the field."

Moves by former rebel states toward keeping down former Black slaves, who were declared US citizens in 1865 with the ratification of the 14th Amendment to the Constitution, began almost immediately. Lincoln's assassination and his replacement by a weak and corrupt Andrew Johnson were harbingers of things to come. Not long thereafter, black codes, sharecropping, and the Ku Klux Klan sprung up, followed decades later by Plessy v. Ferguson, Jim Crow laws, the Southern Manifesto, and "separate but equal" state and local policies, mainly–but not exclusively–in the South.

These discriminatory activities, policies, and laws all contributed to seriously delaying full social and economic equality for America's Black citizens, thought Fortina.

As General Grant described in his memoirs, completed just one week before his death in July 1885, he regretted that the South had not been as committed to national healing, "Reconstruction," and true freedom for the emancipated slaves as he and most Union veterans were. It would take until June 2020 for the state of Mississippi to finally remove the symbol of hate, division, and to many people, white supremacy fluttering on the dome of its state capitol.

This is gonna be one hell of an interesting get-together tonight, thought Fortina.

CHAPTER 26

TRUTH SERUM

JAKE FORTINA ARRIVED AT FELLINI'S BAR on time. Fortina looked through the barely transparent, smoked glass entrance door. Fortina observed Beau Bragg seated at a small round table for two, holding a drink. Fortina did not know that Bragg had been there for forty-five minutes already and was halfway through his third whiskey and coke.

It appeared Bragg was the only customer in the place. Fellini's had a shiny mahogany bar and could seat up to 40 people around small, four-top tables. It was Rome, so most people wouldn't start coming in until about 9:30 or 10 p.m. The latest would come in around 10:30 or 11 p.m. Giancarlo "Gianni" (pronounced Johnny), the bar's owner, normally closed around 1 a.m., sometimes a bit later if he had a good crowd.

Fortina opened the door and walked toward Bragg.

"Hey Jake, have a seat," said Bragg.

Before seating himself, Fortina nodded to the stout, 50-something Gianni standing behind the bar.

"*Buona sera*," said Gianni, beating Fortina to the punch.

"*Buona sera, signore*," responded Fortina.

Fortina and Bragg exchanged pleasantries as Gianni approached the table.

"What would you like, sir," asked Gianni of Fortina in English.

"I'd like a glass of the house red wine, a bottle of noncarbonated water, and a ham and cheese *panino, per favore*," replied Fortina in Italian.

"*Con piacere*," responded Gianni in Italian, then adding in English, "With pleasure."

Fortina had adopted the Italian tradition of always ordering water (served without ice) with his drinks or meal. Although potable everywhere in Italy (unless specifically indicated to the contrary), restaurant water was rarely served from the tap unless patrons specifically asked for it *dalla spina*. Two choices of bottled water were always offered: carbonated and uncarbonated. Fortina preferred uncarbonated. Fortina understood that water helped with hydration and, truth be told, could even help stave off a state of drunkenness and, ultimately, stupidity. If the water helped dilute the alcohol, the sandwich would help absorb it.

Fortina had attended well over a hundred official diplomatic receptions and dinners in Baku and Paris over a combined five-year period. He knew that at most events (less so in Baku), alcohol usually flowed freely. But if its intake was not prudently managed, it could make one diplomatically ineffective or worse. As a military attaché, Fortina knew he had to keep his observation and "bullshit-filtration" skills sharp. Too much alcohol and those skills significantly diminished. Fortina always avoided drinking to the point of getting tipsy. Except for those couple of occasions during his much younger "stupid years." He was not proud of them.

"You eating anything, Beau?" asked Fortina.

"Nah," Bragg burped. "I'm going with a liquid diet tonight."

Fortina thought Bragg was joking. He hadn't heard talk like that since he was a lieutenant. Turned out Bragg was serious.

After Bragg washed down another drink, Fortina took a breath to ask Bragg about the Confederate flag he had seen stuck to the inside of Bragg's padfolio. But Bragg engaged first.

"So, where do you call home, Jake?"

"Michigan," responded Fortina.

"Michigan, huh?" replied Bragg. "I've heard they've got some good militia up there."

"You mean ... the National Guard?" responded Fortina. "Yes, the Michigan National Guard is an exceptional organization."

Fortina knew something about the Michigan National Guard. He'd met its commander at a one-week senior executive seminar at the George C. Marshall Center for European Security Studies in Germany. He was familiar with the Guard's training area near Grayling and had also met some of its soldiers in Iraq.

"No, I'm talkin' about a real militia," said Bragg. "Not government-owned weekend warriors. Folks who are ready to take up arms and defend their state and country when things get stupid."

Fortina had never heard the term "government-owned weekend warriors." He was surprised to hear it from an officer who served in the National Guard. Fortina's only thoughts of the National Guard were that since the late 1990s, the National Guard had deployed thousands upon thousands of soldiers and airmen to places like Bosnia-Herzegovina and Kosovo as enforcers of the international peace, as well as to Afghanistan and Iraq after 9-11. According to the reports during the conflict, the National Guard played a pivotal role in each conflict, accounting for about 45% of the total force sent to Iraq and Afghanistan and more than 18% of the casualties among US forces. Almost 1,000 National Guard men and women had made the ultimate sacrifice in Afghanistan and Iraq. Tens of thousands had also served in the Balkan Wars and conflicts of the late 1990s and early 2000s. Fortina knew full well there was no way the United States could have executed a simultaneous two-war strategy without the National Guard.

"Stupid? As in …?" responded Fortina searchingly.

"Stupid, as in the feds wanting to take our guns or giving those Black Lives Matter people a pass while they loot, burn, and destroy our country." Bragg was just warming up. "But then they turn around and prosecute those patriots who peacefully tried to enter the capitol to stop the steal of the election." Bragg's arms went wide in a questioning, frustrated gesture.

Well, thought Fortina, *Bragg does not appear to be holding back.*

"Hundreds if not thousands of BLM and Antifa people who rioted, destroyed, or stole property in the summer of 2020 have been prosecuted," replied Fortina calmly. "Besides, how is it that the very same people who complain about federal overreach into the affairs of states and cities expect the feds to intervene at the first bit of rioting–or even protesting–in our cities?"

Bragg ignored the comment and the question.

"The feds' reaction to the peaceful Capitol demonstration by real American patriots was a huge overreaction by those socialist bastards who stood–and still stand–in the way of making American great again."

With his previous statement ignored, Fortina gave a slight non-committal nod–not an "I agree with you nod" but an "I am listening" nod–in return.

"We got some good militia in Mississippi, too," continued Bragg.

"I understand you served in the National Guard there?" offered Fortina, trying to take the subject down another path.

"Yep, sure did, until I got the call for this crazy assignment. It's not one I could easily turn down. Seems there was serious political pressure at the state level to get me here."

"I wouldn't have any idea," responded Fortina.

"Yep, there was. I'm not going back to the Guard after this assignment, though." He paused to take a swig of his drink. "I do speak a little I-talian (Beau pronounced it "eye"-talian, placing a huge accent on the "I"), so that's why I got the call to active duty." He shrugged. "Rome is not that bad of a place, actually, except for the crazy-ass drivers ... and I mean *crazy*. But there sure as hell is no good huntin' and fishin' around here like back home." He looked wistfully at his drink before shrugging and taking another swig.

"Nope, not near Rome," replied Fortina. Jake was an avid fly fisherman and was glad he finally had something he could agree with Bragg on. But Fortina knew that if Bragg met the right people and learned about the right places to go, both good hunting and fishing were possible in Italy. Fortina had fly-fished for world-class grayling in the Italian alpine regions. He'd also fly-fished in the Piedmont region, not far from the French-Italian Alps. Fortina had also fished in Slovenia, which bordered northeastern Italy. The fishing in Slovenia rivaled the best places in the United States for catching rainbow trout and grayling. But Fortina was not exactly interested in sharing that information with Bragg since he realized Fortina was in no mood and, increasingly, in no condition to hear it.

Bragg gulped down his fifth whiskey and coke. This latest one was a double shot of whiskey into an otherwise empty stomach.

He looked at Fortina squarely and asked, "Hey man, you want a *grappa?*"

Grappa is a popular grape-based Italian brandy that varies between 35 and 60 percent alcohol content. The alcohol content depended on who was making it, a licensed distillery or grandpa down the street.

Since Bragg had arrived in Rome a few months before Fortina, it was not surprising that Bragg had already sampled the strong Italian drink.

"No, thanks. But I *will* have a *limoncello*," responded Fortina.

Limoncello, as the name implies, was a lemon-based alcoholic drink first distilled on the Italian island of Capri, home to an abundance of lemon trees that produced lemons the size of grapefruit. Limoncello's alcoholic content is about half that of grappa.

"Aw, limoncello is for lightweights," responded Bragg.

Fortina ignored the comment as Bragg signaled to Gianni. Bragg knew Gianni spoke good English, so he ordered the two drinks in English.

Within minutes, Gianni brought over two shot glasses, one filled with room-temperature grappa and the other chilled limoncello. Italians considered both drinks a *digestivo* or "digestive," believing they were an "aid to digestion" after meals, particularly heavy meals consumed at Sunday family get-togethers. Those big Sunday meals were still a tradition for many families in Italy.

Fortina jokingly referred to Italian digestives as Drano, the American clot-busting product used to clear clogged drains and pipes typically found under kitchen sinks.

Gotta give the Italians credit, Fortina often mused. *The Italian digestive concept seems to work pretty darn well.*

By this point, Fortina figured Bragg had already washed down several drinks beyond the ones he'd witnessed. Fortina had yet to observe Bragg consume a single morsel of food or drink any water.

He's gonna have one helluva headache tomorrow, thought Fortina.

Fortina could not believe what he'd heard so far, and frankly, it was challenging to keep his composure as his stomach began to churn at Bragg's crazy talk. It was becoming clear that the alcohol that Bragg had consumed was acting as some kind of truth serum.

Not that what Bragg is saying is true, thought Fortina, *but the booze is bringing out Bragg's true, innermost beliefs and feelings.*

Fortina took a final bite of his sandwich. Looking at Bragg, Fortina wondered where this conversation would go next. He did not have to wait long to find out.

As he chewed, Bragg burst out, "Kennedy upset the status quo, with blacks in their place and whites in theirs."

"You mean John Kennedy?" Jake got an absent nod for an answer. "And when you say 'status quo,' do you mean the separate-but-equal policy of many Southern states of that day?" asked Fortina.

"Exactly," replied Bragg emphatically. "Them in their place and us in ours. Nothin' *unequal* about that. Just *separate,*" he waved his hands expansively, "and equal."

Fortina knew the "separate-but-equal" phrase was derived from a Louisiana law of 1890 (although the original law used the phrase "equal but separate"). The legal doctrine was confirmed in the Plessy v. Ferguson Supreme Court decision of 1896, which essentially sanctioned state-sponsored segregation. The case stemmed from an 1892 incident where Black American train passenger Homer Plessy refused to sit in a car designated for "colored people only."

"Ever hear of Plessy versus Ferguson?" asked Fortina.

"Plessy, *who*?" replied Bragg. "Never heard of it. Like I could give a shit about some court case."

The two men took a long, awkward look at each other.

The conversation then pivoted, with Bragg mentioning John Kennedy's brother, Robert Kennedy.

"His brother Bobby Kennedy was no better. He got what he deserved in 1968. That guy that shot him…what's his name…?"

"Sirhan?" replied Fortina.

"Yeah, that guy," continued Bragg. "That A-rab said he shot Robert Kennedy because Kennedy supported Israel in the Arab-Israeli war of 1967. Hell, in the South, there were a whole bunch of Americans—at least white ones—who woulda shot that liberal son-of-a-bitch Robert Kennedy themselves."

"Why's that?" asked Fortina.

"Because he *way* overstepped his bounds as Attorney General under that jackass brother of his, JFK. Robert Kennedy did his brother's bidding by trying to desegregate schools in the South. Our schools were just fine." Bragg's voice got louder. "We got along just fine with them n…"

As drunk as he was, Bragg caught himself, not saying the ugly word Fortina was expecting to roll off Bragg's tongue.

"…with them colored people," continued Bragg.

The statement was the first time in the conversation when Bragg even remotely tried—or was able—to exert a measure of self-control.

"They *had* their freedom, and we had ours." He sounded almost reasonable until he continued. "We did not need Kennedy interfering with our perfectly normal and happy way of life," Bragg finished, the subdued anger evident in the clipped twang of his speech.

"No kiddin'?" was all Fortina could manage.

Fortina figured what he said mattered little since Bragg seemed to be getting to the point of drunkenness whereby Bragg would not remember his hate-laden words—nor Fortina's responses—the next day. The thought also occurred to Fortina that Bragg just might be testing Fortina to see if Fortina had similar views to his own.

After Bragg mentioned Robert Kennedy's assassination, and given what Fortina had been hearing, Fortina thought Bragg would try to justify the assassination of Martin Luther King, too. The world-famous Black civil rights leader had died at the hand of a White gunman, James Earl Ray, in the city of Memphis in that tumultuous spring of 1968. King's assassination led to an even more turbulent and violent summer of '68 throughout the United States. But Bragg did not mention King.

Probably because he's getting too stinkin' drunk to remember, thought Fortina.

Fortina knew that many, if not most, White Southerners (and many in the north) were not enamored with the forced integration of public schools, so Bragg's comments provided no shock as far as that was concerned. But what was disturbing was Bragg's callous attitude about two assassinated American political leaders.

But then came the ultimate Beauregard Bragg disclosure.

"Hell, when his brother, the President, got shot, my grandparents, who were Mississippi landowners at the time, they cheered." Bragg almost laughed.

Fortina couldn't believe what he'd just heard and wanted to be sure he'd heard it correctly.

"You mean when President John Kennedy was assassinated ... your grandparents *cheered*?" asked Fortina.

"Yep, when JFK got taken down by that ole grassy knoll," responded Bragg with a chilling chuckle, "everybody in the Bragg clan was happy."

He was referring to the small, often-referred-to hillock in downtown Dallas near the assassination. The "grassy knoll" and the activity on and around it at the time of John Kennedy's assassination had become the subject of much speculation, conspiracies, and many inquiries and investigations.

Fortina sat stunned. It was all he could do to look Bragg in the eye as anger built in his chest.

For the first time in the conversation, Fortina did not know what to say. But Bragg did.

"And what about all this Army woke shit?" asked Bragg.

"What is *woke shit*, exactly, Beau?" asked Fortina, the anger leaking out in his tone. He took a deep breath to steady himself as Bragg responded.

"All the bullshit the Army worries about, like making a big deal about inclusivity, like bending over backward to accommodate colored people and queers and ragheads. It's the reason I'm leaving the Army after this tour. You know what I mean, don't ya, Jake?"

"Actually, I don't," responded Fortina, his patience for this man and conversation expended.

Fortina's thoughts flashed to the US Army of the 1950s. Already it was far ahead of the rest of the country in terms of equal opportunity and racial integration. Fortina thought of Colin Powell, the senior ranking Army general of Powell's day and a future Secretary of State. Fortina thought of Sergeant First Class Manny Alvarez, his current assistant, a man Fortina loved and respected. Fortina thought of Sergeant Dennis M. King, the Black engineer sergeant on the Special Forces team Fortina had led. King was recommended for, and awarded, the Bronze Star with V device. Fortina thought of family stories passed down by his great-grandfather about early 20th-century Italians (and other southern Europeans, like the Portuguese and Spanish) who were looked upon as lazy, lower life forms by their northern European and fellow American citizens.

"They called us *dago*," his grandfather had said. "Every day, we had to prove that we worked every bit as hard if not harder than they did—and that we were just as clever—to achieve the American dream."

I'm proud of my Army, a meritocracy and brilliant mosaic of Americans, where respect and every promotion must be earned. And where dignity and respect for each other matter. In Beauregard Bragg's Army, there is no way Powell would have made it beyond the rank of lieutenant, thought Fortina. *Hell, he probably would have been unjustly court-martialed, just like Jackie Robinson.*

Fortina had heard enough. Fortina, who had placed third in his weight class in West Point's annual Brigade Open Boxing Championship, visualized grabbing Bragg by the shirt collar, jerking him up from his chair, and punching him in the face. But Fortina, whose rebellious spirit, even at 40, still required occasional tamping down, knew that was an irrational and juvenile thought.

With Bragg as drunk as he is, it wouldn't be a fair fight either, he thought.

Besides, Fortina had already received a Letter of Counseling after punching out a derelict Army captain in Afghanistan. That letter had almost kept Fortina from being promoted to lieutenant colonel.

Fortina got up from the table and walked over to Gianni. Gianni, standing behind the beer taps, greeted Fortina with a smile.

"I'll take care of the bill," said Fortina as he pulled out a credit card.

As he paid, Fortina looked at Gianni. Fortina's eyes conveyed empathy.

"I hope we weren't too loud," said Fortina.

Two customers had come into the bar within the previous few minutes. Fortunately, they didn't seem overly concerned with the boisterous Americans. Being located close to an international diplomatic enclave on the via Cassia, it was known by locals that Americans occasionally hung out at Fellini's. Most Americans were quiet and subdued, but occasionally their voices would get louder than anyone's in the bar.

"Thank you, sir," said Gianni, "it's all good. I think you came in once before, right? When we had a full house? I hope to see you back here again. You are welcome any time."

"*Grazie, signore*," replied Fortina. "Yes, I came here once before with my beautiful Florentine bride. You can't miss her."

"I didn't," chuckled Gianni with a wink.

Fortina laughed.

"But remember, she *is* a Carabinieri officer," Fortina winked.

Both men laughed out loud.

Fortina walked back to the table.

Looking down at the still-seated Bragg, laying back in his chair with legs spread-eagled, Fortina said, "I think it's time to go, Beau."

"Don't you want another drink?" asked Bragg.

"Nope. I'm good. Let's go."

Bragg reluctantly stood up. Bragg may have wanted another drink, but Fortina knew Bragg was already two or three over the line.

Stepping outside, Fortina stood close to the shaky Bragg in the event Bragg lost his footing. Fortina walked a few steps with Bragg to confirm he could move under his own power without face-planting.

Bragg passed the test, but not exactly with flying colors.

"Look, man, I got this," slurred Bragg, looking back at Fortina.

"I believe you do," replied Fortina.

Fortina was not lying. He had learned during his pre-command training–before taking command of an Army Special Forces A-Team– that it was difficult to spot alcoholics in the Army's ranks. Some soldiers developed a high tolerance for large amounts of alcohol. Others learned to cover their excessive drinking by always making sure they showed up at work in the morning sober. To do otherwise might blemish their reputations and careers, the very things that paid for their heavy drinking habits.

Bragg turned around and walked toward his apartment. Fortina judged it best to fall a bit behind and follow Bragg to make sure he safely reached his apartment building. Once Fortina saw Bragg reach the apartment building's front door, Fortina turned around and headed back to the via Cassia. He found a taxi stand and was soon on his way to his home, farther north of Rome.

What Fortina did *not* witness was Bragg stumbling his way up the stairwell and into his cold, sparsely furnished apartment. Bragg's ex-wife, unable to live with the heavy drinking and his extreme views on race, had left him some four years earlier.

Alone in his apartment, Bragg sat on his couch, helped himself to more whiskey, and blacked out.

CHAPTER 27

THAT LONER AMERICAN GUY

JAKE FORTINA ARRIVED HOME by taxi. It was 8:37 p.m. when he walked through the penthouse apartment door. Sara was seated in the living room.

"How'd it go? How about I make you some *spaghettata*?" asked Sara, referring to the simple garlic, olive oil, and red pepper spaghetti dish that Sara knew Jake loved.

"I had a sandwich at the bar, but that pasta sounds wonderful," replied Jake. "I'd be happy to make it for us."

"Nope, Jake, I got this," Sara said, moving to the kitchen. "But if you could find us a bottle of red wine, I'd appreciate it." She started pulling ingredients from the cabinets. "I want to hear all about your time with that loner American guy."

Jake and Sara had promised each other that they would not bring their work home, and, in many cases, they were prohibited from doing so. The security classification of some of their work demanded that it remain classified as "US only" or "Italy only." In this case, Sara's interest was purely personal. She thought this American guy was a strange bird. Sarah had become friends with some of the wives of the military attachés, and they occasionally gossiped about Beauregard Bragg.

Jake poured Sara and himself a modest glass of *Valpolicella* wine. Jake thought the medium-bodied red wine was a good match that wouldn't overpower the simple *spaghettata* dish. He'd discovered the Veneto region Valpolicella during his early days in Vicenza. Jake's American father, of Sicilian heritage, had always touted the health benefits of consuming red wine *in moderation*.

While Sara prepared the pasta at the stove, Jake recounted much of the entire evening's discussion with Beauregard Bragg.

Sara was not surprised at most of what Jake had said. She knew America had dealt with racism for a long time. In the past ten years or so, it seemed to be resurging. However, she had limited knowledge of the racially tumultuous American '60s because she was born in the mid-'80s.

Then Sara dropped a comment that Jake was not expecting.

"You know, Jake," she glanced over her shoulder at him, "we have racist people in Italy, too."

"*Racist?*" asked Jake incredulously.

"Yes, racist. Maybe it's not the same as in the US," she paused to consider, "I don't know, but we do have racism here." Sara sliced garlic cloves as she continued, "much of it emerged from the backlash to the waves of Black and Arab immigrants, mainly from North Africa, landing on our southern shores at all hours of the day and night over the past few years." Another considering pause. "Well, at least those who survived the journey across the Med landed on our shores or were fortunate to be picked up at sea by Italian naval forces. At the same time, we have many, many Italians who have employed and even taken people of color into their homes. But to say Italy is devoid of racism would be wrong." She turned to him, "furthermore, to say Europe is completely devoid of it would be wrong, too."

"Dang, Sara, I guess if I had really thought about it and done some research, I might have reached a similar conclusion. But you're Italian, so I'll take what you say to the bank." He smiled at his beautiful wife as she moved around the kitchen.

"By the way, *cara mia*, your English is getting *really* good," added Jake.

"How so?" responded Sara, sprinkling sea salt into the pasta water.

"You used the word 'devoid.' Heck, I didn't use that word until I was about 35." The recently-turned-40 Jake chuckled.

Sara, standing at the stove with her left hand on her hip, wearing tight blue jeans and a simple white V-neck t-shirt, turned and looked lovingly at Jake.

Jake thought how blessed he was to be married to this bright, passionate, beautiful, and athletic woman.

"Are you trying to flatter me?" she asked.

"Maybe ... just maybe," responded Jake, grinning. "Wait. Let me answer that differently," he continued. "Yes, I am trying to flatter you. But let me say that you are an exceptional lady and truly beautiful ... and I'm not saying that because you are making me a dish of my favorite pasta."

"Speaking of your special pasta, how hungry are you *really*, Jake?" Her eyes were hooded. "Because at this moment, I'm not that hungry." Sara locked eyes with Jake. "This pasta can wait," she said, turning off the stove. Warmth spread from her belly as she sashayed over to Jake, who stood up from the kitchen table.

Sara drew close enough to reach around his waist. She grasped his shirt in her hands and pulled him roughly against her.

Jake warmly embraced her, matching her heat in his kiss.

Sara, flushed from his attentions, heart pounding in time with his, took Jake's hand, broke their kiss, and pulled him to the bedroom.

CHAPTER 28

FADING

THE RUSSIAN PRESIDENT'S POPULARITY was in decline. But this was not something you could measure by some poll. In a country where a poll might have some degree of legitimacy, one could–at least marginally–depend on the results, with the almost standard "plus or minus three or four percent accuracy" caveat. But not in Russia. Such a poll would never be sanctioned by the government. If, by some chance, a "poll" was to be government-sanctioned, that normally meant one could not trust its results.

The reasons for Puchta's decline were many. He had made a strategic blunder in leading Russia to an illegal and brutal war against Ukraine. He had severely damaged Russia's economy and depleted its armed forces. On more than one occasion, he had called for the conscription of young men for his losing military cause, only to see them try to escape Russia in droves rather than serve as cannon fodder in a senseless conflict. No one knew the precise number, but over one hundred thousand Russian boys and men had been estimated to have died in the war, as did tens of thousands of Ukrainians, both military and civilian.

Unless he was getting a piece of the financial action, Puchta had tried to make it hard for wealthy oligarchs to thrive outside Russia. Inside Russia, Puchta was far more successful, having had many of them murdered for either getting in his way or not fully supporting his cause.

Puchta had exposed Russia's military weaknesses to the eyes of the world. Because of the Ukraine debacle, many oligarchs hated or distrusted Puchta. Russian mothers despised him. Young men feared him. It had been almost a quarter century since Puchta was voted into power as Russia's leader. Even the Russian people, who seemed to have a proclivity for needing or wanting an authoritarian ruler, believed it was time for Puchta to go.

The Wolf pondered this, knowing his time to return to Russia was drawing near. With Puchta's popularity at rock bottom, he knew the great majority of Russian people wanted a replacement.

"My time is approaching," he said to his confidant, Boris Stepanov. "I must return to Russia within the next few months. Over half of the wealthiest men at the meeting with Puchta on the eve of the war with Ukraine support my assuming the presidency. The Russian people know the great things I have accomplished. After Puchta, I am the wealthiest Russian alive. The economically struggling people of Russia will support me as the Americans did their supposedly wealthy American president in 2016. I will have great power, and Russia will go the way I choose for it to go. I will make Russia great again."

CHAPTER 29

SLEEPLESS IN ROME

IT WAS ALMOST 4 A.M. Jake Fortina didn't need to ask himself why he was wide awake. Fortina knew why. Everything hateful, everything against US Army values, everything against his notions of "duty, honor, country," everything against his commissioning oath, including "defend the Constitution of the United States of America, against *all* enemies, foreign and domestic," *everything* that Beau Bragg had said the night before kept coming back to Fortina. Each hate-oozing word and statement that had come from Bragg's mouth and slurred speech gave Fortina a jolt.

The 4 a.m. wakeups had happened before. Fortina's anguish and pain from losing his wife Faith, daughter Kimberly and son Jake, Jr. on a rainy Texas road woke him up often. The wakeups continued for years after his precious family had departed this earth. His realization that his Army Special Forces A-Team had been compromised in the Korengal Valley and was about to be attacked by a greatly outnumbering force woke him up, too. The loss of Sergeant First Class Johnson in that same ugly, God-forsaken valley and the wounding of three of his soldiers during his first combat tour caused him to sometimes break into a sweat and sit bolt upright in his bed.

Those events all tugged and pulled Fortina away from what should have otherwise been restful sleep. Once awake, with thoughts about past crises and traumatic events having begun, there was no turning back. He was not returning to restful slumber.

The age-old military trick for falling quickly asleep that he'd learned early in his career didn't work, either. He'd tried mentally saying to himself, "Don't think, don't think, don't think," until he fell asleep. It didn't work.

What woke him and kept him up on this calm morning in his and Sara's apartment was different. Nobody had died. Nobody had gotten maimed. There was no tragic, soul-crushing loss of the people he'd held dearest on the planet.

It was only deep and troubling concerns about what he'd heard from a senior officer in the United States Army, *one who was at one time—and perhaps might be again*, thought Fortina, *responsible for leading American soldiers.*

What kept Fortina up more were his thoughts about *what to do*. And moreover, *how* to do it. This situation was not like when he had observed an Infantry School classmate, an Army second lieutenant (like Fortina at the time), cheating on an infantry tactics test. In that case, Fortina simply went straight to the cheating officer and confronted him.

Convinced that the officer was sufficiently ashamed and sincere in his willingness to change, that was all Fortina decided he needed to do.

Out in the real Army, thought Fortina, unlike at West Point where Fortina would have been duty bound to report an offending fellow cadet, *Army officers, especially green-behind-the-ears junior Army officers, police themselves. If the offending teammate does not correct him or herself, that's another matter.*

No, this situation concerning Beauregard Bragg was different. Jake perceived it to be a deep and persistent problem, resistant to anything Jake might say or suggest. Jake wrestled with the situation as he left his apartment. It was 6:49 a.m. He was still deliberating with himself about Bragg when he drove through the US Marine-guarded gate and onto the US embassy grounds at 7:13 a.m.

Soon, Jake Fortina would know what to do.

CHAPTER 30

A STRATEGIC RESERVE

"I NEED A STRATEGIC RESERVE for my plans, my vision," said the Wolf to his personal chief of staff and confidant, Boris Stepanov.

"What do you *mean* by strategic reserve?" asked Stepanov.

"I need the ability to threaten or influence NATO and its failing Western democracies at a time and place of my choosing," answered the Wolf.

Boris Stepanov was frustrated. After twenty years of being close to the Wolf, Stepanov normally knew what Volkov would say before he said it. This time, he didn't know what the hell the Wolf was trying to say.

"What kind of strategic reserve are you considering?" asked Stepanov.

"Do you recall those suitcase nukes that we procured from that former nuclear engineer? What was his name? Popov? And his former FSB partner, Koz-something?" asked the Wolf. "It was about fifteen years ago or so."

Stepanov chuckled at the Wolf's use of the word "procured". It made it sound like Stepanov had conducted some kind of upright business deal which concluded with a handshake and celebratory vodka. Instead, Popov and Kozlov, who thought they were about to earn $2 million for selling all five of the suitcase nukes, ended up in the iron safe that had formerly stored the well-hidden nukes.

Lucky for them, thought Stepanov, *we killed those idiots before stuffing them in that safe.*

"I do. They are still secure and viable."

"I want to put two of them in play," replied the Wolf.

"Put them into play as in ... set them off?"

"Yes and no," said the Wolf.

I'm losing my touch with this guy, thought Stepanov. *This conversation is about as abstract as I've had with Volkov. What's he thinking?*

Both men looked at each other. They were equally poker-faced. The Wolf knew he had Stepanov's attention.

"You mean…," said Stepanov. Before he could finish, the Wolf interrupted him.

"I mean, I want one low-yield nuke to be pre-positioned in Finland, in a remote location, up in the northern part of the country. At the right time, we will set that nuclear weapon off with minimal–and preferably no–damage to infrastructure and people." He considered a moment. "I think that is possible. Finland is one of the least densely populated countries on the planet. We'll need to ensure everything is right, including prevailing winds. But Finland, the United States, NATO, and the world will know that a nuke–although a small one–went off in Finland, on NATO soil. We'll frame our buddy."

The Wolf paused and laughed.

Stepanov figured he knew to which "buddy" the Wolf was referred, but he wanted to be sure.

"Which buddy?" he asked.

"You know, the so-called Russian *president*," continued the Wolf, "and we'll have most of the world thinking he did it. The Cyberkid will be magnificent in developing a strategic cyber and social media campaign to make sure everybody thinks that crazy KGB sonofabitch did it."

The Wolf paused. Stepanov nodded his head affirmatively.

"And the second nuke?" asked Stepanov.

"I want it brought to Italy, to the Farm," said the Wolf, referring to his "Farm" and Pack operations center southeast of Rome. It was the same place from where Blake Conners had directed the great Caravaggio painting heist in Rome's San Luigi dei Francesi church.

"And?" asked Stepanov.

"And…if I need to, I want to deploy it against the US Navy stationed in Italy," said the Wolf. "I also want it under our immediate control in case the Italians get stupid, more stupid than they have been. I have some thoughts, from nuclear blackmail to setting one off in Italy after I land in Moscow. Keeping it safely hidden in Russia does not enhance my options."

The men paused again.

"And what about the other three suitcase nukes?" asked Stepanov.

"We keep them in Russia, ready for my return. They will add options for my future courses of action against NATO and the West," a wide grin stretched across the Wolf's face.

CHAPTER 31

THE TALK

JAKE FORTINA WAS UNCHARACTERISTICALLY ANXIOUS as he waited outside the senior Army officer's door. Fortina knew he was about to have a tough conversation with Colonel Seaton. The conversation would be about what Fortina had heard from another US Army officer and peers within the US embassy's ranks.

Jake Fortina never wanted to be thought of as a snitch. West Point's honor code, at least when Fortina was a cadet there, had stated, "Cadets will not lie, cheat or steal, nor tolerate those who do." Fortunately, he never witnessed nor had firsthand information of anyone who violated the Honor Code while he was at the academy. But he occasionally wondered if he would have turned someone in for a violation. It was more Jake's rebellious style to have confronted that individual directly and gotten them to change their ways.

Fortina again thought about his Infantry Officer's Basic Course days at Fort Moore (formerly Fort Benning), Georgia. During his first months in the Army, newly minted second lieutenant Jake Fortina was taking a written exam on infantry small unit tactics. While taking the exam, he noticed a classmate seated to his right front, copying exam answers off another officer. After the class, Fortina confronted his fellow lieutenant about what Fortina had observed.

"Hey, man, I saw what you were doing during the exam," he began. "That wasn't right. But you know that, don't you?"

Fortina observed the officer's countenance. The officer's face turned a pale white. The 23-year-old newly commissioned Army officer knew he'd been caught red-handed. His facial expression conveyed shame and fear.

"Are you going to say anything to anybody, Jake?" asked the young officer. "I'm sorry, man, it was wrong … and I know it was wrong."

The essence of a Biblical passage flashed into Jake's thoughts: mercy over judgment. Jake looked at his fellow soldier.

"Nah," he replied. "I'm sure it will never happen again, right?"

"You are right, Jake. It won't," replied the young officer. "I swear, man."

"I believe you, man," replied Fortina.

Fortina indeed believed the officer. Five years later, out in the Army, Fortina came across the same officer again. The officer, then a captain, had a stellar reputation as a strong leader with unshakeable integrity.

But this situation concerning Lieutenant Colonel Beauregard Bragg felt different. Fortina had lost a lot of sleep thinking and praying about it. Sure, Bragg's words were filled with hate. But Bragg had not actually *done* anything wrong.

Nonetheless, the thought kept coming back to Fortina: *almost everything Bragg told me that night at Fellini's ran directly counter to the Army values of loyalty, respect, and integrity.*

Fortina thought about another Army value but not as it applied to Bragg, but rather, as it applied to Fortina himself. That value was personal courage and, moreover, *moral* courage. Jake had demonstrated personal and physical courage in combat, but now he needed to show it differently.

The words of the Holocaust survivor Ellie Wiesel kept popping into Fortina's thoughts.

"The opposite of love is not hate; it's indifference. The opposite of art is not ugliness; it's indifference. The opposite of faith is not heresy; it's indifference. And the opposite of life is not death; it's indifference."

Fortina considered those words.

I will not be indifferent, he thought.

Jake believed deep in his soul he needed to say something to someone who mattered. That someone who mattered, fortunately for Jake, was his immediate boss, the US Army Attaché to Italy, Colonel Marion Seaton. Fortina respected Seaton and felt blessed that Seaton—a former artillery officer and now an Army Foreign Area Officer—was his supervisor.

Colonel Seaton has a backbone of steel, the integrity of Abraham Lincoln, and a heart of gold, Fortina thought.

As Jake waited outside the colonel's office, he resolved to tell Seaton *almost* everything he'd heard from Lieutenant Colonel Beauregard Bragg. The part he would leave out was Bragg's heavy drinking. The drinking concerned Jake, but Fortina thought mentioning the drinking to Seaton would be a cheap shot at Bragg. After all, Jake had only observed the heavy drinking on one occasion, that one night at Fellini's Bar.

Anybody can have a rough night now and again, thought Jake.

And truth be told, Jake was impressed how Bragg got himself home as handily as he did after consuming a boatload of alcohol. But as the to the rest—Jake's sighting of the confederate flag inside Bragg's padfolio, Bragg's white supremacist comments, his praise of the assassination of two national political leaders in America, and his worship of burgeoning militia forces in America—Jake would not hold back.

Finally, Colonel Seaton's door opened.

"C'mon in, Jake. Sit down and tell me what's on our mind," began Seaton.

"Sir, there are some things I need to talk to you about concerning Lieutenant Colonel Bragg," began Fortina. "My concerns began when I saw this Confederate flag sticker inside his portfolio. It annoyed the hell out of me, but I didn't want to overreact. And then, recently, we had some drinks together."

Fortina paused. Seaton observed Fortina's concerned countenance.

"Put all your cards on the table, Jake," replied Seaton.

With that response by Colonel Seaton, Fortina told his boss everything, only leaving out Bragg's excessive drinking.

As to the rest—Bragg's comments praising militia groups, his bigoted comments about Black, Hispanic, and Islamic Americans, his empathy with the assassins of the Kennedy brothers—he mentioned it all.

Seaton was the one that now had a concerned look on his face.

"Jake, I appreciate this. I know this was hard as hell for you to do, but you did the right thing. I'm going to let the Defense Attaché know, and I'm also going to speak with Bragg's boss, Colonel David Chapman. Do you know Colonel Chapman?"

"Other than seeing him in a couple of embassy meetings, I do not," replied Fortina.

"Colonel Chapman's a standup guy, a Citadel (The Military College of South Carolina) grad, and a straight shooter. He'll be very interested in what you just told me. As the only two Army colonels in this embassy, David and I talk from time to time, as you can imagine. Chapman has mentioned to me once or twice that he's not enamored with Bragg. That's all I'll say about that. Just understand that Chapman might want to speak to you personally."

"Roger that, sir," replied Fortina.

"Again, Jake...you did the right thing. Don't give this another thought. I'll take it from here."

CHAPTER 32

SLOVAKIA

IT WAS THE SECOND OF THREE daily trains which crossed the Ukraine-Slovakia border. This train—unlike the first and third trains of the day, which were passenger trains—carried ore slag and ash. The two commodities used for cement and insulation production constituted about 45% of the $948 million (2021) in annual exports from Ukraine to Slovakia. Other cars in the train carried iron ore and steel.

Unknown to the train conductor and engineer, this train carried two additional metals: a small amount of weapons-grade plutonium and uranium. The metals were contained in a suitcase nuclear bomb which had made its way from their hiding place in a heavily forested area just outside of Shapki, Russia, through Russia and Ukraine, and onto the Slovakia-Russia border. The bomb, non-threatening until activated by human hands, was bolted to the bottom of car 14 of the 15-car train. Once inside the Slovakian border and the greater European Union, the Wolf had a plan for getting it to Italy.

The Slovakian train inspector at the border had accepted a handsome sum from the Mafia operator in lieu of having one of his children disappear. The Mafioso was a self-described representative of a Ukrainian oligarch. The Ukrainian oligarch story was a ruse since the true source of the offer was the Wolf's right-hand man, Boris Stepanov. But Stepanov knew that one always needed to make sure that things appeared to be different than they really were, ensuring that no trace of a crime ever made its way back to the Wolf.

In exchange for 15,000 euros (about $16,000), the customs inspector would not inspect—"nor count, for tax purposes," he was told—the last three cars, numbers 13, 14, and 15 of the train. It was a deal the inspector literally could not refuse. The sum "offered" was worth a year's wages for the Slovakian border customs official.

Besides, the oligarch's frontman said it was "to keep the Slovakian government from taking too much of a tariff from the oligarch's hard-earned money and that of his hard-working ore miners."

"That ore is mined by hard workers—just like you—in Ukraine," said the man who made the offer. "Don't you think it's unfair that the Slovakian government and EU take so much money from the pockets of good workers like you? The tax we'll save from those three cars will be put back into their pension funds; I promise you."

The customs inspector thought about the man's statement for about three seconds. The thought that he would help a struggling and fellow Slavic worker from across the border appealed to him. It made him feel good. He gladly accepted the man's offer. It was a bargain. But he knew it was a lie.

CHAPTER 33

ANNIVERSARY DINNER

JAKE FORTINA WAS LOOKING FORWARD to the night out with his beautiful Italian bride of 20 months, Sara Simonetti-Fortina. While having "a little fun" in Rome, they hoped to reach two years of marriage before she and Jake got serious about having a child, even though Sara was increasingly anxious to move·up that timeline. On this night, Jake and Sara had made an impromptu decision to head out, without reservations, for a good Italian meal in Rome. They had decided to try the *Ambasciata D'Abruzzo*, located on *Via Pietro Tacchini*.

Well before social media sites like Trip Advisor and Yelp came along, the "Embassy of Abruzzo" restaurant had a good reputation among US diplomats and international businesspeople residing in Rome. As its name implied, its food was representative of the Italian region of Abruzzo. The Italian family who ran the place made sure of it. Jake had heard about the restaurant at the US embassy and thought it was worth a try.

As they entered the restaurant at 7:30 p.m.–which was early for Romans–Jake and Sara were optimistic. They both said a smiling *buona sera* to the waiter that greeted them. But knowing that Sara spoke native Italian with an authentic *Veneto* accent backed by her cute smile, Jake let her do the talking.

"Do we have a chance to get a good table tonight, sir?" she asked the lively young waiter who greeted them.

"Where would you like to sit?" he replied.

"Perhaps in the back room?" asked Sara.

Sara knew the back room was the nicer part of the restaurant, with a huge wooden wine cabinet and white tablecloths on the tables.

"Please follow me. I think I have one table left back there," he said.

As the three entered the room and got about halfway into it, it became apparent that the table that the waiter thought was available had a "Reserved, 20.15" card on it, indicating an 8:15 p.m. reservation time.

"My apologies," said the waiter, "I thought that table was available. I have a nice corner table still available in the front of the house … if that's OK?

"Sure, that's fine, *grazie*," replied Sara.

As the three turned to exit the back room, Fortina stopped. Seated at the table to his right was a man that Fortina was sure he recognized. The man was seated across from a beautiful, fair-skinned woman with long black hair and dark eyes.

Fortina's extensive travel experiences prompted his next thought.

She does not look Italian. Perhaps Kazakh, thought Jake almost instantly, having once trained with Kazakh Special Forces in the mountains outside of Almaty.

If the man was who Jake *thought* he was, it had been about eleven years since he had attended the US Army Special Operations Qualification Course–unofficially known as the "Q Course"–with the man seated at the table. There were dozens of soldier-leaders in the course, but Jake was sure he recognized the man.

Fortina decided he couldn't leave the room without introducing himself.

"Blake Conners? Is that you?" he asked.

The man coolly averted his eyes from the woman and looked at Fortina. The man's blank expression did not change. He conveyed disinterest in Fortina's question.

"I'm not sure if you remember me. I'm Jake Fortina. I think I attended a military course with you quite a few years ago."

Fortina could have said "Army Special Operations course" or "US Army course" or just "Army course," to be more specific, but he was aware that there were other people, none of whom he knew anything about, within earshot.

Conners was mortified at Fortina's approach. But he kept his straight face. He never thought in a million years that he'd be recognized by someone in this restaurant, in Rome of all places, even if it was known to occasionally have Americans as guests. Conners knew he needed to keep his cool.

Doing his best to feign a Russian accent, Conners replied.

"I'm sawry meester unless you attended a Russian Spetsnaz course, haha," he said, trying to deflect and lighten the mood, "I have never met you."

At this point, Conners' paid Russian-Kazakh escort for the entire evening, who was sitting directly across from Conners, realized what was happening. She responded to Conners in Russian.

"Who is this guy? Why is he interrupting us?"

Conners took the impromptu help and the clue, continuing with a mix of a few basic Russian words and fake Russian-accented English in his reply to the woman. It was all meant to be a ruse for the benefit of Fortina.

"It's nothing, my darling," he said in Russian.

"He has mistaken me for someone else," he added in English, making sure Fortina understood.

Conners turned his gaze back to Fortina. They looked at each other for about five seconds.

"I'm sorry for the interruption, sir," said Fortina before tacking on, "You remind me very much of someone."

"No problem," replied Conners promptly, rolling the "r" in problem, again trying to sound Russian by speaking English with a Russian accent.

117

As Jake turned to follow Sara and the waiter, he realized they had already gone out to the main dining room to secure the corner table the waiter had promised.

Sara, seated at the table as Jake approached it, faced the room. Jake seated himself to Sara's right rather than across from her, ensuring both had a good view of the restaurant. Jake and Sara had learned long ago that having a broad view of an entire public establishment was a good personal security practice.

"What was that all about?" asked Sara.

"I could have sworn I attended a US Army training course with that guy," answered Jake. "It was about 11 years ago, though, so maybe not. Some people can change a lot over a few years."

"Well, that's quite a while ago, isn't it, dear?" replied Sara.

"It is, and it was." Jake hesitated. "But…I rarely forget a face. Names? Yes. Faces? Rarely."

The more he thought about it, the more it bothered Jake.

Why the hell did he mention a Russian military course? thought Fortina. *How many people in this world know what the hell Spetsnaz is or means?*

The food and wine were good. But try as he might, Jake couldn't help thinking about the encounter with the guy in the back room. Worse, he couldn't hide his distraction from Sara, who had been hoping for an intimate evening with Jake.

"Jake, where is your mind tonight?" she asked gently, her hand resting on his arm.

"I'm sorry, sweetie. It's stuck on that guy in that room," he replied. "My gut keeps telling me something is not right. And my gut is usually right. I'd like to pay the bill now and then to go to the car. Please follow my lead, OK?"

Jake asked for *il conto* from the waiter. When the waiter brought the bill, Jake let the waiter know he wanted to pay for it immediately, and he did so. Jake did not want the waiter to drop the bill on the table and then walk away for 20 minutes, as restaurant servers were known to do.

As he got up, Jake took Sara's hand and led her to the restaurant's front door. She was curious but not nervous. She and Jake had already trusted their lives with each other in pursuing a couple of Iranian terrorists in Italy two and half years prior. Jake was cautious but happy because he knew Conners was still in the restaurant.

After they departed the restaurant, Jake and Sara walked down some gradually inclined steps toward the sparsely lit street below. Reaching the sidewalk, they turned left and walked to their car. It was parked curbside about thirty yards from the steps they had just descended. Their car was parked so that it had a clear view of the bottom half of the steps.

Jake opened the passenger door for Sara. She got in, and Jake went around to the driver's side door and let himself in.

As soon as Jake sat in the driver's seat, Sara spoke.

"Is this the moment you tell me you are CIA?" she asked, only a little teasing in her voice. "Is that what you are going to say? Because that was a weird dinner. Your head was in the conversation maybe half the time we spoke."

"I know, I know. I'm sorry. I'm not CIA, Sara. I am the soldier you thought you married, even though I'm no longer doing conventional soldier stuff." He sighed deeply. "You are right, it was a weird dinner, and that weirdness was entirely my fault." He leaned over and kissed her olive cheek. "I love you, sweetie, and I apologize for being spaced out for most of that dinner."

"Whew. You had me concerned there for a minute, Jake. I love you, too," responded Sara, leaning over to return the kiss.

Jake smiled at her gesture. "Listen, I know that guy in there is Blake Conners. There is absolutely no doubt in my mind. His whole Russian act was BS ... but it was also very perplexing." Frustration laced his tone. "I–we–need to stay in this car until he comes out."

"What do you plan on doing when he does?" asked Sara. "Do you plan on following him?" There was no anger, just professional understanding.

Damn, but I love my wife, he thought. "I thought about it, but, no, I don't. My gut tells me I need to see how he and that woman leave this place. We have a good view of the steps and the street from here. This might take some time, Sara. If he doesn't come out in 30 minutes, we'll leave. We are in no danger if we stay parked on this semi-darkened street and stay in this dark car."

"Danger?" laughed Sara.

"Zero danger," replied Jake. "It's just…well…you never know. But we are *not* in any danger here."

"Well, you know that I still carry this pistol in my purse, so if I need to be more alert than usual, let me know now." Her teasing turned serious.

Fortina hadn't forgotten about Sara's Beretta PX4 Storm Subcompact pistol. As a Carabinieri officer, she was authorized to carry it while off duty, as were most Carabinieri in Italy.

"There is no threat, at least not that I am aware of. And I don't think it will take much longer than 30 more minutes or so to see what car this guy and his *donna della notte* (lady of the night) get into when they leave," replied Jake, a little tensely.

"OK, you got it, my dear. I'll give you a bonus of 45 minutes, too. But don't try to pull any James Bond stuff, OK?" Sara's voice drifted into concern. "I don't want to lose you. I almost lost you a couple of years ago. We've only been in Rome a few months, and the fun is just starting," said Sara, trying to lighten the mood.

"OK, you got it. No James Bond."

Sara laughed.

"How many James Bond films have you seen, *cara mia*?" he asked, peering out the windshield toward the steps at the restaurant's entrance.

"I've seen many," she said. "And you, Mr. Bond?" she asked, her voice amused.

"I've seen 'em all," replied Jake seriously.

"They haven't had an American Bond yet, though," said Sara as she playfully put her hands on Jake's inner thigh.

Jake could feel every finger of Sara's hand touching him.

"You'd make a good Bond, Jake."

"Are you flirting with me?" asked Jake a little breathlessly.

"Could be," Sara intoned huskily.

Jake smiled and sighed.

"Listen, if we fog up these windows, what will we be able to see if that so-called-Russian guy walks out with his high-priced date?" replied Jake, his heart racing.

"Nothing." Sara said as she rubbed Jake's inner thigh. "We will be able to see nothing, at least not from inside this fogged-up car. But that's your problem, Mr. Bond," Sara's voice caught as her heart raced too.

As Sara said, "Mr. Bond," Jake turned his head toward the windshield.

Through the glass, he saw Blake Conners and his escort come down the last three steps and reach the sidewalk. Jake checked to ensure the flash on his iPhone camera was off. He then adjusted the camera's focus to ensure any image could be enlarged if needed.

As Conners and his attractive, short-skirted female friend crossed the street in front of him, about thirty yards away, Jake pressed his cellphone's white photo button three times. Once on the other side of the street, Conners led his date around the back of their car to the passenger side of a late model Alfa Romeo Giulia. It was too dark for Jake to be sure if the Alpha Romeo's color was black or dark blue. After closing his date's passenger door, Conners came around to the driver's seat and fired up the engine.

Jake lowered his driver's side window. Conners began to pull out of his curbside parking place. In the opposite lane from Jake's parked car, Conners' car began rolling toward Jake's car. It was obvious that Conners' car, in the opposite lane, would pass right by theirs.

Jake turned and pulled a pleasantly surprised Sara to him. In between kisses, he quickly let her know what was going on.

"Please play along," he whispered as the Alfa Romeo's headlights began to shine at him and Sara through the front windshield.

"Oh, I'll play along all right," she giggled. "We've done this before, haven't we?"

Jake missed that Sara was referring to when she had played Jake's lover in front of the Verona train station, helping to run off some Iranian guy who realized he'd misjudged who Jake was.

As soon as Conners drove by, Jake turned to the left in his seat, stuck his iPhone out the window, and took three more photos with his right hand, this time of the Alpha's back license plate. Thankfully, it was a narrow street, limiting the Alpha Romeo's speed to 10-12 miles per hour.

Conners had no idea he had just been in a scene from Candid Camera. One former US Army Special Forces guy had just beaten another, and the loser had no clue. That was just as Jake had intended it.

Sara looked at Jake, flushed from their impromptu make-out session.

"Nice job, Mr. Bond," Sara reached for him again, "I, I mean Fortina. Thanks for the warmup. So, you were saying something about getting these windows steamed up?"

"I was. But I must close this window first," said Jake, a little hoarsely. "It's getting quite chilly out there."

"Well, it's about to get quite warm in *here*," Sara whispered as she pulled Jake back to her lips.

CHAPTER 34

THE CONFERENCE

NOT ONE OF THE THIRTEEN "conference" attendees had their passports checked at the Italian border. That's because there were no border checks once inside any of the 28 European Union (EU) countries, much like traveling on the interstate highway in the United States.

Not that, at least in these instances, having their passports checked once inside the EU would have mattered all that much. With each traveler representing a highly-placed–and in some cases *the* most highly placed–autocratic or authoritarian-leaning politician of their home countries, getting a perfectly authentic-looking passport with a perfectly false name was easy. The fact that the travelers had been sent by top-ranking, authoritarian, and in almost every case, corrupt government officials made acquiring perfectly forged passports entirely too easy.

The Serbian representative came in through Slovenia, crossing Italy's northeastern border with the former Yugoslavian country. The Hungarian, representing Hungary's far-right prime minister, came through Hungary's western border with Austria and traveled through the Austrian Alps and into Italy's mountains for a relatively short but very picturesque trip. The Brazilian entered the EU through Portugal. Then traveled through northern Spain and the French Riviera before crossing into northwestern Italy.

Boris Stepanov, the Wolf's right-hand man, had personally approved the location of the meeting. It would be held in the Italian Dolomite mountains, in a part of Italy where German, Italian, and a local, intra-mountain dialect called *Ladin* were spoken. In this part of north-central Italy, city and village signs displayed names in German and Italian, representing the region's Austrian-Italian heritage dating back to the breakup of the Austro-Hungarian Empire after World War I. The Treaty of Versailles (1919) established the region's political boundaries.

Even the area's dual names highlighted its mixed cultural and international heritage: in Italian, the region was *Alto Adige* (High Adige), and in German, it was called *Süd Tirol* (South Tyrol). People with a long-standing heritage connected to the region were still quite sensitive about what the region was called.

Stepanov chose the picturesque mountain village of *Colfosco* (Italian)–*Kolfuschg* (German), in the municipality of *Corvara in Badia* (Italian), for the site of the "conference." It would be the *Jaeger Haus Hotel* (German) specifically that would host the event.

The manager and personnel of the Jaeger Haus Hotel thought the small group of attendees was coming to discuss "global energy security." This type of international conference was quite ordinary for the five-star Tyrolian-style hotel. The hotel had developed an excellent reputation among European corporate leaders and Europe's rich and famous for being more discrete than a Swiss bank.

The hotel staff was led to believe that this group was coming to discuss fossil fuel energy security from a global perspective. So, of course, people from Kazakhstan, Nigeria, Russia, Saudi Arabia, Venezuela, and perhaps Iran were expected to be present.

The Wolf and Stepanov had discussed the Wolf's personal appearance at the event. The Wolf had decided his arrival would effectively get the attendees' attention, but it needed to be brief. The Wolf asserted that to make a serious first impression–and expression–of his commitment to founding this first-ever, far-right, and far-reaching global political network, he had to physically–not virtually–be there to address the attendees.

With some modifications to his hair and makeup and the addition of stylish Euro-eyeglasses, Anatoly Roman Volkov, aka "the Wolf," would look nothing like the photos of him splashed across Italian and European newspapers and tabloids after the Italian government seized his yacht. The disguise was necessary for the security of the operation. It would ensure no errant persons would easily identify the Wolf.

As to the meeting itself, the Wolf would make sure he made his mark.

"And the beautiful thing, Roman," said Stepanov to the Wolf as they planned the meeting, "is that the group will not expect you. They are each coming to the meeting believing that I will be the one representing you. When you walk into the room and discover you are there, in the flesh, they will be impressed. They will then know just how serious you are about this new alliance. It will mean a tremendous amount to these interlocutors representing some of the world's most powerful authoritarian leaders and families."

Just as for all operations he had directed, Stepanov oversaw the planning for the meeting and the validation of its venue. He had members of the Pack, led by Blake Conners, of course, stay overnight in the hotel and conduct a thorough reconnaissance and investigation of everything: the security of the venue itself; sweeping for electronic bugs; the backgrounds of the people employed there; the high-level and highly discrete events that had already been hosted there; the access roads in and out; the location of nearby emergency medical services, etc. Stepanov would account for all contingencies.

Stepanov had learned from Conners that the best time to bring the Wolf into the hotel was at 2:45 p.m. That was 15 minutes into the kitchen and dining staff's mid-day 90-minute break. The kitchen and dining room were closed from 2:30 p.m. to 5:30 p.m. The front desk was almost always unoccupied then, too, with a bell at the front desk for summoning assistance if needed. With the Wolf in a formidable disguise, bringing him into the hotel at the optimal time added an additional layer of security to the operation. If a hotel worker ran into the Wolf, the disguise substantially lowered the probability he would be recognized.

***

On the appointed day, the attendees were told the conference would begin at 2:30 p.m. sharp, but they were all asked to be inside the conference room before 2:15 p.m.

"Anybody trying to enter the Conference Room after 2:20 p.m. will not be allowed in," Conners told his Pack teammates. "Those are direct orders from Stepanov."

Two Pack members in front of the conference room guarded the entrance. Two other guards were posted inside the room in case someone tried something stupid. Each guard carried 9mm handguns equipped with silencers.

At 2:03 p.m., the first of thirteen international "conference representatives" arrived. As with those representatives who would follow him, he was checked for weapons and told to leave his cell phone outside in the compartmented wooden bin next to the entry door.

"No electronic devices of any kind allowed in the conference room," a guard told each representative as they entered the room.

Not a single representative was late. The last arrival, representing the Myanmar military junta and the four-star general who led it, arrived at 2:14 p.m.

Once seated inside the room, a guard again checked each attendee for electronic bugs. The bug check was a surprise to most in attendance. That's exactly how Stepanov wanted it. If there were any enemies in the crowd, Stepanov wanted numerous opportunities to flush them out.

The Venezuelan was next-to-last for the bug check. *Why the hell am I being checked for electronic listening devices?* He wondered. *I know we will talk about other things besides energy security, but this seems a bit over the top.*

After the guards cleared the Venezuelan, only the Myanmar representative was left.

When the former Russian Spetznaz soldier passed his electronic wand over the pocket of the Myanmar colonel's breast pocket, his wand beeped. Just to be sure, the Russian passed the wand over his breast pocket again. The wand beeped again.

"Come with me," said the guard.

The Myanmar military officer tried to think of a protest, of something to say.

"Don't worry," said a second guard, a Belorussian. "It's OK. We just need to check you out a bit further."

The sweating Myanmar officer turned pale. Pack guards grabbed him by each arm and forcibly walked him out of the conference room. They

126

led him to a guest room at the opposite end of the hall. It was the farthest room from the hotel's front door. The Pack had reserved the room for contingencies just like this. The room next to it and the two rooms across the hall were also reserved for the Pack. They were empty as an additional security measure to ensure nobody could eavesdrop from next door or across the hall. The officer from Myanmar did not return to the conference room.

The Wolf entered the building precisely 17 minutes after the Pack members removed the Myanmar official from the conference room. His disguise was "Professor Sebastian Borowitz." Professor Borowitz was advertised to the conference attendees as a Polish expert on the security of global oil and gas supply lines. At least, that's what the one-page conference program said. All the attendees expected the "professor" to be Boris Stepanov, not the Wolf himself.

And Boris Stepanov indeed walked first into the room. The seated conference attendees thought their expectations were confirmed. But just behind him came the "professor," and behind the professor, two guards, adding two more Pack members to the two already in the room. The professor took his assigned seat at the head of the table, and Stepanov seated himself next to the professor. The professor took off his faux and slightly shaded eyeglasses. His colored contact lenses changed his eye color from blue to brown, but he did not remove these.

Slowly, the Wolf eyed the room. He successively looked each "energy security conference participant" in the eyes. He let them see him. During the silence, one by one, they realized this was not a Polish professor. This was the second richest and second most powerful Russian on the planet.

The jaws of a couple of the international attendees dropped. The Wolf completed his observational survey of the room's occupants and cleared his throat. The Wolf was direct, confident, and firm in his remarks. He had thought about them dozens of times before this meeting.

The Wolf's last words concisely summarized his 8-minute talk.

"The Western world's version of government, of *democracy*," he said mockingly, "is not working. The best and only way for national governments to work in this world is with governments led by strong, resolute, and uncompromising leaders like me and the leaders you each represent. Russia will regain its prominent position in the world, using *whatever means necessary,*" he said with emphasis. "And when we do, I will *remember* who our friends are. And you, gentlemen," he gestured to each of the attendees, "represent leaders and countries who will be Russia's close friends. I will personally and individually speak to each of your leaders via teleconference within three weeks of this conference concluding."

The Wolf stood, and then Stepanov stood. As a sign of respect, the Venezuelan stood. Then the Nigerian stood. The two stood isolated for about three seconds, and then the other attendees joined them, one after the other, until the whole room was standing. It was as if the Wolf was their military commander. The Wolf went around the room, looked each person in the eyes, and shook hands with them. The Pack guards watched and followed closely as the Wolf made his way around the room. After completing the circuit of the room, he approached the exit door. Before leaving, he turned to face the group.

"We are going to change the world, gentlemen."

CHAPTER 35

THE GAME GETS HARDER

THE SLIGHTLY BUILT, SEMI-NAKED Myanmar Army colonel and intelligence officer weighed no more than 150 pounds. He'd had his suit coat and overcoat taken away around three hours earlier. At gunpoint, he had been forced to remove his shoes, socks, pants, belt, dress shirt, and t-shirt. He was left wearing white jockey-style underwear in the brisk and damp 44-degree Fahrenheit autumn mountain weather. The colonel was doing his best to keep from shivering.

The temperature was dropping rapidly because the sun had disappeared over the nearest mountain to the west twenty minutes ago. Before the sun came up in the morning, the cold was expected to dip below freezing. The colonel's hands were zip-tied behind his back as he sat cross-legged on the cold, damp, mossy forest floor. He had been busted four hours earlier for carrying an electronic bug into the conference room.

The spot was perfect for an interrogation. Nikolai had chosen the spot deep in the thickly wooded alpine forest. It was two miles from the nearest paved road and 7 miles from the nearest dwelling.

Nikolai had done his duty as a lookout during the big heist in Rome. But Boris Stepanov hired Nikolai because he thought Nikolai might be useful. Conners didn't like it but was forced to work with Nikolai anyway.

Nikolai was a sadistic former GRU operator rumored to have tortured people in Syria. Nikolai liked to leave people guessing—it built more mystery and fear. He didn't bandy his torture skills about, but he relished the domination in the role of Interrogator.

"I'm going to ask you–*nicely*–one time," Nikolai cajoled. "Why did you bring that electronic bug into the conference room?"

The Myanmar officer was shaking from fear and cold. He did not answer.

"Fire up the woodchipper," Nikolai shouted to Enzo. Enzo was the Italian 'Ndrangheta local mafia clan "liaison." He worked under the umbrella of "Vulkovich and Sons," a mafia cover company whose leader promised Stepanov whatever he needed, "including having people disappear," *for the right price.*

So far, Stepanov had only asked for simple stuff, like a small fleet of five Italian-plated vehicles for the Pack, a Mercedes eSprinter van, and lots of silk sheets. Enzo also delivered on the woodchipper. He helped Nikolai secure the industrial, tractor-mounted woodchipper days before the conference.

"The chipper is in case of a contingency," Nikolai had said with a wink to Enzo after Enzo located it. "One never knows if we'll need woodchips to start a fire in these cold mountains."

Dmitri Dunay, a 220-pound former Crimean petty criminal, stood with his Glock 19 Gen 5 semi-automatic pistol pointed it at the Myanmar Army officer's head. A fourth Pack member stood watch for distant headlights.

The woodchipper, capable of making sawdust or larger wood chips out of 15-inch diameter logs, began to whir. Nikolai nodded to Enzo. Enzo grabbed a 6-inch diameter, three feet long piece of wood and shoved the log into the chipper's intake compartment. Sawdust flowed like a waterfall out the other end, creating a shallow pile of wood dust and chips. It covered the forest floor in an area of about four feet in length by two feet wide.

"Did you see that?" asked Nikolai. "You have a choice: tell me who had you wear that listening device, or you are the log." When the colonel didn't immediately respond, Nikolai pressed him, "*Why* were you wearing it?"

The officer was resolute. He would not—could not—divulge what Nikolai was asking.

Once the officer's boss, the Myanmar Army Chief of Staff, learned of the conference, he decided to inform his oil and gas industry contacts in Beijing, China. Myanmar (Burma before the name change) had long been an oil and gas supplier and junior trading partner with China. The Chinese, upon learning of the Wolf sponsoring the conference, offered to pay the Army four-star general $100,000 if he brought back all the information.

Like the other invited leaders, the Myanmar general, who also headed the military government, decided to send one of his intelligence experts. But the colonel's mission was not only to serve as a dependable representative for his general. The colonel's real mission was to gather as much intelligence as possible from the conference for his boss and, ultimately, the Chinese.

The Wolf's notions of forming an international alliance of authoritarian leaders intrigued Myanmar's leader. But that is not what interested him most. What interested the general most was to stay in China's good graces and make an easy $100,000. That was a small fortune in Myanmar, even for a four-star general and Myanmar's self-appointed head of government.

The Myanmar army colonel had been caught in the middle: either go on the intel gathering mission to Italy for a $10,000 cut (almost three times his annual salary) and be promoted to brigadier general if successful or be retired immediately two ranks lower, at the rank of major. The colonel realized he had chosen poorly.

The officer from Myanmar met Nikolai's question with shaking silence.

The fourth Pack guard came up behind the seated colonel and injected him in the neck with a mild dose of propofol.

"He should be very woozy for about 20, maybe 25 minutes, and he'll be out cold for maybe 15 of those minutes," said the guard.

Boris and Nikolai waited two minutes for the propofol to take effect. They and Enzo dragged the deeply sleeping colonel to the woodchipper. With Boris and Nikolai holding the unconscious colonel upright, Nikolai carefully stuck the officer's right arm just far enough into the woodchipper's intake funnel to contact the sharp blades whirring inside.

The blades made a brief, high-pitched squeal like a band saw when it cuts wood.

Nikolai pulled the officer's arm back out and examined the officer's hand. The blades cleanly cut off the three smallest fingers of the colonel's right hand, leaving his largest forefinger and thumb partially mangled.

"I got it right on the first go! Can you believe it?" Nikolai chuckled, childishly gleeful. "Perfect, don't you think?"

Enzo, the Italian mafia man, was unmoved. In southern Italy, he had seen the Italian mafia throw people into vats of acid. Dmitri Dunay, the Crimean, thought he was going to vomit. He had done some bad things, but never anything like this. It turned his stomach.

"Enzo, turn off the chipper," Nikolai commanded.

Enzo complied while the larger and stronger Dunay held the slight man upright.

"Lean him in a seated position against that tree," Nikolai pointed, "with his torso and head in the upright position," he ordered.

Dunay did so with ease.

Nikolai pointed at the colonel's pile of clothes nearby and addressed the Crimean.

"Grab his t-shirt and wrap up his hand. We don't want him bleeding out and croaking before we have the chance to have another sweet chat." Nikolai's voice held anticipation.

Dunay, despite his roiling stomach, again did as he was told.

After fifteen minutes, the colonel stirred. Nikolai directed Dunay to zip-tie him again, "only this time do it with his arms in the front, so he can see his hands when he wakes up."

The colonel sat hunched against the tree with his bare legs stretched out on the cold, wet ground. The group heard the colonel moan. They watched as he looked at his hands and the improvised t-shirt bandage around his right hand.

"Remove the bandage," Nikolai directed Dunay.

The Crimean did so. As the bandage fell away, the colonel saw his bloodied and mangled right hand. The colonel winced. Only his mangled right thumb and index finger were attached to his hand. Where his three smaller digits should have been was a mass of bright red blood and three white bony stubs. The Myanmar colonel felt the scream build. But he swallowed it back, wincing instead. Tears flowed down his cheeks. The colonel now understood the searing, otherworldly pain he felt.

With his head down, the colonel mumbled something unintelligible in his native language of Burmese.

Nikolai kneeled in front of the colonel. Nikolai's put his face eye-level with the colonel's. Feigning empathy, Nikolai addressed the colonel.

"Listen." He sounded almost apologetic. "I didn't want to have to do that. I'm just doing my job here. I'm sure you know that. Right?" The colonel could make no response. "Now, you can *help* me do my job or make things harder for both of us. Please don't force me to completely cut off both of your hands." Some of Nikolai's excitement at the prospect slipped through the conciliatory tone in his voice. "This game only gets harder as it goes along, *mon colonel*. I really don't want to see that. But if you force me to, I *will* make the game harder ... *a lot* harder."

Nikolai paused. He let his words sink in.

Nikolai believed everyone had a breaking point. He just needed to find it.

"Now, I'm going to ask you one more time: who is behind that electronic bug you were wearing in the conference room? Why were you wearing it?"

The colonel looked at Nikolai.

"It was me, just me," replied the colonel, hoarse with pain and the need to scream. "Nobody else was behind it."

"Bullshit," replied Nikolai, replacing the placating tone with cruelty. "You are lying! Now, I'm going to give you one more chance to answer the question: who was behind it? *Why* were you wearing a bug?"

The colonel did not respond. He continued to sit stone-faced. He looked down at the ground. He tried not to grimace from the pain, but it was impossible not to.

"Enzo, fire up the chipper!" directed Nikolai.

Nikolai grabbed a tuft of the colonel's short hair and jerked the colonel's head back, forcing the colonel to look at Nikolai, who now stood over the poor, mostly-naked man.

"Last chance, my friend," said Nikolai.

The colonel was unmoved.

Nikolai released his grasp of the colonel's hair.

"To *hell* with him, let's go for both hands," shouted Nikolai to Enzo and Dunay. He warmed to the idea instantly, glee dancing in his voice. "If he wants special treatment, we will give him what he wants!"

Above the din of the chipper's motor and whirring blades, Nikolai's directives were easily loud enough for the colonel to hear.

"Get him up and over to the chipper. If you shove both arms in at the same time, this will work *beautifully*. Should only take a few seconds to leave him with a couple of bloody stumps," shouted Nikolai.

Enzo and the Crimean complied, dragging the colonel to the woodchipper. They forced the colonel upright. After Enzo and the Crimean stabilized the colonel in position, they worked together to slowly push the colonel's zip-tied hands and wrists into the woodchipper's funnel.

The colonel squirmed and tried mightily to retract his arms from the funnel. But his hands inexorably inched their way to the whirring blades.

With all his strength, the colonel screamed.

"Stop! I will tell you everything! Stop!" Panic and pain in every syllable.

Enzo and Dunay looked at Nicolai for direction.

Nikolai hesitated for only a moment.

"I think we should put his entire arms in there. What do you think, Boris?" asked Nikolai.

"That's up to you, boss," responded Dunay.

Nikolai walked into the colonel's field of view. Nikolai rubbed his chin as if pondering a profound decision.

The colonel's legs began to shake uncontrollably as he wet himself.

Nikolai looked at Enzo and Dunay.

"Put him back on the ground," said Nikolai. "Let's see if he's truly had a change of heart."

Enzo and the Crimean complied.

Seated back on the ground, his soul relieved of having avoided imagined yet unimaginable trauma, the colonel did exactly what he said would. Leaning forward from the tree, he told Nikolai everything about the real reason he had traveled to the Italian Dolomite mountains.

After the colonel finished, Nikolai, satisfied, nodded to the fourth guard, the one who had been pulling security and keeping an eye out for approaching headlights. The guard understood the nod's meaning.

He walked to a spot three feet behind the seated colonel, extended his right arm, and aimed his pistol at the back of the colonel's head. He fired two quick shots in succession. Once the colonel's body rolled to the side, the guard fired a third shot–the *coup de grace*–into the colonel's temple.

Nikolai looked at Enzo.

"Finish the job."

Enzo and the Crimean laid the colonel's body across the back of the woodchipper's metal frame, where it connected the chipper to the tractor. Enzo drove the mobile, tractor-mounted industrial woodchipper forty yards down a slight incline to an 8-foot-wide creek while the Crimean walked behind it. Enzo stopped the tractor at the creek's banks. He switched the woodchipper's setting from the "wood chips" to the "sawdust" mode.

Enzo got out of the driver's seat to make sure the chipper's exit funnel was properly positioned over the flowing creek water. He returned to start up the chipper. Enzo and the Crimean fed the colonel's body into the chipper. They couldn't see it under the starlight, but the creek got pink, almost red.

Enzo turned off the chipper.

Enzo and the Crimean took a few minutes to clean the chipper's blades and funnel with a bucket and some water from the creek. They drove the tractor back to the original interrogation spot. Nikolai stood there, his hands on his hips.

"You see, boys. Never. Ever fuck with the Wolf," said Nikolai.

It was clear to Enzo, the Crimean, and the guard that the message was not only meant for the Myanmar general who had sent the now-pulverized colonel to Italy. It was also meant for them and all the Wolf's Pack members.

CHAPTER 36

A CASUAL LUNCH

IT WAS NOT THE FANCIEST EATERY in Rome. The place sold fried cod filets in brown paper wrapping, so they could be eaten by hand, on a plate, or while walking along the Roman streets. What made the *Filetti di Baccala*, located at Largo di Librari 88, a great place for a confidential meeting was its narrow entry door with only about a dozen small tables inside. A few tables were in the back room. After entering the restaurant's main door, the back room had to be accessed through another narrow door. In that backroom was a back corner table with sightlines of the entire room through to the bar area.

If a Russian goon tries to follow me, thought Ukrainian Colonel Hennadiy Kovalenko, *he won't get near me without me spotting him first.*

Kovalenko knew that Russian spies stationed in Rome were very interested in Kovalenko's military attaché business. So were other spies, like the Chinese and Iranians. It was almost an open secret among Western intelligence agents working in Rome that *Iran Air*, Iran's nationally owned airline, 100% owned by the Iranian government, was staffed exclusively by Iranian intelligence agents. Kovalenko figured the Ukrainian embassy in Rome was under constant surveillance, too, and most likely, so was the entrance to the gated Roman compound where he resided.

Kovalenko thought about the restaurant.

The restaurant would not, however, be a good place for a hunted mafia capo to have lunch, he thought. *No, signore. There is no way out!*

Their meeting time was set for 11:30 a.m. Kovalenko knew that no local Roman in his right mind would have lunch for at least another hour or two. Perhaps a British, German, or American tourist might come wandering in between 11:30 and noon. But since it was a beautiful, if brisk, day outside, they would likely take one of the outside tables first.

Kovalenko walked in the Filetti da Baccala at 11:28 a.m. Right before Kovalenko went through the restaurant's entrance door, a waiter offered

Kovalenko an outside table. Kovalenko declined it. He told the waiter he was meeting a friend waiting in the restaurant. As the waiter led him to the table, Kovalenko noticed only one patron standing at the bar. The patron was ordering takeout, a *baccala da portare via*.

Within two minutes of sitting at the back corner table, Jake Fortina walked in. Fortina had ditched his Charles Tyrwhitt, English-cut business suit–his US embassy "uniform"–in favor of slim-fitting black Levi jeans, black leather loafers, and a white Massimo Dutti open-collared, long-sleeved shirt. A lightweight, dark blue goose-down vest he had picked up in Barcelona rounded out his "Roman casual" ensemble. Kovalenko also dressed casually.

After each ordered a fried cod filet with some sides of grilled vegetables and *aqua naturale*, Kovalenko got down to business.

"Jake, things are going–how do you say it in English," he paused a moment, searching, "to hell in a handbasket. Yes, that's it, hell in a handbasket–in Russia."

Fortina admired Kovalenko's command of colloquial American English. He recalled Kovalenko's former duties and extensive contact with Americans while representing the Ukrainian Joint Staff to US military and government officials stationed in Europe.

"I know things are not good," replied Fortina.

"They are beyond not good, my friend. The Russian presidency is hanging by a thread. Puchta's popularity is in the gutter. His oligarch buddies are jumping ship. Those oligarchs who are still with him are sleeping with one eye open. They are also avoiding balconies and hospital windows like the plague."

Kovalenko chuckled ironically at the otherwise serious matter of numerous Russian oligarchs, who, having gotten in Puchta's way or not fully demonstrated their loyalty, "fell" off balconies or out of hospital windows.

Fortina chuckled with him.

Kovalenko continued. "Most of his generals can't stand Puchta. He might also be quite ill, but we can't confirm what is causing it. But his physical weakness is not what worries our intelligence folks the most. Look, I know my national intelligence people regularly engage with your people. But our Ministry of Defense Intelligence Office has authorized me to cross a line with you and only you, Jake."

"Oh, crap," replied Fortina. "Why does my Spidey sense tell me I'm about to be thrown into a briar patch?"

"Your what?" asked Kovalenko.

"Haha, never mind, Hennadiy," responded Jake. "I'll explain the next time we can share a Ukrainian vodka. Sorry for the interruption. Keep going."

"OK, as I was saying," continued Kovalenko. "Puchta's oligarch buddies are distancing themselves from Puchta as best they can. But among those former 'buddies' are two, maybe three, who would love to replace him, and not necessarily with the intent to make things better for Russia or to make nice with the rest of the world. We think the top contenders for replacing Putin include one oligarch living in the UK, one in Russia ... and one right here in Italy."

Fortina nodded his head affirmatively. "Who, might I ask, is the Italy resident you're speaking of?"

Kovalenko cast a glance at the entrance door from the backroom where he sat, just to make sure nobody was standing there or walking in.

Kovalenko whispered anyway. "His name is Roman Anatoly Volkov, otherwise known as 'the Wolf.' Ever hear of him?"

"I was not aware of that 'Wolf' moniker, Hennadiy." Jake dropped his voice too. "But I know who Volkov is. I saw the news after they seized his yacht. That yacht seizure made a big media splash, pun intended."

"Yes, it did. I don't think that part of the saga is over yet, by the way. The Wolf normally doesn't let anyone–not even a foreign government– get away with something like that without payback. But what we in

Ukraine are really worried about is if the Wolf takes over in Russia. We have evidence that suggests he will be worse than Puchta. I don't have to tell you what that will mean for Ukraine, Jake."

"No, you don't," responded Fortina. "If your assessment is that it would be worse for Ukraine than with Puchta at the Russian helm, that means it would be beyond description."

"Jake, we Ukrainians heard about what happened here in Italy a couple of years ago. The word among our intelligence circles is that you had a big hand in stopping that Iranian virus threat."

Kovalenko referred to Fortina's involvement in stopping a tier-one national security threat against the United States and Israel. It had emanated from Iran and could have killed hundreds of thousands, if not millions, of Americans and Jews.

"I can guarantee you I didn't even have a small part in that," replied Jake.

Kovalenko knew that was exactly what Fortina was supposed to say. Fortina was a quiet professional. But Kovalenko also knew the US Army officer had been critical in stopping the Iranian national security threat aimed at Americans, Israel, and Jews worldwide. An Italian intelligence agent with loose lips had divulged that fact at a recent official visit with his Ukrainian intelligence counterparts. The Italian intelligence agent had assumed that the Ukrainians had already known about it, except they hadn't.

"Jake, listen. We—my government—we need your help. We are asking that you help us keep an eye on this Volkov guy. By that, I mean whatever intel that you are authorized to share here on the ground, in Rome, please share it. We're not, of course, asking that you drop everything and make this your number one priority. But you know as well as I do that if somebody worse than Puchta takes over, it will be horrific for the United States, the Western world, and even the Russian people, many of whom do not want this Russian mess either."

"I don't think I can do much more than keep a casual eye on this," said Fortina. "This is more in line with what our other national US intelligence agencies should be doing. My lane is military stuff and especially Italian military and NATO stuff. My job in Rome is to focus on US Army cooperation with the Italian Army. A whole bunch of people above my pay grade will have to OK my involvement with what you are asking."

"Look, Jake, you know I can't share *everything* that we Ukrainians think we know about this Volkov guy, this, *excuse* me ... Russian asshole, this 'Wolf.'"

Fortina smiled. "No excuse needed."

"The Wolf has assembled an international para-military force to enforce his power and to achieve his goals." Kovalenko continued. "If he manages to take over the Russian government, I believe nothing—and I mean *nothing*—would be off the table militarily for this guy."

At hearing Kovalenko's "nothing off the table" comment, Fortina's thoughts immediately went to weapons of mass destruction—biological, chemical, nuclear, and perhaps cyber.

There was a long pause as the two military professionals looked at each other. It was clear that weapons of mass destruction were indeed what Kovalenko referred to.

Finally, Kovalenko spoke again.

"We are looking at someone and something that could be catastrophic for the United States, Europe, and even the world, Jake. We could use your help, buddy."

Fortina held his silence for several seconds before responding. "I will see what I can do, Hennadiy. You know darn well I'm not the captain of my own ship in this city. I've got a bunch of people I work for who would need to say that it will be OK to add this to my 'to do' list."

"Thank you. That's about all I can ask, my friend. And ... the baccala is on me."

CHAPTER 37

TOO EASY

"SOMETHING FEELS WRONG," said Yuri, a Pack member and former Army Special Operations soldier from Moldova. Yuri had deserted his Army and country to find fame and fortune abroad, ending up, like others with his background, in the Pack.

"What do ya' mean?" replied his Pack partner, Ivan, who was Lithuanian and also on the run from his home country.

"This seemed way too easy. It was too easy to take off that suitcase from the bottom of those train cars, even if it was 3 a.m. and the train tracks were almost completely dark. The lights near the train tracks probably haven't been replaced since the Russians occupied this place forty years ago."

The Lithuanian laughed.

"You always overthink things, Yuri," replied the Lithuanian. "Do all you Moldovans think that way? We were given clear instructions. We have all the right papers for our vehicle. We know where to deliver our suitcase. From right here in Bratislava, we have established checkpoints all the way to Rome. I'm not sure what's in the suitcase—diamonds, other precious jewels, a cure for cancer … *shit*, I have no idea, and I don't care. I just know that when we complete our mission and get this thing delivered where we're supposed to, I'll be able to take an extended vacation on the island of Majorca. Beautiful women will be everywhere, and my pockets will be stuffed with euros. I'd say whatever the hell we're delivering to Italy will be well worth it."

"Yah, you are right," said Yuri.

Just like Yuri, Ivan had no idea that the suitcase they were transporting was, ounce for ounce, pound for pound, the deadliest and most destructively powerful suitcase in Central Europe.

CHAPTER 38

THE "SOLDIER"

LEE ROLAND COULD SEE the hay bales. They were stacked over twenty feet high. Every time he was driven deep into the northern Michigan forest by his militia "sergeant" Jeremy Buckhalter, and Roland spotted those hay bales, he got excited. On the other side of those hay bales was a makeshift firing range.

The 34-year-old Buckhalter owned an AR-15 semi-automatic rifle, and today, Buckhalter would again let Roland fire it. Roland loved the coaching he got from Buckhalter. Coaching of any kind was something Roland's life had lacked.

If it weren't for the UP Boys, my life would suck, thought Roland as Buckhalter wheeled his pickup truck to the backside of the firing range.

Roland's alcoholic father left Roland and his mother when he was eight. Despite his father's erratic behavior and maltreatment of him, little Lee Roland clung with all his might to his father's pantleg as his father stormed out of the house. His father practically kicked the crying child, like so much mud, off his boots and leg.

"Don't act like a dog!" said Roland's father. "Grow up!"

The man was never seen or heard from again.

Roland's emotionally distant mother had her own bouts with alcohol and drug abuse and on-again, off-again, minimum wage employment. Were it not for an aunt that took Roland in when he was 15 and just about to go off the rails, he would have been on the road to a lengthy stay in prison or worse. Now, at age 23, he still lived in his aunt's basement. His part-time job at the local convenience store helped his aunt with the heat and water bills and put a few bucks into Roland's worn pants pockets, too.

Sometimes, his aunt let him use her twelve-year-old car. Most of the time, Roland had just enough gas money to get the gas tank to half full.

But then Roland found the UP (pronounced ewe-pea) Boys. Or rather, the UP Boys found him. The Boys gave Roland a sense of belonging, a sense of family, and some sense of meaning in life. The AR-15 he got to fire occasionally made him feel like a real man. It was a feeling he'd been searching for since he was 14, maybe even as early as 12.

And after some previous instruction by Buckhalter, Roland thought, *I'm pretty damn good at firing this weapon.*

It was the first thing in his life that Roland felt good about and could call his own.

Buckhalter had told Roland, "Firing an AR-15 requires real skills: focus, concentration, controlled breathing, self-discipline, a soft touch, and a good eye."

I will soon own my own AR-15, he often thought. *And then I'll really be somebody.*

Roland had learned from Buckhalter, "Never call the AR-15 a "gun. It's a weapon, plain and simple," Buckhalter had said. "It's meant for killing."

Roland had wanted to be a soldier. He went to a parade in Marquette once. He saw the respect and adoration the people had for military veterans, young and old. He had considered enlisting in the Army, but the thought of drill sergeants screaming at him gave him extreme anxiety, driving him to haunting thoughts of his missing father. The triggering emotional pain was too much. Plus, having to deploy with the US Army to foreign places was a daunting thought, as was the disgusting idea of having to share a bunk bed—or worse, a pup tent—with anybody of color.

Roland had been out of Michigan's Upper Peninsula (UP) only once, and that was on a trip downstate to Grand Rapids. After he turned 18, he took the trip in a Greyhound bus from Munising. The trip's purpose was to see a distant cousin. It would be the farthest Roland had ever ventured from home.

The trip, however, ended abruptly, with Roland leaving early. He discovered that he had little in common with his 19-year-old smart-ass cousin. Roland also learned that he hated big cities, preferring the isolated forest of Michigan's upper peninsula over any other place on the planet, a planet that Roland knew very little about.

It was in Grand Rapids where Roland saw his first Black Americans. He'd heard bad things about them from his mother, who had heard bad things about them from Roland's father, who had heard bad things about them from *his* father. However, none of Roland's family members had ever met a Black person. As to the seasonal Mexican migrants who had come up to the UP to work picking berries on its blueberry and strawberry farms, the Rolands kept their distance from *those* people, too.

I could never live here, thought Roland during his visit to Grand Rapids. *Too many niggers.*

He recalled hearing the terms *nigger* and *spick* a couple of times from his father. After his father had left, he'd only heard the terms once more, in passing, from another schoolmate. But the labels stuck with him, creating his own images and world of just how bad *those* people must be. Those thoughts also gave Roland a sense of well-being and superiority.

As an adolescent, when he felt the rest of the world was passing him by and seeing other kids riding in new cars, wearing new clothes, acting more confident, and seemingly happier, he would always think, *well, at least I'm not a nigger or a spick.*

Given the low population density and sheer geographic size of Michigan's Upper Peninsula, it provided a lot of secluded places for an anti-government militia group to be formed. The group included a handful of white supremacists who sought common anti-government cause with others. Indeed, many militia organizations in the United States were not white supremacist based, but some were. One of the more notorious militia groups was the Aryan Nations group, an antisemitic, neo-Nazi, and white supremacist hate group that was originally based in northern Idaho and later spread to other states.

While the UP constituted 29 percent of Michigan's land mass, only three percent of Michigan's citizens inhabited the area. Twice the size of New Jersey and larger than Switzerland, the UP's vast forests were thick, and the roads leading into them were sparse. In the winter, which started as early as October and could last well into late April, the peninsula received some of the heaviest snowfalls recorded in the United States.

After exiting the truck, Buckhalter led Roland to one of the simple firing range's four designated firing positions. Paper silhouetted targets containing black and white images of a human torso and head were tacked to hay bales about 80 yards away. Buckhalter laid out a well-worn Army poncho on the ground. Buckhalter had gotten it from his father, a Vietnam vet who had died of Agent Orange.

"He got cancer from that shit after serving in the 'Nam," Buckhalter told whomever he thought might care.

Buckhalter blamed the US Army for his father's miserable death. But Buckhalter decided to "try" the Army anyway, only to end up hating the Army even more for rejecting him after they discovered during Basic Training that Buckhalter had attention deficit syndrome. Buckhalter's disdain for pretty much anybody who did not share his white skin color also became apparent.

Screw it, thought Buckhalter when he got back home to the UP, *I'll learn this Army stuff by studying on my own, on the internet, and talking to vets about their experiences.*

After Buckhalter came back home to northern Michigan, the local boys, many of whom had never left the UP, let alone the state of Michigan, held Buckhalter in high respect. Buckhalter had made up a pretty good story about why he came home unexpectedly from the Army.

"My drill sergeants thought I should become an officer, that I had too much potential to be a regular GI Joe. So, they let me come home and try a different route for serving in the Army."

Even if some of his friends knew the story was complete bullshit, they also knew Buckhalter had served in the Army, even if for only a few weeks. After all, when he had enlisted, the local newspaper published that

Buckhalter was going off to join the Army. That gave Buckhalter an added air of respect and a leg up among his few friends. Now, at age 34 and one of the designated "sergeants" with the UP Boys, Buckhalter had consolidated that respect. He, in fact, knew more about "Army stuff" than most new UP militia Boys did.

"Today, Lee, my man, we're going to focus on headshots," said Buckhalter to Roland. "We're gonna start you out in the prone position. Try to put every round right between the eyes of that silhouette. Remember, at this range, you're going to have to aim slightly above your intended target. You'll soon figure out where the sweet spot for aiming is. At longer ranges, like 300 yards, it might be a few inches above the target; could be a bit more, could be less, depending on the range. And always remember to apply some Kentucky windage, especially for the longer distance shots and again, depending on the range. If you have a breeze from the right or left, adjust your sight picture accordingly. If you keep getting better with your accuracy, Roland, we'll move you up to using a scope. I've got a Barska model that you'll love."

Roland beamed with pride, knowing that Buckhalter had confidence in him.

Wow, a scope, thought Roland. *That would be freakin' awesome. So, this is what being a real soldier must feel like.*

Roland had never been shown trust like this by anyone. He would not let Buckhalter down.

Buckhalter, for his part, thought, *this kid is a natural. For sure, he's the best marksman among the UP Boys.*

CHAPTER 39

WEAPONS

"HOW MANY WEAPONS CAN YOU GET ME?" asked Lieutenant Colonel Beau Bragg.

Brigadier General Cadorna paused, looking at his office door. It was cracked about two inches open. That didn't concern him. His aide-de-camp, whose desk was just outside the entrance door to the general's office, was not expected in the adjacent office for another twenty minutes or so.

"I can get you thousands," replied Brigadier General Cadorna.

Bragg raised his eyebrows.

"Thousands? How many thousands are we talking about, Constantino?"

"At least three thousand, maybe five thousand. But listen. I think we should make a trial run with a few weapons first. In the long run, it will be safer that way."

General Cadorna knew that "safer" included his side of the bargain, too. If his scheme, about to be proposed to Bragg, did not work, he and the mafia organization he was working with would not be out that much cash, all things considered. A trial run was prudent business.

"How so?" asked Bragg.

"You've heard of the Great Lakes Waterway, haven't you, Beau?" asked the general.

"Vaguely...sort of," replied Bragg. Bragg had heard about the Great Lakes but had no idea of a Great Lakes Waterway.

"It's also called the Great Lakes-St. Lawrence Maritime River Shipping System," Cadorna said.

"General, how the hell did you know that?" asked Bragg.

"You forgot, Beau. I was the top logistician who graduated from my military academy class at Modena. I'm ... how do you say in American English ... a geek? Yes, I am a logistical geek." Cadorna laughed.

Bragg nodded his head affirmatively.

"Listen, here is what I propose. We ship thirty AK-47s, with 5,000 rounds of ammunition, to Munising. One standard shipping crate is all we need for shipping. Munising is right on the front doorstep of your UP Boys, isn't it?"

"Holy shit, Constantino, are you serious?"

The Mississippi-born and-raised Bragg wasn't a geography expert when it came to Michigan's Upper Peninsula, but he had learned a lot from the UP Boys' leader at a recent meeting between the Four M state militia commanders from Michigan, Mississippi, Missouri, and Montana. While he was back in the US on leave for a week, Bragg had organized a Four M meeting in a neutral location, a non-descript Holiday Inn Express just off the highway near Omaha, Nebraska.

The Michigan and Missouri militia commanders traveled the least distances, with the Montana commander having traveled a bit farther. Bragg had reserved two adjoining rooms in the Holiday Inn, using them as a temporary Four M command post. Their sleeping accommodations were reserved elsewhere in the hotel. Over one long, 10-hour day, they briefed the makeups of their organizations and talked about what they needed to make them more operational. During those meetings, Bragg had first heard about the Upper Peninsula cities of Marquette and Munising. The militiamen also drank their fair share of booze at the meeting.

Bragg couldn't believe what he was hearing from Cadorna. Since Four M had been formed, the UP Boys of Michigan thought they'd test the validity of this interstate-militia "partnership" mentioned by their new overall commander, this active Army Lieutenant Colonel Beauregard Bragg. They were skeptical. As a test of their new Four M commander's abilities, they decided to ask for AK-47 assault rifles ... lots of them.

In a meeting with Cadorna three weeks prior to this one, Bragg had mentioned the need for "small arms" and AK-47s specifically. Some Michigan militia guy had seen the physical damage and wounds the weapons caused his buddies in Afghanistan. The AKs had the added benefit of being simple to use, easy to maintain, and ubiquitous. They fired the easy-to-find and deadly 7.56X39 mm round. Bragg had done some research and discovered that about 100 million AK-47 weapons existed on the planet.

"I'm deadly serious," replied Cadorna. "It normally takes eight and a half days of sailing from Quebec City to Duluth in a small cargo ship. To Munising, Michigan, it will take closer to a week to get through the St. Lawrence Seaway and to Michigan's northern peninsula. So, the entire trip from Reggio Calabria, including getting out of the Med and crossing the Atlantic, will take about four weeks. The ship–ahem–owned by some friends of mine, will make some stops and drop off some crates carrying other stuff along the way. So, conservatively, it will take six weeks to make the entire journey from Italy."

The *'Ndrangheta* leased the cargo ship Cadorna mentioned. The 'Ndrangheta was Italy's largest and most powerful mafia organization. In 2013 a Swiss research group assessed that 'Ndrangheta made more money than Deutsche Bank and McDonald's put together, with annual revenue of over 60 billion dollars. Along with the other major Italian mafia organizations–Sicily's *Cosa Nostra,* the *Camorra* in Naples, and *Corona Unita* in the Puglia region–the 'Ndrangheta combined for about 165 billion dollars in revenue in 2008. Organized crime was, in effect, one of Italy's largest businesses.

"Because I like you and your cause, I will make you a good deal," continued General Cadorna. "Six hundred dollars per rifle and five thousand dollars total for all the ammunition. That's $100 less per rifle than what the Afghan market charges. If this first run works well, I'll cut the prices of everything by a third for the next shipment, which will include more rifles and much more ammo."

Bragg ran the numbers in his head. It was $23,000 for the entire deal. He considered whether he should make a counteroffer. As a used car buyer, Bragg never paid the asking price. He also knew this deal would set the bargaining precedent for any future deals. But Bragg also didn't want to offend the general. He pondered the issue and decided he would ask.

"Sir," he began, emphasizing his respect for the general, "that sounds like a good deal. I don't want to sound ungrateful, but how about $500 for each rifle?"

Cadorna hesitated. He looked straight into Bragg's eyes. Cadorna chuckled.

"Look, I'm from the south of Italy. I *expect* you to haggle. Let's call it $540, and we're done," he said, deciding to meet the American officer more than halfway.

"Done deal, Constantino," replied Bragg.

Lieutenant Colonel Beauregard Bragg left the general's office on a cloud.

My plan is coming together beautifully, he thought. *Tonight, I'm going home early to celebrate.*

CHAPTER 40

GUT INSTINCTS

JAKE FORTINA WALKED TO HIS DESK in the embassy's Defense Attaché office spaces. It was still early in the US embassy, with only a handful of people in the building. The thought of having spotted a guy the night before who looked exactly like someone he had completed the Army's Special Operations Qualification Course with many years ago still bothered Fortina. He'd spent a restless night feeling "99% sure" the guy was Blake Conners, although the guy denied it. Fortina's gut instincts were rarely wrong.

If that was Conners, why the hell would he deny knowing me, and who was that woman who seemed to speak excellent Russian? thought Fortina.

Fortina's mind ranged through possibilities.

Perhaps he was cheating on his wife and did not want me to know about it?

Then he thought about why two Russian-speaking people would be sitting in a Roman restaurant known to be frequented by US diplomats and businesspeople.

Were the two watching for US patrons and trying to listen to their conversations? That seems possible but not that probable. Almost makes too much sense.

On *this* morning, Fortina had left his apartment complex shortly after 6 a.m. It was earlier than he usually went down Rome's via Cassia. But he knew it was useless laying wide awake in bed. Realizing he wouldn't get another minute's rest thinking about his encounter with Conners, he decided to make an earlier-than-usual trip to the office.

Upon arrival at his embassy office, Fortina grabbed a rare second expresso from the DAO office espresso machine. He started his email triage earlier than usual while awaiting Sergeant First Class Manuel Alvarez's arrival in the DAO office spaces. Fortunately, he did not have to wait long.

After the usual morning pleasantries, he showed the former Army Green Beret sergeant a photo of Conners.

"Manny, does this guy look familiar?" Fortina asked the former Army Special Operations medic.

Out in Regular Army units, it was quite rare—and unprofessional—to address a subordinate by other than his or her rank and last name. But here in the US embassy, among very senior military service leaders—commissioned, warrant, and noncommissioned officers—it did occasionally happen, especially in private company and after establishing great trust.

Sergeant First Class Alvarez stared at the photo of the soldier displayed on Fortina's iPhone. Fortina took the photo after the "Conners guy" had opened the door on the passenger side of his parked car, then moved around the back of the car to his driver's side, across the street from the *Ambasciata d'Abruzzo* restaurant. As the guy approached his driver's door, Fortina had about three seconds to get a decent frontal shot of the man's face. The streetlight provided just enough light to make out some facial features.

"I'm not sure, sir," replied Alvarez bluntly. "In fact, the longer I look at the photo, the more I'm not sure."

That was not the answer Fortina was hoping for. He pulled his phone back from Alvarez's view.

"In your, what—seven years as an Army Special Forces medic—did you ever come across a guy named Blake Conners?" asked Fortina.

"Eight years, actually." Alvarez smiled. "Did I ever work with him?" he continued. "No, I didn't. But I'd heard of him. When word got out that he had tried out for the Task Force and didn't make the cut, a few folks were talking about it. Conners was known as a helluva competent soldier and NCO who had some personal problems. Too bad. But you know as well as I do, sir, that you not only have to be an absolute top-tier warrior to make TF, but your stuff must be straight in your off-duty life, too."

"Yeah, too bad," responded Fortina. "And yes, I agree, the TF entrance bar is pretty freakin' high."

Fortina pondered his next move.

I must confirm Conners' military status, he decided. *Is he still on active duty, or did he retire? That would at least give me another piece of information for figuring out the "Conners" puzzle.*

Right after Fortina presented Alvarez with the information concerning his encounter with Conners in a Roman restaurant, Fortina took the information directly to the Army Attaché, Colonel Marion Seaton. The Russian connection, however flimsy, made the incident of interest. Seaton was intrigued by it. It didn't take him more than a few seconds to reflect on it.

"Jake, you have the green light to check on Conners' military duty status," said Seaton. "If nothing else, our counter-intelligence people will be interested that you came across a Russian-speaking couple in that restaurant. Their presence there does not exactly mean they were up to no good, but as you know, you can't be too safe with this stuff. I'll talk to the Defense Attaché for her thoughts on this. Given the Ukraine-Russia war and the sensitivity of just about any information that smacks of Russian presence, I believe Captain Cheman will want to know about your encounter in that restaurant. I hope the food was at least good," added Seaton, chuckling.

Seaton's instincts, as usual, were right. Cheman formulated a plan with her assistant defense attaché to follow all leads concerning this strange–but quite interesting, she thought–encounter between Alvarez, Conners, and some woman who spoke Russian.

After presenting Seaton with the information on Conners, Fortina brought something else up to his boss.

"Sir, I need to tell you about my encounter with an old friend who is now the Ukrainian Defense Attaché to Italy," began Fortina. "He asked me–*us*, actually–for help. It concerns the Russian oligarch, Anatoly Roman Volkov, aka the Wolf."

"Oh? Now this sounds *interesting*," replied Seaton. "You're just full of all kinds of information today, aren't you, Jake?"

Seaton and Fortina laughed. Fortina nodded affirmatively.

"Let me have it," said Seaton.

Fortina detailed his meeting with the Ukrainian colonel at the *Filetti di Baccala* restaurant. The most significant part of what Fortina told his boss was the request by the Ukrainian–backed by the Ukrainian Defense Intelligence Agency that stood behind him–to pass any US intelligence it had on the Russian oligarch to the Ukrainians. The Ukrainians also wanted Fortina to serve as the principal US embassy contact for any information collection activity involving Volkov.

"This sounds intriguing, too," replied Seaton. "We'll have to run it by the Defense Attaché, the US Ambassador, and probably the Army Staff in the Pentagon. It's a bit out of your primary lane for you to be focusing on the Russians here in Italy. But that doesn't mean it won't enhance US national security."

Seaton paused. He smiled at Fortina.

"Jake, I know all about the work you did in France and Italy to help quell that Iranian virus threat."

Jake was not surprised at the colonel's statement. He figured Colonel Seaton had done some homework to find out who Jake Fortina was before Fortina showed up at the embassy.

"If we get approval for this, are you ready for another similar mission?" asked Seaton.

Fortina hesitated. He thought about Sara. They were trying to have a child. They were beginning to enjoy Rome socially. But when duty called, that got his attention. The West Point motto, "duty, honor, country," and his US Army oath to "defend the Constitution, against all enemies, foreign and domestic," meant something to him. They were always there, like twin north stars guiding his military service.

"I am, sir. If it helps our national security posture in dealing with an increasingly unstable Russia and ongoing threats from Russia, I'm in."

CHAPTER 41

MORAL COURAGE

THE YOUNG CARABINIERI CAPTAIN, PIETRO BONDANELLA, had been terribly concerned by what he'd heard. The military aide to Brigadier General Cadorna had returned to his desk, just outside Cadorna's office, fifteen minutes earlier than normal from his lunch break, which he took before the general took his. The adjoining door to Cadorna's office was cracked only two inches. But that was enough for the young captain to hear more than he wanted.

It was not in the captain's nature to eavesdrop on his boss's conversations. But this time, for some reason, perhaps because of the nature of the conversation, he couldn't help himself. And what he'd heard–or at least thought he'd heard–bothered him greatly. The conversation between Cadorna and an American officer had been about illicit weapons. About selling, buying, and shipping illicit weapons. About AK-47s. And about the two senior officers' preferences for "glorious" fascist leaders.

After three sleepless nights, the captain decided he needed to say something to somebody. But who? Whom could he trust?

He decided to seek out a Carabinieri lieutenant colonel, who, as a captain, was posted to Modena when Bondanella was a cadet there. Besides being the birthplace of Italy's world-famous opera tenor, Luciano Pavarotti, and home to Italy's perhaps equally famous balsamic vinegar, Modena was the home to Italy's West Point equivalent.

Established in 1678 and the oldest institution of its kind in the world, *L'Accademia Militare di Modena* produced officers for Italy's Army and its Carabinieri forces. The Italian military academy's academic, character, and physical standards were exceptionally rigorous. Less than seven percent of all applicants were admitted.

While at the academy as a captain, the now-lieutenant colonel Sara Simonetti-Fortina mentored and befriended Cadet Bondanella. Bondanella trusted her like a good and honorable aunt. Bondanella decided to tell her everything he'd heard pass between the Italian Army brigadier general and the US Army lieutenant colonel.

That conversation landed the captain in front of the three-star general Deputy Director of Italy's Carabinieri forces. Lieutenant Colonel Sara Simonetti-Fortina also sat in on the conversation.

The Italian general was gravely concerned. The overheard conversation indicated connections between Brigadier General Cadorna and an Italian mafia organization, of which there were four major ones in Italy. The conversation Bondanella overheard implicated an Italian-government-issued, badge-holding American officer with easy access to Italian military headquarters in weapons trafficking through his high-level Italian military contact.

But it also concerned the three-star-general from another perspective. Cadorna was known by his peers to be far-right in his thinking, although Cadorna had never gone so far as to publicly espouse his admiration for fascism. Furthermore, Cadorna was known to have cultivated friendly relationships with a handful of high-level Italian politicians in the Brothers of Italy. The Brothers of Italy were the most far-right political party of the far-right. In Italy's 2022 election, the Brothers surged in popularity. Where previously they received 4% of Italy's elected parliament representatives, they obtained 26% in the 2022 election.

As Italian politics went, the three-star-general wondered if his fellow Italian general officer might not be in a position of invincibility. But the general wanted to hear what the captain had to say, and the young captain told him everything he'd heard between the Italian and American military officers.

When the captain finished talking, the general looked at the captain and said, "That took a lot of moral courage, son."

CHAPTER 42

SOMETHING IMPORTANT

"SHE'S A SOCIALIST BITCH," said the Michigan militia "sergeant" Jeremy Buckhalter. He referred to Michigan's governor. "But having that darkie lieutenant governor replace her as governor would be a lot worse. That can never happen. Lee, *he* needs to go!"

As to the governor, Lee Roland had an idea of what *bitch* meant. He knew, however, that the word triggered trauma from his past. At the mention of the word, Roland recalled his raging father screaming, "You bitch!" at Roland's mother right before his father left, never to be seen again.

But Roland wasn't quite sure what a *socialist* bitch was. Nor did Buckhalter, for that matter, when he'd read the characterization of Michigan's governor on Truth Social. Roland, on the other hand, had heard the term "socialist" on One America News and occasionally from a couple of older UP Boys. It was clearly a negative term. But socialism's application in Michigan did not turn out to be so negative for Roland nor Buckhalter.

When Buckhalter got Covid, missed work, and finally lost his construction job, he found himself a few hundred dollars from sleeping on the street. That is until he stood in the unemployment line for a few months and received the Covid "Economic Impact Payment" from the Trump Administration to get back on his feet.

When Roland's mother had bouts of depression and couldn't work, the only nutritious meal Roland consumed each day and week as a nine- and ten-year-old boy came from his school's hot lunch program. And Roland had no idea that his benevolent aunt, who still provided him with a low-cost room in the basement of her house, had received life-saving treatment from Medicaid. Without Medicaid and unable to afford other health insurance with a Social Security check as her sole source of income, her only option would have been to face a slow, painful, and debt-ridden death from her disease.

Buckhalter and Roland also had no idea that capitalism and socialism had coexisted with some balance in the United States of America—and wealthy Western Europe—since the days of President Teddy Roosevelt. Roosevelt had rounded off the sharp edges of capitalism by siding with poverty-stricken and abused American workers in establishing an 8-hour workday and fair wages. Roosevelt also fought monopolistic practices, practices that had shoved the American worker into the dirt while filling the pockets of a half-dozen of America's robber barons. And Teddy Roosevelt's distant cousin, President Franklin Delano Roosevelt, had created thousands of "make work" jobs for destitute Americans to lift them out of the Great Depression.

But Roland knew none of this mixed capitalist-socialist economic US history, nor did he care to know it. Buckhalter had called the governor a "socialist bitch," and that was enough for Roland to know that the governor was utterly evil. And if *his sergeant* said that "bastard lieutenant governor has to go," Roland would be the one to take care of business.

After all, Buckhalter said it would be "very, very important" for Roland to do so.

***

I'm finally doing something important, really important, thought Lee Roland. *Sergeant Buckhalter has confidence in me, and so does my militia commander. Yes, today, I, Lee Roland, will finally do something important. Sergeant Buckhalter will be proud of me.*

Roland quietly and slowly improved his concealed position on the hillside.

Just like Sergeant Buckhalter taught me, he thought.

Roland's observation point was well-concealed under the thick brush. He was lying on his stomach with a good view of the house on the edge of the same southern Michigan forest that provided his concealment. The forest wrapped around and through most of the local 5-year-old housing development. The development was about 12 miles northeast of Lansing, Michigan's capital.

The driveway and house Roland was observing, slightly below and about 100 yards from his position, were located near a cul-de-sac. Tall maple and beach trees from the original forest were in the house's backyard and in those of most of the other homes.

Roland was proud to be wearing a Ghillie suit. Its natural brown and olive colors provided excellent camouflage. A person could walk within ten feet of Roland and never know he was there.

I'm just like a real Army sniper, he thought.

Jeremy Buckhalter told Roland that Buckhalter and the commander had been observing and tracking Roland's intended target for weeks.

"During the week, he usually comes home between 6:45 and 7 p.m.," they had said. "You can set your watch to it."

Roland checked his watch. It was 6:43 p.m. Roland's heart rate began to increase. In two minutes, the 15-minute window would open when the car was expected to pull into the driveway.

Roland peered through his rifle scope. He could see through the large bay window at the front of the house, adjacent to the front door. He could see the living room, too. Through the living room, he could see the kitchen light was on toward the back of the four-bedroom, two-story home. In the living room, he could see a young girl. He put his crosshairs on her head. Roland followed her movement until she left his site picture, taking her small plate of cookies and happily ascending the staircase to her bedroom.

Roland shifted the scope's crosshairs back to the driveway. Intermittently, he surveyed the target area with his naked eye instead of the rifle's high-powered scope.

At 6:49 p.m., a late-model white Ford SUV slowly approached the house. It turned to the left and crept up the slightly inclined driveway. The vehicle stopped about four feet from the closed garage door.

Just like Buckhalter and the commander told me, thought Roland as he tried to measure his breathing.

Buckhalter had told Roland exactly the type of vehicle he was to look for, adding, "he always parks outside, in the driveway."

What none of the three UP Boys knew, though—not that they cared—was why the Michigan Lieutenant Governor did that. He used half of the two-car garage to store things, like his 8- and 11-year-old girls' bicycles and his riding lawnmower. He left the other half of the garage clear for his wife to park her minivan. That was especially important in the wintertime. She used the minivan to shuttle the two girls to soccer games in the fall, and during the winter, to basketball games.

Even near Lansing, in the southern part of Michigan, winters could get rough. The husband and father of two girls did not want his wife to have to scrape ice off the minivan every time she drove it. He didn't mind scraping the ice off his own SUV windshield every morning, though. Nor did he mind riding in an ice-cold vehicle for the first five minutes until the heat kicked in. With the minivan parked in the garage, his wife and the girls would not have to endure that. They could go from the kitchen hallway right into the garage and into a warm car.

Roland observed the car's rear brake lights come on. They remained on for four seconds. Roland's heart was slamming in his chest so loud he could hear his heartbeat. But then he remembered the thought Buckhalter had repeatedly put in his brain.

"You are ready for this. You trained for it. You are skilled. You are the best damn marksman among the UP Boys. We are proud of you. What you will be doing is *really important*."

Roland swelled with pride. The positive thoughts steadied his heartbeat, shooting hand, and trigger finger.

A 39-year-old, six-foot-tall Black man in a business suit and no tie stepped out of the vehicle. The man did exactly what Buckhalter and the UP Boys commander predicted he would: he shut the driver's door and turned toward the rear passenger door. His intent was to open the back door and collect his gym bag and briefcase from the back seat before entering the house. The man knew his girls would come running downstairs when they heard the front door open.

The man shut his driver's door and turned toward the rear passenger door, facing directly toward Roland. Roland softly exhaled and gently squeezed the trigger. The silencer at the end of his rifle barrel did its job. The .30-30 caliber bullet, with which Roland had killed many a white-tailed deer, hit its intended target. The bullet ripped into the man through his torso's left side. The man arched backward to his left and fell on his back in the cement driveway.

Got that son-of-a-bitch, thought Roland. *He'll never be governor of Michigan now. He'd be a lot worse than that socialist bitch we have as governor. Buckhalter will be proud of me.*

CHAPTER 43

WHAT ARE WE DEALING WITH?

FBI SPECIAL AGENT LAUREN SANDERS stared at the day's intelligence summary. Sanders had a reputation among the Intelligence Community (IC) as a brilliant and morally courageous law enforcement analyst. She had a keen eye–a gift, even–for seeing patterns where others only saw pieces of disparate information or nothing at all. Her ability to make connections between seemingly unrelated events and facts was exceptional.

The FBI's former Legal Attaché to France was now serving as the FBI's Senior Special Agent in the US National Counterterrorism Center (NCTC or CTC) in McLean, Virginia. The CTC was established in the aftermath of the 9-11 attacks. In the investigation that followed the attacks, it became woefully obvious that the 9-11 attackers had exploited information and intelligence gaps between the major–and overly independent–intelligence agencies of the day.

Since its founding on May 1, 2003, the CTC's mission–like finding and putting together pieces of a puzzle–was to integrate and fuse information and intelligence from all federal agencies engaged in the fight against terrorism. This included agencies with federal employees located within America's homeland and beyond its shores. In other words, in the fight against terrorism, its mission was to eliminate the information and intelligence gaps that had existed between the major US intelligence agencies before the 9-11 attacks.

Sanders was widely respected throughout the CTC as well as the broader IC. She had no qualms about ruffling bureaucratic feathers if she had to. If Sanders even *smelled* that a US intelligence analyst–from the FBI, her own organization–or the CIA, Defense Intelligence Agency, or the State Department's Bureau of Intelligence Research or *any* analyst from you name the intelligence organization–tried to gain some form of one-upmanship over another agency, she would mercilessly and publicly call out the offender.

"Country first!" was her well-known motto throughout the Center.

When Sanders was angry, she would remove her reading glasses, and her response to her subordinates would be, "Country first, *dammit!*"

Sanders had cut her professional teeth on countering domestic and international terrorism. But she also had twice volunteered to serve overseas in a combat zone, ending up in Afghanistan both times. Her first tour there took her to Regional Command–South, in Helmand Province. RC-South, as it was more commonly known, was one of four International Security Assistance Force (ISAF) regional commands in Afghanistan. It was in Helmand Province where she tried to get the Afghans to stop growing countless tons of poppies for heroin production.

The Afghan farmers would grow the poppies, and the corrupt local warlords–and some corrupt Kabul government officials–would export the resulting heroin to Europe and the United States for massive profits. They then took the exorbitant profits after the warlords and Afghan government officials got their cut–no pun intended–and used them to fund the Taliban.

On her second tour of duty in Afghanistan, Sanders was assigned the mission of serving in the Major Crimes Task Force. It was a major international effort, led by the United States, to bring the rule of law to Afghanistan and to stem the most heinous and widespread crimes in the country. These crimes often involved the mass killing–or massive financial theft–of Afghanistan's people and treasure.

"This is a big deal," said Sanders to a subordinate as she continued to stare at the intelligence reports.

Whenever Sanders used the term "big deal," her Deputy knew she was onto something of significant national security intelligence value.

"This is the third politician someone has tried to kill in the United States in the past four months. Each served in state governments. The most recent one was a Black man who was a heartbeat away from the Michigan governor's office; a second was an out-of-the-closet gay man in Montana; and the third was an Islamic woman from Missouri. I'm not yet

165

sure what it all means. But a hundred—heck, even fifty—years ago, they would not have had much of a chance being in US politics."

Sanders paused. Her Deputy remained silent, knowing his boss had more to say.

"Is someone trying to turn back the clock—or send some messages—with these attempted killings? I'm concerned that there might be something more ominous afoot here."

CHAPTER 44

A GOOD DAY

JAKE FORTINA ARRIVED HOME early. It was a September second summer's late afternoon. With a 6:30 a.m. start at the embassy, it had been a long day. Jake walked through his apartment to the back kitchen and grabbed a bottle of San Pellegrino spring water from the refrigerator. He looked through the kitchen window and out on the balcony. The verdant Roman hills beyond it would begin showing fall colors in another week or two. The balcony had a majestic view of the hills, with no other apartment buildings obstructing the view.

Fortina looked at his bronzed, athletically fit wife of almost two years on the balcony. She was lying topless on a double-thick yoga mat, soaking up the late afternoon Roman sun. A bikini bottom and Italian *Persol* sunglasses were her only accessories. When she was single and living next to a vineyard near Vicenza, she would go out on her top-floor balcony with only the sunglasses.

Fortina thought back to his days at the Marshall Center after he'd first met and gotten to know the Italian beauty. During lunch hour one day, he'd entered the Center's gym. He'd heard somebody upstairs pounding a boxing speed bag. It was the teardrop-shaped kind that hung on a small chain and boxers used for training to throw quick and rhythmic punches.

Expecting to see a hulk of man pummeling the bag, Fortina was surprised to see a soaked-in-sweat Sara Simonetti. He was stunned by her athleticism and beauty. It would be another five years after departing the Marshall Center before Fortina would see her again. A year after teaming up with Sara in Italy to defeat an emerging biological threat from Iran, they were married.

She hasn't changed a bit since I met her almost eight years ago, thought Fortina. *How was I so blessed to meet this woman?*

It had already been a good day for Fortina. Like every day, he began his early morning routine with a double espresso and some quiet reading time with *Jesus Calling,* the *Holy Bible,* and *The Economist.* By 6:03 a.m., he was on his way to the US embassy on Rome's storied *via Veneto.* Jake never left his apartment at the same time and never returned at the same time, at least not in the same two-week period. He departed his apartment complex somewhere within a broad 45-minute window, always mixing up the departure (and return) times. It was, however, important that he departed his apartment complex each morning before the Roman traffic got crazy. He savored the opportunity to take early morning drives down the via Cassia in light traffic and the emerging Mediterranean sunlight.

Arriving at the embassy before most other employees did, Fortina spent a good hour reviewing emails and embassy cables in his office. They came in overnight, mostly from Washington, D.C. The Pentagon and US State Department were six time zones behind him, so occasionally, an overnight surprise or two would land in his email inbox while he was safely tucked in bed at home. Fortina checked first for high-priority emails, then lesser stuff. He also got caught up on the relevant geo-political news from the preceding 12 hours and confirmed his daily calendar.

Shortly after 8 a.m., the phone rang. The call was atypical for that hour. The earliest calls normally would not come in until after 8:30 a.m.

"*Pronto,*" said Jake with the standard Italian "hello" greeting.

"*Buongiorno,* Jake," came the friendly Italian male voice on the other end. "This is Dario Raffinelli. I'm the Carabinieri officer Sara introduced you to at the German ambassador's reception a few weeks back."

"Oh, *buongiorno* Dario" responded Jake. "How are you? To what do I owe the pleasure of your call?"

"Jake, we ran the license plate number Sara provided me. You probably saved at least a week of red tape by taking the personal route through her."

Raffinelli laughed.

Fortina laughed, too.

"Well, I appreciate you checking it out," responded Fortina. "What did you find out?"

"The license plate tracks to a legally registered Serbian company called 'Vulkovich and Sons.' It's in the cement business based out of Naples."

Fortina thought for a moment. What Raffinelli said did not add up. Unless Conners was working for a cement company out of Naples, Fortina had made a mistake in misidentifying that guy in the restaurant, after all.

"Were you able to find out anything else?" asked Fortina.

"No, my friend. That car and its license plate seem to be completely legitimate."

"OK, *tante grazie*, my friend," responded Fortina. "I owe you a bottle of your favorite wine!"

"Haha, no stress," replied Raffinelli. "I hope it helped."

Jake Fortina had no idea that "Vulkovich and Sons" was a mafia money laundering operation cover. He also didn't know the cement company was on the payroll of Boris Stepanov and, ultimately, the Wolf.

Hours later, Fortina received a phone call from a US Army personnel (HR) official in the Pentagon.

"Sir, you remember that sergeant you asked about?" asked the Army master sergeant. "His last name was Conners."

"Yes, of course. What did you find out?" asked Fortina.

"He retired from the Army two years ago. He was honorably discharged. Nothing else exceptional is noted in his records."

"Roger that," responded Fortina. "Thanks much for the follow-up."

That's the first piece of information I've received, thought Fortina, *that makes me think I may not be crazy. There is at least a good chance that the guy I saw the other night was, indeed, Blake Conners.*

***

Jake's eyes turned back to the large, marble-tiled apartment balcony. He walked to the balcony's sliding glass door and opened it.

Sara heard the door open. She turned her head toward Jake.

"*Ciao, bellissima,*" said Jake.

"*Ciao, caro,*" she replied.

Sara felt the warm Mediterranean sun and caressing breeze from the Roman hills flow over her breasts, her nipples erect.

"Listen, big boy," she intoned, "if you don't grab us each a glass of red wine or your beverage of choice and come out here and join me under this beautiful Roman sun without that banker's suit you're wearing, you're wrong."

Jake chuckled. When he'd arrived home, he hadn't even bothered to remove his business suit coat or his tie, part of his daily US embassy uniform.

"Gosh, Sara, you're not even going to ask me how my day went?" Jake pretended to sound hurt. "What kind of greeting is that? You're just going to bark out orders like some Carabinieri lieutenant colonel? You're hurting my feelings," he teased playfully.

Now it was Sara's turn to laugh. Jake did too.

"Yep, that's me. I love barking orders at an American officer." She laughed. "So, listen. Here is another order: go get those drinks. We have a family we need to make." She arched her back against the floor in a cat stretch, her arms over her head. Her lithe form set a fire in Jake.

Jake's heart leapt in his chest at the sight of his stunning wife; he stripped as he headed back to the bedroom to shower. Freshly scrubbed, he stopped in the kitchen for some chilled Prosecco before joining Sara.

She took her glass from him, eyeing his clothing choice as she sipped. "Ah, yes." she purred, "this birthday suit, I like it much better."

She put down her glass, took his to set it aside, and pulled Jake in for a sun-warmed kiss.

A good day was about to become a great day.

CHAPTER 45

A MYSTERIOUS PACKAGE

BLAKE CONNERS PEERED THROUGH the 14-inch high by 16-inch-wide bulletproof window he had insisted be installed in the Farm's operations center. He liked to maintain real-time situational awareness of the weather and time passing outside. When the operations center managed an operation like the painting heist, they blacked out the windows by lowering electronically controlled metal shutters outside the bulletproof glass. Once the shutters were down, the center was practically sealed.

Today was a slow day, and Conners was now peering through one of his windows. Conners didn't like what he saw. His gut asked him why he hadn't been informed about what he was observing. Through the window of the converted cinderblock farm building, a van's appearance caused Conners to raise his eyebrows.

A metal storage shed, about the size of a two-car garage, was located about 60 yards from the operations center. A utility van had pulled up to the shed's garage-sized door. Conners observed two Pack members come out of the shed. A former Crimea-born Ukrainian soldier and a former Russian soldier maneuvered a large pallet jack up to the rear opening of the van. Another Pack member assisted them from the back of the van. The three men offloaded an object. It was about the size of a large, rectangular, floor-mounted freezer, the kind Conners used back home for deep-freezing venison and fish.

That UPS paint job on that van looks fake as hell, thought Conners.

He thought of how military special operators would sometimes use commercial vehicles such as this, real or painted over, for their operations.

And why the hell have I not been made aware of this delivery and what that object is?

Conners understood it was not his place to know *everything* that took place at the Farm's compound. But it *was* his job to run operations for

Stepanov and the Wolf. Conners prided himself in knowing *almost* everything that occurred within and outside of the compound. This activity around the shed was strange.

The van departed, and Conners walked out of the operations center and approached one of the three Pack members he'd observed handling the large object. Conners didn't personally know the Pack member because he wasn't part of Conners' operations team. The Pack member was with two other logistics guys who also worked for someone else, someone else who worked for Stepanov.

"What the hell did you just offload?" Conners asked.

The man was coy. "Look, I cannot tell you what it is," he said in a thick Slavic accent.

"You know who I am, right?" asked Conners.

Conners rarely used hubris-filled language like that. Throwing around his elevated position in the Pack was not his style. But after pulling off the phenomenally successful painting heist at the Saint Louis of the French church, Conner's stature had grown immensely among the Wolf's Pack. Conners knew it. He thought perhaps this man knew it, too. And Conners was right.

"Yes, of course, I know who you are," replied the man. "Almost everyone around here, except for maybe some of the newer people, knows who you are."

"Look, I'm sure you understand that to be successful, and I'm speaking of our *entire* team," said Conners, "I need to know what the hell goes on in this compound. I'm in charge of operations, as you know. I'd appreciate it if you could help me with that."

The Crimean, whose mother was Ukrainian and whose father was Russian, looked at Conners.

"Look, like I said, I can't tell you, alright?" said the man. "I—we—were told to keep quiet about this. But … the door to the shed is unlocked. My partner and I have uncrated that thing. I have no idea what that heavy ass thing is for but go ahead and look for yourself if you want."

173

Conners nodded affirmatively.

"I appreciate it, buddy," he said.

Conners walked up to the shed's unlocked side door, turned the metal handle, and walked through the door. In the sparsely lit room, he could see the object sitting in the center of the shed's concrete floor.

Well, how about that, Conners thought. *It's an iron safe. Looks brand-spankin' new.*

The safe was about four feet wide, six feet long, and about three feet high. It had a combination lock for the top door, but the combination had not yet been set.

Conners turned the door's brass handle and pulled open the safe's door. The door was heavy, but not as heavy as he expected. It seemed made of a composite of iron and lead, *but mostly iron,* Conners thought.

The safe was empty. Conners pondered its utility. His initial thought was practical enough.

Maybe Stepanov wants to add to the weapons arsenal we already have on this compound, thought Conners. *Every member of the Pack has an assigned weapon. A few more couldn't hurt. That kind of safe wouldn't be my first choice for storing small arms or ammunition, but I guess it would work. Or maybe we're adding more teammates to the Pack,* Conners posited, *and Stepanov wants to preposition a few rifles and pistols before their arrival.*

Conners walked away, not knowing much more than a large safe had been dropped off at the shed. But he continued to ponder it.

***

Two days after the safe had been dropped off, Conners observed an armored Mercedes Benz G63 AMG pulling up to the shed. The Mercedes was a bit larger than an American Jeep Cherokee. That was not evident at first glance. But Conners knew his cars, armored or otherwise. At first, Conners didn't think twice about the vehicle being there.

Looks like Stepanov might be getting a nice new ride for himself or the Wolf, he thought.

He observed two armed men, neither of whom Conners recognized, get out of the Mercedes. Both went around to the back of the vehicle. One of the men opened the back hatch. He reached inside the vehicle with both arms and pulled something out. It was a bit larger than an airplane carry-on suitcase but not quite as big as a mid-size suitcase. The man didn't seem to be struggling with the weight of the object and easily moved it inside the shed. The second man followed the man carrying the object into the shed and shut the door behind him.

Why all the secrecy? Conners thought.

Conners looked at his fellow Pack member standing beside him. He was casually observing the same scene. A Frenchman, he had served with France's *Le Commando Hubert*, a commando unit widely considered the French equivalent to the British Special Boat Services (SBS) and the US's SEAL Teams. Commando Hubert specialized in hostage rescue, counterterrorism (focusing on maritime environments), direct action, and underwater special operations.

Conners had personally recommended the Frenchman—whom Conners fondly called *LeBeau*, after the blue-bereted Frenchman in the 1960s US television series *Hogan's Heroes*—be hired by Stepanov. The embittered LeBeau left the French special operations command after he'd lost two teammates in Africa. Both had died in a super-secret French special forces operation gone wrong and had subsequently been abandoned and disavowed by the French government.

LeBeau knew the two special operators were great soldiers who loved their country.

But they were compromised in a sticky operation while working with the special forces of an African country. Innocent people had died, many unnecessarily. The African country's government blamed the deaths on the French special operators. LeBeau knew the facts to be different than what the African government had claimed. In his eyes, his men were blameless. To keep good relations with the African country government, the French government scapegoated the two French warriors, disavowing all knowledge of them.

What was worse, LeBeau often thought, *was that their two families were left with nothing.*

LeBeau was heartbroken by the incident. He decided to take his exceptional martial skills elsewhere.

Conners trusted LeBeau more than any other man he served with in the Pack.

Conners thought LeBeau had a good heart, was extraordinarily competent, could be funny as hell, and always told the unfettered truth.

Conners looked at LeBeau.

"LeBeau, my man," Conners said, "would you mind doing some checking around for me?"

"Not a problem, boss," replied LeBeau. "What do you need me to find out?"

"I'm curious as to what it is that just got placed in that building. Keep this on the down low. Find out what you can without making it a big deal of it."

"I hear you loud and clear," replied LeBeau. "Give me a few days, and I'll let you know what I find out."

"*Merci, mon ami,*" replied Conners.

CHAPTER 46

OPERATION CLEAR VIEW

THE TWO MEN, wearing head-to-toe hunter's camouflage, were lying on the soft earth and in the brush. Popular in this part of Michigan, camouflage was standard attire by archery (bow or crossbow) hunters who needed to get close to their prey, certainly closer than hunters with high-powered rifles. On Michigan public land, hunters with rifles, on the other hand, were required to wear a color called hunter orange. The bright color was not worn so that Michigan game wardens could monitor their activity, as some Michigan hunters typically joked. It was required to be worn by hunters with firearms because, over many decades, a few hunters were wounded or killed each year ... by other hunters.

Before they squeezed the trigger, the shooters failed to recognize that the motion they were observing in the brush some 200, 100, or even 50 yards away was not the trophy buck they dreamt about: it was a 66-year-old grandfather or someone's 16-year-old daughter. The results were tragic. But for the two FBI special agents lying in the brush, wearing "hunter orange" on this day was a complete NO-GO.

The two G-men were well-concealed. Concerned that they might give off a glint or flash of reflective light to the Michigan militia members they were observing, they preferred to operate without field glasses. That meant they had to get uncomfortably close to the firing range, like seventy or eighty yards close. If they were discovered by the men they were observing, their story was well-rehearsed.

"We're hunters from Marquette who just stumbled upon you guys and wanted to know what all the shootin' was about," repeated Special Agent Joe Clairey to his junior partner.

The two men had been assigned to the FBI's highly classified national law enforcement mission, Operation *Clear View*. It was a rather unimaginative name for the FBI's effort to figure out, according to the FBI's Deputy Director, "what the hell is going on with the increased communications chatter among militia groups from across the United

States, but particularly in places like Michigan, Missouri, Montana, Wyoming, and Idaho."

Joe Clairey, the lead agent of the pair, was well-suited for this reconnaissance mission. By this point, the 44-year-old, 18-year FBI veteran and former police officer had been assigned to the FBI's office in Marquette, Michigan, for a year. Clairey quickly fell in love with northern Michigan's many year-round outdoor sports opportunities. Its waters were gin clear and frigid, and some of its vistas, like those along the idyllic coast of Pictured Rocks, on Lake Superior and not far from the port town of Munising, rivaled the most beautiful coastlines on earth. The fact that Marquette was home to Northern Michigan University, with an excellent basketball team, was also a huge plus for the basketball-loving FBI Special Agent. The city of 22,000 "Yoopers" (people who live in the Upper Peninsula or UP) suited him perfectly.

While other FBI agents had sought to avoid "the long winters and deep snow" of this area, Clairey knew that some of the most beautiful lakes and forests in the world were a short drive from his front door. A world-class hunter and fly fisherman, he knew how to be "one with nature," as he often joked with his family and colleagues. The well-read FBI agent knew, too, that Ernest Hemmingway had once chased trout in the UP and had spoken highly of his having spent 21 summers there.

New York Times author John O'Connor wrote the following about Hemmingway's time in northern Michigan:

"He spent his first 21 summers there, fishing, hunting, drinking, and chasing girls. It was where men lived hard and lean, ran trotlines, and considered bilge water a beverage."

Clairey recalled that Hemingway also said, "The best sky was in Italy and Spain, and northern Michigan in the fall."

For a moment, Clairey and his partner froze. They observed the same thing. One of the UP Boys militia members had cast a glance in their direction.

"Don't move," uttered Clairey, barely moving his lips.

Twenty excruciating seconds passed before a large jack rabbit, apparently finally spooked enough from the gunfire to scoot from its well-concealed position, crossed the area between Clairey, his partner, and the curious UP Boy. With the rabbit soon clear from everyone's vision, including that of the UP Boy, the militia member returned to his business.

After waiting ten minutes, Clairey and his partner managed to slowly pull away from their concealed observation position, eventually putting over 300 yards between them and the Michigan militia men they had observed firing at the shooting range.

Walking on a dirt trail and taking the lead, Clairey was shaking his head.

"What's up?" asked Clairey's partner.

"That did not make sense," replied Clairey.

"You mean all those AK-47s?" asked the younger, 31-year-old Special Agent, who was only on his second posting with the Bureau.

"It wasn't just the AKs, amigo," said Clairey. "It was how they were firing them."

"What do you mean?" asked Clairey's partner.

"They were firing them on fully automatic ... and as you saw, they expended *a lot* of ammo in a short time."

Not knowing how much his partner knew about AK-47s, Clairey waited for a response.

"And?" the man replied.

"And ... fully automatic means you pull the trigger, and the weapon keeps firing until it runs out of ammo. In the United States, the vast majority–like 99 percent, if not 99.9 percent–of the AK-47s sold are *semi-automatic*. One pull of the trigger and only one bullet leaves the barrel. Said another way, you must pull the trigger for each round fired. On fully automatic, however, one steady pull of the trigger, as you observed, and you can empty an entire 30-round magazine in several seconds."

The young agent shook his head affirmatively.

"But here's the part I don't understand," continued Clairey. "Every one of those nineteen yahoos was carrying and firing their *own* fully automatic weapon. In the United States today, you gotta jump through serious hoops and pay some serious bucks to buy an *original, fully automatic* AK-47. Original automatic AKs can only be bought if you pass a background check, and that usually takes a year to complete. Then you must pay the $200 tax stamp and, for those who can afford it, pay upwards of $25,000-$30,000 for each weapon. That's what they cost in the US. Now, you could probably buy one of those AK-47s for $500 to $800 in Afghanistan or $2000 in Mexico, but those aren't exactly readily accessible or optimal shopping areas for most Americans."

Clairey chuckled.

"So, in the good ole US of A," he continued, "if you want to *legally* buy a fully automatic AK, you must pay the equivalent of a new car price for it. How many of those wannabe soldiers do you think could afford a new car?"

The two men approached their office's older model pickup truck. They had left it parked in a stand of pine trees, just off the two-track road they had been walking on. The older model truck helped them blend in better with the locals.

In some cities, FBI agents drove "standard issue" black SUVs with blackened windows or plain blue or black sedans. Not in Michigan's Upper Peninsula. When Clairey arrived at the Marquette FBI office, he convinced the Bureau to let him procure a 12-year-old Ford F150 pickup to serve as the local FBI office car. In a rare case of government frugality, the Bureau agreed, saving it at least $30,000-$35,000.

"Driving one of those black SUVs around town, we'd stick out like a prostitute in church," Clairey told his fellow agents in Marquette after the Bureau originally offered to provide the Marquette office with a black SUV.

Clairey's partner stopped just short of the parked truck. He gave Clairey a hard look.

"Up to thirty thousand dollars per AK-47? Are you kiddin' me, man? They had nineteen guys out here today. Each one was shooting their own fully automatic weapon. And each had to pass a one-year background check to acquire their weapon? No, no, I don't think so," he said. "Something's not right. That does not add up."

Clairey appreciated the thoughtful summary by his less-experienced partner.

"You got it," replied Clairey. "Something is definitely wrong."

Clairey rode shotgun in the truck back to Marquette while his curious FBI mind began to think of why and how those men at the makeshift firing range were able to acquire fully automatic AK-47s. His mind drifted to Canada, just across Lake Superior, as a possible source. Its proximity to Michigan's UP made it a prime candidate as a source for the weapons. Time would tell soon enough if he was right.

CHAPTER 47

LEBEAU

"CHEF," BEGAN LEBEAU to Conners, whom LeBeau respected and was very fond of, "I checked out that item you asked me about. The one moved into the shed."

"And?" replied Blake Conners.

"To be frank, I couldn't get a straight answer. But I was able to get a look at the item for a few seconds."

"How the hell were you able to pull *that* off?" asked Conners.

"Don't ask, boss," replied LeBeau. "What you don't know can't hurt you."

Conners knew what this phrase meant. Sometimes, under interrogation, torture, or the threat of death, it's better to know less. It might save your life. Conners didn't like being kept in the dark, but, for now, he would accept LeBeau's response. He figured it was just LeBeau's resourcefulness and his concern for Conners' wellbeing.

"Were you able to find out anything … *at all?*" asked Conners.

"I was. For one thing, that big iron container is not filled with small arms (weapons) or anything else like that. The *only* item in there…is basically a metal case with a couple of latches. Had some Cyrillic letters on it, too. I think you know the Cyrillic alphabet points to origins like Russia, Bulgaria, Serbia, Ukraine, and a few other places. The case didn't look very modern. It was a bit smaller than your grandmother's old leather suitcase, only with more metal in the outer structure than suitcases of her era."

"Hey, how did you know my grandmother had an old leather suitcase?" asked Conners.

Both men laughed.

Conners was pensive. He had some thoughts about what could be in that suitcase-looking container. But he wanted to ask LeBeau's opinion first.

"Any idea what could be in that thing?" asked Conners.

"Look, you and I both know that the way they have stored it, with a guard posted outside the shed now, it's *not* being hidden away as somebody's Christmas present," replied LeBeau.

LeBeau considered what he'd just said. He promptly followed up, his tone darkly mocking, "Then again, maybe it *will* end up being somebody's Christmas present." He shook his head. "*Merde*, for all I know, it contains the keys to Rome. But there *are* a couple of things that come to mind." Gravely he said, "One, it could be some kind of biological agent. As you know, it doesn't take much of that nasty bio stuff to do a lot of damage to things like reservoirs, city water systems, shopping mall air filtration systems, and the like. However, as you also know, most military-use bio agents often need some kind of refrigeration, and that iron container had no visible refrigeration."

"Interesting," replied Conners.

"Another possibility is a nuclear device," LeBeau's voice, beyond the professionalism he always displayed, held an edge.

Conners looked directly at LeBeau. Conners nodded his head affirmatively. Both men got quiet.

Conners knew France had its own nuclear weapons arsenal. During the Cold War, France's nuclear weapons—along with those of Great Britain and the United States—were widely thought to have been one of the major deterrents to Soviet Warsaw Pact forces (led by Russia) attacking NATO's central and Western European countries. So, in Conners' eyes, the nuclear weapon idea had merit.

As for his part, having served with France's best-in-class special forces outfit gave LeBeau more than casual knowledge about these weapons.

"I have seen versions of these weapons," said LeBeau. "During the Cold War, NATO referred to them as atomic demolition munitions (ADM). They were intended to fill alpine valleys with nuclear radiation to channel Soviet tanks and troops into radiation kill zones. Today, you can find pictures of the ADMs all over the internet. Hell, I saw a photo on Google where one of your US Green Berets allegedly had one strapped between his legs right before a parachute jump. I presume it was inert," laughingly, he continued, "for training purposes only!"

Conners chuckled with him.

Conners thought back to his last years serving on active duty with the US Army. In January 2019, the *Army Times*, the weekly newspaper subscribed to by active, National Guard, Reserve, and retired soldiers, published an article about atomic demolition munitions. The article featured a former soldier from Wisconsin whose job it was to serve in an atomic demolition munition platoon in the late 1960s. By the late 1970s, these platoons were all disbanded.

"Yeah, during my last couple of years in the Army, I remember seeing an article about those things," said Conners. "Delivering and setting off those small nukes would have been a one-way suicide mission. Those Cold War days were freakin' crazy times."

The Frenchman nodded affirmatively and smiled.

"Almost as crazy as the times we live in now," he said.

Conners returned an even broader smile but then became serious.

"So, *monsieur* LeBeau, what do you think? What is your gut telling you about what's in that container?"

"I give a big edge to it being a nuclear device. Little else makes sense. If it was a bioweapon, that type of container does not make sense. I haven't even talked about chemical weapons, but as you know, boss, it takes a lot–and I do mean A LOT–of chemicals to make an effective weapon against troops or large numbers of people." LeBeau considered for a moment. "If you are going for pinpoint application or have a tightly enclosed area, like a subway car, that's a different story," said LeBeau.

"Roger that," replied Conners.

"But a small nuclear device is the thing that makes the most sense. Allegedly, the Russians stopped making them after the Cold War ended. So, the thing in that container would have to be from the 80s or maybe even the 70s. A nuclear weapons scientist would know how to 'refresh' the plutonium or uranium in the intervening years, if necessary. The container makes sense, too. A device like that will give off traces of gamma rays. Limited human exposure to the device in its current state is not a problem, but prolonged exposure to the gamma rays it produces, even just sitting still, could be harmful in the long run. So, the heavy metal container, in addition to providing some physical protection," he nodded, coming to a conclusion, "does make a lot of sense."

"So, *mon ami*," said Conners, "here is the 64,000-dollar question."

"The *what?*" asked LeBeau.

Chuckling, Conners replied, "It's an old, unimportant American saying." Conners took a deep breath. "How do we *confirm* what's in that thing?"

Conners had his own thoughts about the matter. But he wanted to hear what his French friend and fellow warrior thought.

"The easiest way to confirm its contents is with a Geiger counter. Today you can buy small, inconspicuous models on the open market. Somebody needs to get in there with one for about a minute, two minutes max. If the Geiger counter shows even the slightest levels of increased gamma or radiation emissions, we've confirmed what we're looking for."

Conners looked at LeBeau. Conners had a slight grin on his face.

"Aw, *merde*, you want *me* to go back in there?" asked LeBeau.

"Actually, no, I don't, LeBeau," replied Conners. "You've already done a lot with that scout mission of yours. Thanks for doing it. If anybody goes in there, I'll be the one to go back in. But can you help me do it?"

"I *could* help you, *chef*," said LeBeau. "But I'm not going to. If you go in there—and if the wrong people see it—that will raise some eyebrows. Let me do it. I know one of the guards there. Happens to be a Belgian guy. We hate each other when our countries play each other in football," he switched to a goofy American drawl, "or soccer, as you 'Mericans call it." In his own laughing voice, "But we otherwise get along and even speak the same language!"

"Are you sure?" replied Conners.

"I'm more than sure," replied LeBeau. "Give me a few days, and I'll have our answer."

Conners was about to say *merci, mon commandant*, when LeBeau cut him off.

"But it's going to cost you," said LeBeau.

"Name your price," said Conners.

"French wine. Not any French wine. A good case of Bordeaux. I will make a humble recommendation as to what chateaux to buy it from. Are you sure you'll be able to afford it, *chef*?"

"That's too easy," replied Conners. "If we pull off another heist like the one we did a few months back, I might be able to buy the chateaux ... or ... at least a few vines in the vineyard."

Both men laughed out loud.

CHAPTER 48

LISTEN TO YOUR URGINGS

IT HAD BOTHERED FBI SPECIAL AGENT JOE CLAIREY since he'd first spotted the object. It was during a stealthy reconnaissance of the UP Boys' firing range. He had been with his junior partner on the recon mission. They had counted nineteen militia members, each carrying his own fully automatic AK-47. But it was *not* the numerous fully automatic AK-47s that bothered and engaged Clairey's curious mind now. It was the shipping container that stood off to the side of the firing range. The container piqued Clairey's curiosity. He had been trained to follow up on those curiosities and even urgings which at times seemed to come out of nowhere. All he knew was that he needed to get a better look at that container.

On this weeknight, at 1 a.m., he and his young sidekick decided to take the old Ford 150 pickup truck out for a spin.

The G-men didn't expect anybody to be guarding the remote and makeshift firing range, made mostly of hay bales and paper targets, at night. And they didn't know it as they departed the Marquette FBI office, but they were completely right. Just to be sure, they parked their truck about a half-mile in the woods from the range. They then began walking down a two-track road toward the range and the container.

Each man wore night vision goggles (NVGs, sometimes referred to as NODs–night optical devices or night observation devices). But with the starlight and moonlight reflecting brightly off the snow, Clairey told his partner, "Screw it. We don't need these things tonight. They can be encumbering at times. Let's do this the old-fashioned way."

Clairey took off his NVGs, and his partner followed suit.

Clairey and his teammate approached the container. Clairey knew exactly what he was looking for. Clairey had served in Iraq for a year, and containers like this were a dime a dozen there. Many had been converted for multiple uses, including, in some places, for sleeping.

Clairey took out his switchable filtered flashlight and switched on the red filter. At a distance of a few feet and aided by night skylight and reflecting snow, the flashlight easily illuminated what he needed to see.

"IF there is anyone as close as 70 or 80 yards away, they won't see the red light. But they *can* see white light from several hundred yards away and sometimes farther," he told his partner, who was not exactly an outdoorsman. Clairey's partner had spent his first FBI tour in the urban canyon that was downtown Chicago.

Clairey immediately searched for the serial number. He expected to find it stenciled to one of the two containers' two side-by-side doors, and it was. Seeing that the serial number had been painted over, Clairey wanted to laugh out loud. Instead, he smiled a big grin in the darkness. With the ambient starlight, his partner could see Clairey's white teeth.

"Nothing conveys that someone is up to no good more than when they spray paint something over," whispered Clairey.

His partner suppressed a chuckle.

Like a rock climber, Clairey used the protruding metal hinges on one of the doors to climb to the top of the container, giving it some extra effort to pull himself fully up to the top. He'd been hitting the gym and climbing wall regularly, which helped.

Thank God I can still haul my 44-year-old ass to the top of this thing, he thought.

On the ground, Clairey's thirty-something sidekick thought a simple, *holy crap,* after watching his partner conquer the container like a ten-year-old kid on a Jungle Gym.

Clairey quickly found exactly what he was looking for. Unknown to the UP Boys, there was a second serial number engraved over the top of what was essentially the door frame for the container. Viewing the container from the ground, you'd never know it was there.

"Rookies," he chuckled.

He didn't want to risk a flash from his camera, and he chose not to use the Notes App of his cell phone for the light that his phone might give off, so he took out his notepad and, in the red light from the flashlight, wrote down the container's serial number. Clairey had learned during his early years in the FBI to never go anywhere without a pen and a small pocket-sized notepad. Without the notepad, he would have written the number on the palm of his hand.

His next move was to check for the GPS or IoT (Internet of Things) RFID (radio frequency identification) sensor attached to most shipping containers like this. If one knew where to look, it didn't take long to locate the device, and Joe Clairey knew where to look. He found it near the top left rear of the container. It fit perfectly into one of the container's metal grooves, thereby preventing it from getting knocked off, especially when the container had another container stacked on top of it.

Clairey pulled out his Leatherman tool, loosened a few screws, and easily removed the sensor from the containers' metal composite frame. Clairey let himself down from the top of the container.

"Jackpot," whispered Clairey to his FBI colleague, who was new to all of this. "Tonight, we batted two for three. Not bad. If this RFID sensor is a top-of-the-line version, it will have a memory capacity in it, too."

The FBI Agents took a different way back to the truck than they used to approach the container. They diverged off the trail and walked through the corner of a moonlit meadow and then through some trees. One could never be too sure about the sophistication of the UP Boys in identifying stray tracks in the local area. But given that many of the UP Boys had already been in the area, marking it up with their own boot tracks, the chances were quite slim, if not highly improbable, that the UP Boys would notice any tracks that should not be there.

The next day, Clairey shipped the RFID tracker via United Parcel Service to the FBI's Laboratory (also called the Laboratory Division) at Marine Base Quantico in Quantico, Virginia. He had also sent a classified situation report (SITREP) to his regional FBI supervisor while courtesy copying his old friend, Laura Sanders.

Sanders served as the senior FBI special agent at the US National Counter Terrorism Center (often referred to as NCTC or CTC) in Virginia. Clairey thought Sanders might be interested in the discovery of nineteen fully automatic AK-47s in one location in Michigan's Upper Peninsula. Clairey had enough situational awareness to understand his old friend, grinding away inside the Counterterrorism Center, was in a daily battle to stay on top of the US national domestic terrorism picture.

CHAPTER 49

IT'S THE REAL DEAL

"*MON CHEF*," SAID LEBEAU. "It's the real deal."

"How can you be sure, LeBeau?" asked Conners.

"Whatever Stepanov directed to be put into that box, *franchement* (frankly) … scares me." He took a deep breath before continuing quietly, "Again, don't ask me how I did it, but I was able to get in there with a Geiger counter. I took two measurements with the Geiger counter: one from outside the closed container and the other with the container's door open. The radiation–although slight–that it registered with the door closed was not beyond anything that would suggest stray atmospheric radiation or the iron box's own emission. I took a photo of the first reading."

LeBeau showed his iPhone screen to Conners.

Conners nodded. "Looks like a positive reading, if a slight one."

"Yep. I then opened the steel door and stuck the Geiger counter down into the box, holding it about 20 centimeters (about eight inches) above the device," LeBeau held out his phone to show Conners the elevated reading.

"Damn, Frenchie, are you sure you can still make babies after doing that?" asked Conners.

"Yes, I'm sure," laughed the Frenchman. "I'm not a nuclear radiation expert, but I do remember from my special operations days that limited, short-duration exposure to low-level radiation normally means there is less than a one percent chance of anything bad happening down the road. Heck, people who get radiation treatments for cancer get more exposure than that. So—how do Americans say it—my family jewels will be just fine. Besides, I'm getting too old to father some *bouts de chou* (little tots), don't you think?"

Conners laughed, "Well, from what I've heard about Frenchmen being, how shall I say, prolific lovers, I'm not so sure if you *are* too old."

Both men laughed.

"It's clear that what is in that old case is some kind of nuclear device," said LeBeau.

Now serious, both men looked at each other.

"Oh, *putain*! Let's just say it, Blake," LeBeau said. "Our original instincts were right. It's a nuclear bomb. Nothing else makes sense."

"Shit," responded Conners, "I was afraid you were going to say that. Whatever I told you before about getting you some Bordeaux wine, just double the quantity. It took huge *cajónes* to do what you did. I owe you big time. Obviously, let's keep this between us."

"Obviously, *mon ami*," replied LeBeau.

"Thoughts on what Stepanov is up to?" asked Conners.

"I have no bloody clue," replied LeBeau, remembering some of his British English. "But I have to say, that thing scares … how do you say it?" He cracked a smile, "It scares the *hell* out of me."

CHAPTER 50

PUCHTA DID IT

THE 6 FEET, 2-INCH TALL, 220-POUND RUSSIAN, and former Spetsnaz GRU soldier was a rare form of athlete. The former Russian Army biathlon ski champion had been born and raised in the rugged backwoods of Russia's wild and picturesque Kamchatka peninsula. Traveling on foot there was like living in a dark fairy tale. It was home to one of the densest brown bear populations on the planet. If a brown bear missed having you for lunch, then a pack of Arctic wolves surely would not. The terrain was brutal, and in its northern reaches, lying in a subpolar zone, the sub-zero winter weather would mercilessly kill any careless or inexperienced traveler.

Boris Stepanov had employed the Wolf's massive resources and connections to get the soldier out of a Russian military penal colony. The Godforsaken forced labor camp was in Siberia. Feeling constantly chilled was a way of life there. The soldier still had five years of a seven-year sentence to serve for a minor theft, for which Stepanov thought the soldier was guilty but had received far too harsh of a sentence. And now the former GRU operator was deeply indebted to Stepanov.

The soldier's mission was straightforward: deposit the contents of the large rucksack in the center of a frozen lake on the other side of the Finnish/Russian border. Once at the lake's shore, he was to walk 400 yards out onto the 13 to 14-inch-thick ice. There he would place the nuclear device directly on the ice. Once emplaced, set the timer for 6 hours.

Once the timer was set, the former soldier was to return across the Finnish-Russian border. At a pace of three miles per hour walking through heavy snow with snowshoes, that would give him three hours to get back across the border, meet his escort, and be driven south for another three hours to a remote dacha, away from any stray or curious eyes, before the small tactical nuclear device would explode.

As compared to walking from his parent's cabin to a "nearby" school some 2 miles on foot every day, *this will be as easy as a stroll through Moscow's Kolomenskoye Park,* thought the former Russian soldier.

For having a seven-year prison sentence eliminated and a promised payment of 100,000 dollars? He shrugged and adjusted the straps on his shoulders. *I could live on that for a long time in Kamchatka,* he thought as he trudged across the snowpack.

During the winter of 1939-1940, however, this Finland-Russia border area did not result in an easy "stroll" for the more than half million Soviet soldiers filling the ranks of the 7th, 8th, 9th, and 14th Soviet Armies. The Soviet military's–and Joseph Stalin's–strategic goal was to push the Finnish-Soviet border farther to the west, away from Leningrad (now St. Petersburg). However, the resolute Finns had another idea.

A brutal Finnish winter and the courageous, resolute, well-trained, and well-led Finnish soldiers combined to disastrous result for the undertrained Soviet soldiers in the untested Soviet Red Army. In less than three months, the Red Army suffered almost 300,000 casualties. The Finns suffered just shy of 65,000 casualties. While the Russians eventually subdued the greatly outnumbered Finns, it was at a tremendous cost.

In the decades after World War II, Finland never erected a continuous physical barrier along the vast, 830-mile border with Russia, the physical dimensions deemed too challenging. There were still sporadic, rundown semblances of a barrier along small stretches of the Finnish side of the border in 2022. They consisted of wood-posted, four-foot-high, two-strand barbwire fences intermittently emplaced along the extremely long border. The fences were barely capable of retaining a few cattle, let alone people. Sure, there were checkpoints at the sparse country roads and crossing points near the border, but that was all in terms of Finland's physical border security.

It was not until September 2022, when much of Finland was clamoring to join NATO, that the Finish Border Guard authorities' concerns about the necessity of building a more effective barrier were heard. The first prototype stretch of a new border wall wouldn't be complete until Spring 2024. However, the complete project, as envisioned, would only cover 10-20 percent of the border.

Now, in January, it was a typical white and wintery month along the inter-Finnish-Russian border. The former Russian soldier's journey would begin on foot, three miles north of Kaalamo. Kaalamo was a tiny outpost of a village in northwestern Russia. During the summer tourist season, perhaps 1000 people came north from St. Petersburg to vacation in the area. But in the dead of winter, it held less than 30 inhabitants.

There was an 18-inch-thick layer of snow on the ground. It could easily reach six to seven feet in depth during some winters.

For today's mission, two Russian border guards aided the soldier's journey. The Russian soldier's true mission was unknown to the guards. They had no idea why the soldier would be traveling across the border. For the preceding four months, the border guards' sergeant, an old, paid Stepanov connection, told them to observe the border to find out what they could about Finnish patrols on the other side. The guards did as they were ordered, thinking that they were just performing their routine duties, if perhaps with a bit more focus.

The Russian border guards had observed vehicle-mounted–and occasionally on foot–patrols passing by on the Finnish side. During late fall and early winter weather, a Finnish Land Rover-type vehicle passed by twice a day, once in the morning and once at dusk. During this snowy weather, in the dead of winter, the frequency was reduced to once per day, if that.

It seemed obvious to the Russian border sergeant and to Stepanov that the Finns were more worried about Russian tanks or armored vehicles coming across the border than some crazy former Spetsnaz soldier on snowshoes in a driving snowstorm.

***

The snow was falling and blowing so hard that, within 20 minutes, the soldier's snowshoe tracks were completely covered. A well-trained dog, if it was downwind and nearby, *might* be able to pick up a human scent in those conditions. But on this brutal day, the dogs' handlers saw no reason to venture out, nor did any of the area's handful of inhabitants.

The snow was not only falling hard in big, fluffy flakes, but it was also blowing sideways with variable gusts of winds in a northeasterly direction. The wind gusts were causing the snow to drift in places, creating almost four-foot-high drifts where the snow should only be eighteen or twenty inches deep. The ambient temperature was 15 degrees Fahrenheit. That was not exceptionally cold for January in this part of northern Europe, nor was it as cold as it could get in this part of northeastern Finland. But the wind chill factor made the average human feel much colder.

But the cold-weather-acclimatized Russian soldier did not feel cold. He had grown up on Russia's brutally cold Kamchatka peninsula. He was confident and happy. He had experienced much tougher weather conditions back home. The soldier had been briefed about—and had to back brief to his handlers—his mission a half dozen times. Over the course of several days, while being kept in isolation with no cell phone or any possible communication with the outside world, he had proven to his handlers many times over that he knew exactly how to emplace the bomb and set the bomb's timer.

For 100,000 thousand dollars and not going back to the hellhole of a military penal colony, he had often thought, *this is too easy. What a blessing.*

The soldier had recalled his days of tracking, hunting, and trapping wild game back home, often using terrain recognition to navigate the rugged and heavily wooded terrain. The hunting had helped feed him and his parents, especially through the winter. If the conditions became challenging, such as in a driving snowstorm like this, he would occasionally break out his lensatic compass. Now he carried a wallet-sized GPS device but kept his compass just in case his electronic GPS didn't work.

With GPS, this is almost cheating, he thought as the snow hit his wind-burned face. He was on the Finnish side of the border now.

He arrived at the frozen Finnish lake, his final objective, right on time.

The former Russian Spetsnaz operator didn't know it, but men in positions of much greater authority and means had calculated—or had other experts calculate—that everything was just right for setting off a small, so-called "tactical" nuclear bomb on this day. The snowfall, the wind direction, the humidity conditions, the depth of the lake, the nearby forests, everything that could affect—or mitigate—the thermal blast radius, and, more importantly, the nuclear radiation dispersion pattern of a tactical nuclear weapon had been calculated.

The destructive yield of the bomb would be roughly one-twelfth the power of the bomb that was dropped on Hiroshima, Japan, in World War II. Of the five suitcase nukes that Stepanov had procured from an old Soviet nuclear weapons scientist who lived near Tonso, Russia, this one had the smallest yield. However, the fact that it was nuclear would not only get Finland's, Russia's, Europe's, and United States' immediate attention; it would get the world's attention. In fact, it would shock the world.

"Its purpose is almost entirely political," the Wolf had said to Stepanov. "I want NATO countries and the world—including the Russian people—to think Puchta did it. But I also want to leave some *doubt* that it was *not* him. It will cause chaos, fear, and even panic in the Western world. The explosion will be big enough to be seen from overhead satellites. And the nuclear radiation will be enough to be locally detectable. But it will not be excessively destructive. If we get unlucky, we might accidentally kill a stray hunter in the area or several fish in the lake, but that should be it. One of today's best nuclear weapons scientists has informed me that the bomb's location, the heavy snow, the lake's ice and water, the wind direction, atmospheric conditions, and the negligible population in the immediate area will minimize the bomb's collateral damage. I don't know if you know this, Boris, but Finland is the least densely populated country of the 27 countries in the European Union."

"I was not aware of that," replied Stepanov.

"It's even less populated the farther north you get," replied the Wolf. "There should be nobody within five, even ten miles of that lake. The prevailing winds and predicted ground winds will dissipate any stray radiation in a north-by-northeast direction out to the Barents Sea. There is nothing but water, ice, and the occasional polar bear out there."

Stepanov pondered his boss' plan. The Wolf expected Stepanov to give a thoughtful response. Stepanov was fully aware of his boss' expectations, too. It was a major reason why the Wolf and Stepanov had been close for so many years.

"Roman, you do know, don't you, that the Americans—as well as the Russians—have satellites aloft capable of tracking the launch points, flight trajectories, and impacts of missile launches?" asked Stepanov.

"Yes, I *do* know that," replied Volkov.

"And you do know that once they figure out that the bomb was not delivered with a missile launch, that will create a lot of questions about how it was set off on Finnish soil … correct?" asked Stepanov.

"I know that, too," replied the Wolf. "And that's where our hero comes in. And I'm not talking about the Russian soldier we will employ to deliver the nuke."

Stepanov smiled at the Wolf. Stepanov already knew the name that was about to come out of the Wolf's lips.

"The Kid…our Cyberkid…will create all kinds of international havoc for us. He will feed the chaos by creating two very plausible theories on social media. One theory—the stronger one—will be that Puchta was responsible for it. The other will postulate the *minority opinion*, if you will, that somebody else did it. International governments—and their scared citizens—will be chasing their tails, trying to determine who was responsible for the bomb, a bomb that could start World War III. Meanwhile, it will be instructive to see how the Kremlin responds. Will they disavow the nuke? Because if they do, they will have to show proof that it was not theirs. How willing do you think the Russians will be to do that? And when Russian government officials and generals determine it was set off without Puchta's authority, they'll wonder who was crazy enough–or powerful enough–to do it. Out of that chaos and doubt, I will exploit my opportunity of returning to Russia."

CHAPTER 51

A HERO

THE RUSSIAN SOLDIER SLEPT PEACEFULLY in the remote, snow-covered *dacha*. The dacha, four miles from any other manmade structure, was surrounded by nothing but snow and tall pine trees.

Earlier in the evening, the drive to the dacha from the Russian side of the Finland-Russia border crossing sight had taken just under three hours. In the summer, it took two hours, but the black ice and occasional snow drifts on the road had called for more cautious speeds.

When the two-man escort, a driver and a man riding shotgun in the front passenger seat, dropped the Russian soldier off, the man in the front passenger seat was succinct and direct.

"You will be debriefed tomorrow morning at 8 a.m.," said the man. "We will give you half the cash after the debriefing, as promised. The dacha is stocked with food and drinks. Help yourself. The heat was turned on earlier. You should be comfortable in there. We will see you tomorrow morning."

After the soldier accepted the key to the front door, the two men drove away. The soldier stood silent for a moment. He looked up, admiring the brilliance of a bazillion stars overhead. The northern lights were barely visible on the horizon. The brilliant cosmic light show reminded him of his home on the Kamchatka peninsula, ten time zones–all in Russia–away.

The soldier turned around and approached the building. As he was reaching to put the key in the door, he heard the rumble. It reminded him of distant artillery fire. The rumble had been created by the weapon he had emplaced some six hours before. Its formidable and ominous sound, coming from that far away, surprised him. The way the crow flies, he had left the bomb some sixty miles away on the Finnish side of the border. In a million years, he never thought the sound would carry this far and with so much strength.

Must have worked well, he thought.

The soldier had no idea he had initiated the first Russian nuclear weapon blast on European territory since October 1990. That month the Soviet Union had conducted its last test of a nuclear weapon in its military arsenal. The soldier was told by his handlers that the reason he was crossing into Finland to plant a special bomb was to prove to the Finns that Russia could cross its border and attack Finland anytime it darn well pleased. That made sense to the soldier. But the soldier had no knowledge of the heavy price the Russians had paid for just such an attack in World War II.

"If a single former Russian soldier can just walk across the border and set off a bomb, imagine how much it will show the Finns and NATO just how weak Finland's defenses are? You will be hailed as a Russian hero!" a Pack member told him.

The man didn't know it then, but the only time he would be hailed as a Russian hero was that night, in his dreams.

***

It was easy, at 2 a.m., for the three Pack members to pump the aerosol spray into the Russian soldier's bedroom. The containers of spray were pre-positioned outside the dacha. It was the very same gas that the Pack used on the Carabinieri guards near the *San Luigi dei Francesi* church in Rome. The gas completely immobilized the peacefully sleeping Russian. And, because of the excessive dose the three Pack members pumped into the house through the building's floor-delivered heating system, the gas almost killed him.

But killing was not the gas's intended purpose. That mission belonged to one of the three Pack members.

Twenty minutes after filling the small, one-bedroom dacha with the invisible and silent substance, the Pack trio entered the house. Each man wore a gas mask. For the Pack's former Russian military men, functioning while wearing gas masks was a piece of cake. The trio easily drug the man's limp body outside the dacha before one of them fired three 9-millimeter slugs into his skull.

"It's better to do the dirty work in the deep snow instead of inside the house," said the trio's leader. "The deep snow will dilute the blood, and it will be gone by the spring."

They dragged the dead Russian into the back of the Mercedes jeep and drove him deep into the nearby desolate, if idyllic, winter forest. They dumped him into a 7 feet deep frozen grave prepared two days prior. At that depth, there was no chance that some scavenging animal would dig him up, certainly not through the frozen ground nor in the spring.

Stuffing him inside a rock-filled body bag and dumping him through the ice of a nearby lake had been considered. But when the lead Pack member of the trio had briefed Stepanov on the idea, Stepanov overruled him.

"Too much of a chance that a fisherman will snag him in the spring. You never know," said Stepanov, chuckling, "some vodka-filled fisherman might go out there thinking he's going to catch a record fish and use a fishing line strong enough to catch a whale. And when he snags the soldier's body bag, he might just try to haul up his record-sized fish from the bottom of the lake. I like the burial option much better."

The leader of the three Pack operators, a Russian himself, just laughed.

CHAPTER 52

A COMPLICATED OPERATION

OVER A PERIOD OF TWO WEEKS, the three Pack members studied every move the two Russian border guards made.

"This operation will be a bit more complicated, a bit messier than the last one," said the Pack's leader. "But the Russian border guard sergeant will be of great help to us in understanding the daily routines of his two men."

Indeed, the Russian sergeant did help. He was greatly indebted to Stepanov for saving his life from a Russian mafia hit. Stepanov had subsequently arranged–easily done if one paid enough to the right people–for the sergeant to be assigned to a safe and secluded place, even if the place was considered "a frozen hellhole" by almost every other guard who served in Russia's border guard services. Guards who were posted here, along the northern Finnish-Russian border, were lucky to get mail once or twice per week in the wintertime. Food and other provisions had to be shipped in weekly, sometimes every two weeks. The food's quality was so bad that guards resorted to hunting for local game. The drafty barracks were barely livable. But the Russian sergeant felt safe there, far away from Moscow, where he'd gotten on the wrong side of a criminal organization.

The Pack members had assessed that the two Russian border guards knew too much–or were too curious–about what had happened on the Finnish side of the border and, more importantly, who was responsible for it. After trying to think of sophisticated ways to kill the two guards who had helped the Russian bomber cross the Finland-Russian border, the three Pack members decided to make it as efficient as possible: while the Russian guards were sleeping, they injected the two guards with a lethal dose of propofol. They got the soldiers fully dressed in their winter military uniforms. They drug them out to their military jeep and put them in the back. A Pack member drove the military jeep on a snowy road and through the nearby wilderness area to a point near a river six miles north of their barracks.

Two other Pack guards followed in a second vehicle. With the two unconscious guard members in the back of the jeep, the Pack member driving the jeep created tire tracks off the road. The tracks were intended to suggest that the guards had lost control, driven off the road, and plunged over an embankment 150 feet to the river below.

Having perfectly prepared their ruse, the Pack members placed the two Russian border guard members in the front of the jeep. With a little resourcefulness, like making sure their seat belts weren't fastened and wedging a rock between the gas pedal and the floorboards, they guided the jeep to plunge down a river embankment, hit the river's ice, and plunge through it into the freezing water below.

"That worked beautifully," said one of the Pack members, admiring his work.

Back at the border outpost, the Russian sergeant and supervisor of the two men had rehearsed his story multiple times. He would recount, with feigned anguish—for anybody who wanted or demanded to hear it— how he had lost the two fine young Russian soldiers in a jeep accident.

"Not that anybody gives a shit about a Russian border guard a thousand miles from the Kremlin," said one of the Pack members.

"Mission accomplished," said the trio's team leader. "Nobody except us will know anything about a Russian guard crossing over to Finland and setting off a big firecracker."

"And nobody will suspect it except their sergeant," said one of the Pack members. "And he owes his life to Stepanov."

CHAPTER 53

NEED YOUR HELP

"MA'AM, WE NEED YOUR HELP with some high-priority requests for information (RFIs)," began the FBI's outreach liaison for the US National Counterterrorism Center. The liaison was calling on a secure phone line.

"I just sent you an email on the classified email net. It contains the full report, but I wanted to personally give you a heads up on the gist of the RFIs."

"What can I do for you?" replied the FBI's legal attaché and senior representative to Italy, Jean O'Connor.

"Our analysts at the National Counterterrorism Center have run a trace on a shipping container that began its journey from the vicinity of Reggio Calabria, Italy. It headed through the Med, then followed a northerly route before turning west across the northern Atlantic, and then made passage through the St. Lawrence Seaway. It was allegedly destined for Duluth, Minnesota. But somehow the suspect container got offloaded in Munising, in Michigan's Upper Peninsula before it reached Duluth," stated the FBI special agent.

"Sounds like a cruise I might want to take someday," replied O'Connor.

It was a lighthearted comment by the highly experienced O'Connor. During her early years with the Bureau, she worked for four years to counter transnational organized crime. Before assuming that role, she had studied a Sicilian dialect of the Italian language at the Defense Foreign Language Institute in Monterey, California. The FBI and the US Department of Defense (DOD) had a special agreement whereby FBI special agents could attend the highly specialized DOD school for foreign languages.

For four years after leaving the language school, O'Connor's sole focus was to enforce US federal laws against Italian mafia groups, their activities in the United States, and their connections with Italy's largest island. From that perspective, she was the perfect choice for her role as the FBI's senior representative and legal attaché at the US embassy in Rome, even if it meant she was away from her recently retired husband, Tom O'Connor.

"Me too," laughed the liaison officer. "What's more, the shipping container was coded as containing heavy wood and metal chairs and barstools, ostensibly 'made in Italy.' But somehow, the container ended up in a northern Michigan forest. To cut to the point, we suspect that container was carrying dozens of fully automatic AK-47s that are now in the hands of a Michigan militia group."

"Well, that's a new twist," replied O'Connor.

"It is, indeed, Ma'am. Since the container was allegedly loaded south of Naples, we here at the Center expect Italian organized crime involvement. As to which Italian mafia group it was, we'll leave that to you and your team to figure out. But what really has our attention is *how* some Michigan militia group is or might be *connected* to an Italian mafia organization. It also begs a larger question: is there more of this going on across the United States, with other militia groups?"

For Special Agent Jean O'Connor, that was a legitimate and serious concern. She pondered how much times had changed from when she was mainly concerned with massive drug flows from Italy's mafia organizations into the United States. This implied a more ominous national security threat. In the nature of 21st-century organized crime, international crime organizations not only affected economics and personal security through illicit endeavors such as the drug trade but also impacted national security interests.

"Ma'am? Are you still there," asked the liaison officer.

"Yes, I am. And I appreciate your call and the heads up. We will jump on your email today and get to work. By the way, do you people at the National Counterterrorism Center ever sleep?" asked O'Connor rhetorically.

It was 8:16 a.m. in Rome and 2:16 a.m. in Virginia.

"Haha, of course not," came the reply.

"I didn't think so," responded O'Connor. "I'll get on this ASAP. Thanks again."

CHAPTER 54

BEAUTIFUL CHAOS

WHO, WHY, AND HOW? Those were simple questions. International governments were flummoxed by these questions, national intelligence agencies were scrambling to answer them, military leaders were contemplating the long-term effects presented by them, and national stock markets were losing trillions of dollars at the doubtful future suggested by them. The national and international news media—not to mention social media—were making hay of them.

Who set off the nuclear bomb in Finland? *Why* did they set it off? And *how* was it done?

The great majority of fingers pointed to Vasily Puchta and the Russian armed forces. But Russia's government not only did not issue a message to accompany the alleged attack, but it also denied involvement. NATO was in disarray, with different government theories abounding as to why and how it happened.

"Are the Russians lying? Of course, they are!" was the question and answer posed by many international pundits and in cafés from Seattle to Buenos Aires to Vienna.

Some suggested that the Finns—to garner more NATO and international support for defending their country against the Russians—had set the bomb off on their own soil. The talk about whether Finland should be admitted to NATO after all ran rampant. There was a small minority of voices who thought someone other than Vasily Puchta might have shaken the world order with the bomb, but they had no real evidence, only theories.

Finland was divided between those who knew it could only be Russia and was just more reason to join NATO on the one side and a "leave NATO" coalition led by the Green Party.

Where would it all lead to? Was this the beginning of the dreaded World War III? Was this the first shot in an escalating nuclear exchange that would bring on the global apocalypse?

"Beautiful work," said the Wolf to Stepanov. "Tell the Kid to keep doing his magnificent cyber and social media work. The more conspiracy theories, the better. The United States, Canada, and every NATO country in Europe are running in circles trying to figure out this nuclear weapon explosion in Finland. It's beautiful, beautiful chaos, I tell you! Did you see the New York Stock Exchange drop almost 20% over three days?" Glee was in his voice. "And some Western European stock markets drop by almost 30%? At the cost of billions of dollars, US and European military forces are on full alert. The fear is palpable. If we set off a second nuclear weapon in Italy, the entire NATO house of cards will crumble."

CHAPTER 55

COOPERATION

JAKE FORTINA WAS SEATED at the table when Colonel Hennadiy Kovalenko, the Ukrainian Defense Attaché to Italy, walked into the restaurant. The two military officers had attended a counter-terrorism course together at the George C. Marshall Center in Garmisch-Partenkirchen, Germany. They reconnected in Rome through their official capacities as military attachés.

Prior to the meeting, they had been instructed on what information they could and, more importantly, could not share with each other. Fortina and Kovalenko both understood the rules of the game. For example, sources and methods for how they gained the information discussed were off-limits. Sometimes, broad references could be made, but anything implicating a specific source—a human being—was always avoided. An intelligence source's life was in constant danger.

A small hole-in-the-wall kind of joint, the place for their meeting was secure from the prying eyes and listening ears of foreign intelligence agents. It was a slow Tuesday night at the restaurant in Rome's Jewish Ghetto not far from the ancient church of San Gregoria della Divina Pieta. The Ghetto dates back to the Roman Emperor Titus's sacking of Jerusalem and deportation of Jewish slaves to Rome in 70 AD. In the 16th century, the powerful Catholic popes of the day forced Jews to attend Sunday mass there, with the erroneous intent that the Jews would convert to Christianity. In 1555 Pope Paul IV had the Ghetto walled in, setting it completely apart from other Roman quarters.

Although the physical walls were abolished in 1888, Benito Mussolini walled it in again through his prejudicial and brutal Race Laws directed against Italian Jews. Each of the Fascist edicts, which most Roman Jews thought were unthinkable until they weren't anymore, increasingly strangled, and eventually destroyed Roman Jewish families. Some Jews fled the Ghetto to places abroad or the nearby Vatican. On October 16, 1943, Italian Fascists and German Nazis invaded the ghetto for a *rastrellamento* (roundup). They rounded up twelve hundred men, women, and children and sent them to Auschwitz. Only sixteen survived. Were it not for the Vatican, which ended up housing ten thousand of Rome's twelve thousand Jews, Rome's Jewish population would have been annihilated.

Some families of the Jewish faith—at least those who had family members fortunate enough to live in the Vatican or to outright survive Mussolini's and Hitler's brutal and heinous deportations to World War II death camps—returned to the Ghetto after World War II.

The restaurant—a *trattoria*, actually—was an excellent one. The menu was in the Italian language only, unlike international tourist-frequented places where the menus were printed in four languages and somebody stood outside the restaurant trying to coax tourists to come in for, if they were lucky, an average meal.

Fortina had gotten to personally know the trattoria's owners. An Italian Israeli couple, they were avidly pro-American. But as to their menu, by God, it would remain in the Italian language only.

After warm introductions and talk of their families, Fortina and Kovalenko each ordered *carciofo alla giudia*, the traditional "Jewish style" crispy fried artichoke for which some Ghetto *ristoranti* had become famous.

"How about you pick the vino tonight," said Kovalenko.

"Are you sure, my friend?" asked Fortina.

"Quite sure. You're the one married to the Italian lady, so you should know something about this."

Kovalenko winked at Fortina. Fortina smiled.

"I think I'll get us this 2017 Vermentino from southwestern Tuscany. Should do the trick with the fried artichokes."

Kovalenko nodded.

"Hennadiy, I know it's been a while," began Fortina, getting down to business. "So, it's good to compare notes. How have things been in your part of the world?"

"It is indeed good to compare notes, my friend," replied Kovalenko. Then he sighed heavily. "My world, well, let's just say it's been…interesting. Our sources have been telling us that Puchta is becoming increasingly ill. His cancer still seems to be present, and, on some days, he looks terrible. We don't know if that means he's got a month or a year, but our best medical analysts don't think it will be much more than a few months. Furthermore, one never knows who is plotting to take over, and there are, of course, some contenders and pretenders."

"Well, that begs the obvious question, my friend," replied Fortina.

"It does, Jake," replied Kovalenko. "We still believe there are two, maybe three, individuals waiting in the wings who intend to make a move to replace Puchta when he croaks."

"Is the Wolf still in the running?" asked Fortina.

Kovalenko smiled at Fortina approvingly and nodded.

"He's our prime candidate," replied Kovalenko. "We also see a couple of contenders inside of Russia. One is an old business associate of Puchta. He's about fifteen years younger than Puchta. A second dark horse inside of Russia is a widely respected Russian Army general whom Puchta sidelined early in the war."

"What about the Wolf?" asked Fortina.

Kovalenko nodded.

"We see a lot of signs pointing to the Wolf," said Kovalenko.

"Anything you can talk about?" asked Fortina.

"Let's just say we are able to gain some—how do you Americans call it—inside baseball about him," said Kovalenko.

Fortina deduced from Kovalenko's non-specific "inside baseball" reference that there were some covert—perhaps in the Wolf's Italian organization, perhaps back in Russia helping to prep for the Wolf's return to Moscow—intelligence operators or sources who had reliable knowledge of what the Wolf was up to.

"Yep, inside baseball … I like the metaphor, Hennadiy," responded Fortina.

In fact, the Ukrainian Foreign Intelligence Service (SZRU) had a former Crimea citizen who had made his way onto the Wolf's team. When Russia's "little green men" rolled into and occupied Crimea, enabling Puchta to forcefully "annex" it from Ukraine after the 2014 Winter Olympic Games, the Crimea-born Dmitri Dunay was not happy. His father was ethnic Russian, but his mother was ethnic Ukrainian, putting her in the minority in Crimea. Both parents were Ukrainian citizens, and their loyalty was to the Ukrainian government and the people. They had established a decent life in Crimea. Dmitri's mother was a schoolteacher, and his father was a hard-working farmer and local Mr. Fix It.

"Anything specific you can talk about?" asked Fortina.

"Our sources tell us that the Wolf has been reaching out to autocratic rulers from around the world–some in political office, some out of office–to form some kind of alliance with him after he takes over Russia.

"That's not good," replied Fortina. "What about the nuke that went off in Finland? Any possible connections to the Wolf?"

Kovalenko went silent. He took a long look at Fortina. He casually looked around the room and then looked back at Fortina.

"*Possible* connections," replied Kovalenko. "We have been led to believe that the Wolf might possess a suitcase nuclear weapon." Horror edged his tone, "It might even be in Italy."

Fortina knew Kovalenko had to hold back on some of the information and intelligence he had. Fortina took "possible" connections to mean probable connections.

This last piece of information, while not verified, was the best that Kovalenko had passed to Fortina all evening.

CHAPTER 56

DE OPPRESSO LIBER

SERGEANT FIRST CLASS MANNY Alvarez put the embassy Marine Security Guard on hold. He pressed the desktop phone's transfer button indicating "Assistant Army Attaché."

On his desktop phone, Jake Fortina saw a button light up. He lifted the receiver and pressed the button.

"Good morning, Manny," said Fortina.

"Good morning, sir. The Marine Guard at Marine Guard Post One just called me," replied Alvarez, referring to the guard post that essentially served as the US embassy's security command and control post. "I've got her on hold."

"What's it about?" replied Jake Fortina.

"A guy named Blake Conners wants to see you. The Regional Security Officer is on leave so she called me straightaway, rather than him first. Isn't Conners the name you mentioned a few weeks back, the one you said you saw in the restaurant?" asked Alvarez.

Fortina couldn't believe that Alvarez had just mentioned that name. He hesitated for a few seconds.

"Sir?" asked Alvarez.

"What else did the Marine guard say? Where is Conners right now?" replied Fortina.

"Conners is standing in front of the Marine corporal as we speak. The corporal said she'd checked Conners out. He has all the right personal identification on him—a US passport, a retired US military ID, and even a legit US driver's license. The guard said Conners wants to see you like ... *right now*. Conners told the guard it was *very* important and that it might be a long while before he could make it back to the embassy. The Marine said if you're OK with seeing Conners in your office now, I needed to come down to the front gate and escort Conners up to our office ASAP. If you okay it, I'll go down and bring Conners up here by way of the funky back staircase," said Alvarez.

Given that Fortina had previously expressed some suspicions about Conners, including possible Russian involvement, Alvarez thought it best to play it safe, minimizing Connners' exposure to the physical layout of the embassy. Alvarez expected Fortina would feel the same way.

"That way, Conners won't see much of the embassy grounds or the interior of the embassy. Will that work for you, sir?" continued Alvarez.

"That's perfect. Give me a few minutes to get my stuff together. Tell the Marine guard you'll be down there in seven to eight minutes max, and then bring Conners up to my office exactly as you described. When I sit down with Conners, I want you to be here to take notes. After the meeting, we'll compare what we each thought we heard from Conners. *Capisci?*"

"I understand, sir. I'll head down to the Marine's guard shack in five mikes (minutes). I'll escort Conners through the Marine security checkpoint and bring him on up here. Will that give you enough time to prep?"

"That's perfect," replied Fortina. "I need to sanitize this place."

Besides the initial ID check, Alvarez knew the Marine security guards would require Conners to give up his cell phone and pass through their magnetometer before entering the main US embassy building.

Heck, they might even pat him down, thought Alvarez. *It's not common for someone–not even a US citizen–to just be able to waltz into a US embassy.*

In his office, Fortina reflected on his earlier days at US Embassy in Paris. During his tour of duty there, there was only one time when someone appeared off the Paris streets. That person had asked to see the Defense Attaché. The person was not a US nor a French citizen. He was from the Middle East, and he had some very interesting things to say about the people he'd been incarcerated with while in a Middle Eastern country.

Some embassy impromptu visitors were not worth the time of day. But others might have information they're willing to share about local threats to US security or, in rare cases, national security threats. As a US citizen, Conners' case was intriguing.

***

As Alverez hung up the phone, Jake began "sanitizing" his office. He had no idea what Conners wanted to tell him nor what his intentions were. Fortina would take no chances with what Conners might observe or hear in Fortina's office. He immediately removed two documents marked "SECRET" from his desk's paper inbox and locked them in a nearby iron safe, spinning the safe's dial several times to ensure the safe was locked.

Even though Conners might have caught a glimpse of Sara during the restaurant encounter, Fortina removed her picture from behind his desk to his desk drawer. He shut off both desktop computers. He called the receptionist who monitored the defense attaché office space's front door and told her to hold any calls and not allow any visitors for the next hour.

Fortina heard Alvarez and Conners come up the final three or four rarely used concrete back steps leading to the back door of the Defense Attaché Office spaces. They were for evacuation in case of fire more than anything else. There was a completely different—and official—front entry door to the US Defense Attaché Office spaces. Fortina heard Alvarez's voice outside the heavy metal door. He opened the door as Alvarez was about to knock. Blake Conners walked through the door, Alvarez right behind him. Alvarez shut the heavy steel door behind himself.

Fortina stuck out his hand.

"Sergeant Blake Conners?" asked Fortina.

Conners reached out and shook the Army lieutenant colonel's hand.

"Yes, sir. Retired sergeant Conners now," answered Conners.

"Good to see you again after all these years," said Fortina.

"Likewise, sir," replied Conners.

"Have a seat," said Fortina, opening his right hand while gesturing in the general direction of an office chair.

"Can I get you a cup of coffee?"

"That would be great. Plain black would be fine."

"I got it," Alvarez interjected, not wanting his boss to interrupt what was a cordial beginning between Fortina and Conners.

Conners, oddly enough, was already beginning to feel comfortable. The pain of being rejected by the US Army's elite Task Force was still inside him. But he felt good, *really* good, to be back with two former members of his Army Special Forces tribe. He didn't personally know Alvarez or Fortina, but he knew *of* them. Conners knew Fortina and Alvarez had stellar reputations as US Army soldiers, warriors, and leaders.

After the worldwide news channels and social media filled with news about a nuclear weapon going off on Finnish soil, and after LeBeau had discovered what he thought with 98 percent surety was a nuclear weapon being stored at the Pack's Farm, Conners decided he wanted out of the Pack.

I wanted to use my military and special ops skills for someone who appreciates them, he thought one night after LeBeau reported the discovery of the nuke. *But there is no way on God's green earth I want to be associated with anybody who is thinking about using–or maybe has already used–a nuclear weapon.*

After the encounter with Fortina in the *Ambasciata d'Abruzzo* restaurant, Conners had decided to follow his hunch that Fortina was working in Rome. It took some homework, but Conners was able to learn that Fortina was working at the US embassy. Right now, he felt this meeting with Fortina and Alvarez was his only lifeline for getting out of the Pack alive or without an extended vacation at some frozen hellhole in Siberia.

Alvarez delivered the cup of coffee to the seated Conners. Then Alvarez shut the door and sat down in a chair next to Conners.

"So, Sergeant Conners, how can I help you? What's on your mind?" asked Fortina.

"I'm in deep shit, sir," said Conners. "I need to figure out a way to get out of the complete mess I'm in. I'm here because I think the United States government can help me and because I believe I can help the US government and US national security."

Fortina projected calm and confidence and nodded affirmatively.

"Roger that," replied Fortina. "Tell me about this mess you mentioned and how you think you can help US national security interests."

Conners told Fortina everything about his time with the Pack. Well, almost everything. He left out the part about the great painting heist that took place in the San Luigi dei Francesi church. Conners decided to leave that for later, possibly for a plea bargain with Italian law enforcement authorities or the US FBI stationed in Italy. But as to everything he knew about the Wolf, Boris Stepanov, and about the Pack, and some "conference" the Wolf had held in the Italian Alps, Conners didn't hold back.

When Conners mentioned his strong suspicion of a nuclear weapon being kept in an old farm less than 15 miles from where he and Fortina were seated, Fortina kept his best possible poker face. But to say the news was shocking would be an understatement. Fortina immediately made a mental connection with the nuclear weapon that had exploded in northern Finland just a few weeks prior. It had international governments, their intelligence agencies, their stock markets, and their military forces around the world buzzing. It was not clear who was behind it or why the small nuclear bomb had been set off, but Puchta was strongly suspected by most. Others were not so sure.

In taking notes of the conversation, Alvarez didn't–couldn't, actually–write down the word "nuclear." Its implications for massive deaths and lingering destruction from radiation poisoning were so utterly horrible that he couldn't process them. Instead, he wrote down "n-weapon." Any reference to a nuclear bomb scared the crap out of both

Alvarez and Fortina, especially one that was allegedly being kept on the outskirts of Italy's largest city.

"What do you recommend I do, colonel?" asked Conners. "I need to get out of that place. I've done some bad and pretty stupid shit in my life … but there is no way I want to be involved with setting off a nuclear weapon against innocent people."

"What do *you* want to do?" asked Fortina. "You must have come here having thought about that question."

"I have, sir."

"And?" asked Fortina.

"If I go back there, I might be able to help the US work from the inside until I figure out a way to make a clean breakout. But of course, if I get caught, I'll be flayed alive and then burned to ashes, and no one will ever find my ashes," said Conners quietly.

"What's your *other* option?" asked Fortina.

"You give me refuge. Now. No non-US person or country can touch me if I'm on these US embassy grounds," said Conners.

Conners had done his homework. Article 22 of the Vienna Convention on Diplomatic Relations (1961) made this abundantly clear, essentially stating that the premises of any diplomatic mission *shall be inviolable*. Agents of a hosting State may only enter embassy grounds with the consent of the head of the mission, i.e., the Ambassador. Not only that, but it is the *duty of the host nation* to protect the premises of the mission against any intrusion or damage and that the premises of an embassy were *immune from search*.

With very rare exceptions, these international precepts have been respected around the world for decades. For example, after the 9-11 attacks, the French government immediately deployed a Gendarme police force to form a security perimeter around the outside of the US Embassy in Paris. But the French government did not offer (nor would the US accept such an offer) to protect the embassy from the inside because both parties understood the embassy to be sovereign. They also knew the embassy was well-protected from the inside by US Marines.

"Soldier to soldier," said Fortina, believing that Conners still had some sense of military honor left in him, "let me ask you. If we give you refuge, what in return will US authorities receive through your full cooperation and in your revealing what you have been doing and have observed with this Russian-based organization? You'll need to name names like you just did with me, places like you just named, everything. Will you agree to that?"

Fortina knew he was venturing into unknown territory and that he was, in fact, proposing a deal with Conners.

"Now, let me just add," continued Fortina. "I can't promise you anything except that we'll do our best to protect you from getting deep-sixed by the people you currently work for. But I can't promise you immunity from US or Italian prosecution or anything like that. Only the appropriate US and Italian authorities—way above my pay grade—have that power. Will that work for you?"

Conners thought about Fortina's offer. He then looked Fortina in the eye. Conners had a slight twinkle in his eye.

"I can do one better, colonel," replied Conners. "I have a close French—how shall we say, fellow employee—working with me in the Pack. This French guy and me are close. He's also super concerned about a possible weapon of mass destruction, this nuke. He's a former French military special operator, too. I think he'll help from the inside of the Farm, but we might need to eventually bail him out with me."

Fortina's thoughts flashed back to his positive experiences in working with French armed forces and law enforcement when he was in Paris, also as an Assistant Army attaché.

"I like what you're saying," said Fortina. "But again, I can't guarantee a damn thing about your friend. But if he helps us defeat this nuclear threat—if it is indeed a nuclear threat, as you describe—I'm sure the US and French authorities will look kindly on the French guy risking his life for the United States, Italy, and whoever else might be concerned about the Wolf detonating that thing."

"What you mentioned about a strongly suspected nuclear weapon is, of course, a very serious matter," continued Fortina. "But at this stage, we are going to need to find out more about that weapon. We need irrefutable confirmation that it is indeed a nuke, and the problem is, given what you've been up to for the past year or so, you don't have a great deal of credibility with anybody, perhaps with the exception of me."

Fortina let those words sink in for a moment. He continued.

"I happen to believe everything you just said. But if you *are*, by chance, blowing smoke up my ass right now, you know this will end very, very badly for you, right?"

Conners nodded.

"But," continued Fortina, "If you can work from the inside there for a few more weeks, and we can get someone into the Farm to independently verify that thing is as you described, we should be able to spring you out of there soon thereafter. But just realize, a lot of people– US and Italian–are gonna want to talk to you afterward. And as far as the Wolf will be concerned, you'll be a dead man walking once you leave the organization."

"I understand, sir," replied Conners. "But I'd rather take my chances with the US–or even Italian if I have to–justice system rather than justice by a Russian criminal organization."

"I hear you, *lima charlie* (loud and clear)," replied Fortina, using NATO phonetic alphabet and common Western military vernacular.

"How much longer can you be away from the Farm before the Wolf and his merry little men get suspicious?" asked Fortina.

"I can be here another twenty, thirty minutes tops," said Conners. "And then I'm gonna have to cut bait or fish. By that, I mean I stay here and turn myself and my fate over to you and the USG (US government), or I go back. If I get back late, I better have one helluva good story, or they will get suspicious."

"OK," began Fortina, "let's make sure we're on the same page. You have two choices. Number one is that we take you in now, keep you on the embassy grounds, and await further guidance from the Legal Attaché, Ambassador, the State Department, and, most likely, the US Secretary of Defense, and eventually the DNI's (Direct of National Intelligence) office as to what to do with you. Either way, I expect POTUS (President of the United States) will learn about our meeting during his daily intelligence briefing tomorrow or the day after. Door number two is that you go back in there, help us independently confirm that thing is a real nuclear weapon, and we'll do our best to get you and your French buddy out of there. It's completely your call, Sergeant Conners."

Conners lowered his head for a moment. He stared at the coffee table in front of him.

Meanwhile, Fortina knew he was out on a limb by taking this negotiation into his own hands without guidance from the Army Attaché, Defense Attaché, or Ambassador. But he also understood time was of the essence. If Conners didn't get back soon, Conners would be seriously risking his life. On the other hand, if Conners stayed at the embassy, the chances of verifying that object on the Farm was a nuke without alerting the world and creating all kinds of secondary and tertiary—not to mention unpredictable—effects were greatly lowered.

Conners raised his eyes to meet those of Fortina.

"Sir, I'm going back. As the Operations Chief for the Pack, I am trusted more than your average former military misfit within the Pack. That's a plus. I have a burner cell phone. I will call you on it. Don't call me, ever, unless I specifically change the rules. I will go back inside the Farm and see if my French buddy is ready for one last special operation with me. My gut tells me he will be, but I must be one hundred percent sure of it. I know I have much to account for, but either way, I believe door number two is the best option for me, for the United States and even Italy. *De oppresso liber.*"

"*De oppresso liber,*" responded Fortina.

Those three Latin words—to "liberate the oppressed"—were the motto of the US Army Special Forces, otherwise known as the Green Berets. The words sealed the deal for both men.

The two men stood up and shook hands. Alvarez escorted Conners back down the back stairwell and to the Marine guard post at the US embassy's principal entrance. Jake Fortina's day was about to get crazier than it had already been.

CHAPTER 57

THE TIME IS NEAR

"THE TIME TO RETURN is drawing near," said the Wolf to Stepanov. "Puchta is teetering on collapse, and so is Russia. We must be prepared to return to Moscow within six weeks. Everything has been prepared. Beyond you, my closest political advisors are in Russia, and a handful of military general officers have pledged their loyalty to me."

"I agree," replied Stepanov. "We must take the initiative, what you call in business 'first mover advantage,' correct? To miss the oncoming window of opportunity will be fatal to your plans."

"Concerning my plans," replied the Wolf, "I told you before that I wanted the suitcase nuclear bomb in Italy as a strategic reserve. I am now clear on how to use it."

"You did, indeed, sir," replied Stepanov. "And I am ready to hear it."

"Of course, you are aware that we have a few friends in the Italian government, so this has tempered my thinking on the bomb. Although I am still angry at the Italian government for seizing my yacht, I want to inflict minimal damage to the Italians with the bomb."

"Damage?" asked Stepanov.

"Yes, damage. I want to destroy the US 6th Fleet flagship. The US flagship is one of the most technologically advanced ships in the world. It is anchored just off the Italian coast. I will also inflict some damage on the nearby US naval support base. We will take every precaution to ensure the local nuclear radiation is blown out to the Med. There might be some unavoidable collateral damage to locals, however."

Stepanov was stunned at the Wolf's words.

"How do you plan to initiate the bomb?" asked Stepanov.

"Our mafia friends are connected with Iranian extremists. I'm sure they will be more than happy to execute a suicide mission against the Americans in exchange for taking care of the terrorists' families in Iran.

Much like the attack on the USS Cole in the Gulf of Aden, a single small boat with one or two suicide attackers, the bomb onboard will do the job against the American command ship. The attacker or attackers would not know the bomb is a nuke."

"Do you visualize the small boat ramming the US command ship, like the boat did against the Cole?" asked Stepanov.

"That will not be necessary. The small boat would only need to get within 300 to 400 yards of the command ship to create major damage. Positioned within 300 yards of the ship and with a distance to the shore of about 700-800 yards, the small nuke could take out the ship and some of the US Navy support facility on the shore in one blast. My nuclear weapons friends have verified this. By launching the small nuke more than 600 yards offshore, it would also minimize collateral damage to the Italian civilians living nearby."

In the entire dark scenario that the Wolf had just foretold, trying to avoid collateral damage to the Italians *was the one bright spot*, thought Stepanov. *It's a big gamble.*

It was clear to Stepanov that the Wolf had thought extensively about his scheme. But Stepanov still wanted a few blank spaces of information filled in before agreeing with his boss's plan.

"If I could ask, boss, when would you plan on doing this? And what is your ultimate objective?" asked Stepanov.

"I will have the bombing initiated within a week after my return to Russia. My objective is to completely disrupt NATO and US relations. I will have the Cyberkid standing by, immediately ready to respond after the attack with conspiracy theories and targeted AI (artificial intelligence) that the bomb was set off by a disgruntled, extremist US sailor who had gone rogue. Some people will see it as an absolute lie, but others, especially the uneducated and ill-informed, will take it as gospel. We know how some people take outlandish things they read on the internet as fact. A US sailor jumped ship about three years ago in the Baltic, and a Russian Navy ship picked him up. He has been living in a small town north of Moscow since then. Our Pack boys in Russia will kidnap him in the middle of the night before the bombing and make him disappear. The Cyberkid will then propagate the theory that the disgruntled American died in the nuclear suicide bombing. Unable to find a trace of him and believing the kid was vaporized by the nuke, the Americans and the world will not know what to think."

"Let's face it," continued the Wolf, "the two attackers who initiate the bomb will become vaporized after that bomb goes off, so no DNA evidence will ever be discovered."

Stepanov was impressed at the evil genius displayed by the Wolf. But he wondered if, with this act, the Wolf might be going too far, much too far.

CHAPTER 58.

AN URGENT MEETING

THE US EMBASSY'S DEPUTY CHIEF OF MISSION (DCM) was sitting in the meeting on behalf of the Ambassador. The DCM was intrigued as to why the Italian three-star Carabinieri general had requested an urgent meeting with the US Ambassador to Italy. While impromptu meetings such as this were not altogether rare, they were not very common, either.

The Ambassador was out of town, so his second-in-charge, DCM, took the meeting. Also present at the meeting were the US Legal Attaché, Jean O'Connor, the FBI's senior representative to Italy, and the US Defense attaché, US Navy Captain Rebecca Cheman. Accompanying the Italian general was his aide-de-camp, a Carabinieri major, and Lieutenant Colonel Sara Simonetti-Fortina. The Italian general had specifically requested Simonetti-Fortina accompany him to the meeting.

"She knows the Americans better than anyone on my staff," he told his military aide. "I want her at this meeting."

As to the US side, the DCM was a better choice than the Ambassador to represent US interests at this high-level gathering. A career US State Department diplomat, as a junior foreign service officer, he had volunteered to serve in Afghanistan, where he worked with the US FBI and Afghan provincial governments on law enforcement issues. He had also served a tour at the Hague, where Europol, Europe's international law enforcement organization, was located. The DCM knew his way around the block in working to resolve international law enforcement challenges.

After introductions and opening words by the DCM and general were given, the Italian general did not mince words.

"We believe you have someone on your staff—an Army lieutenant colonel—who has conspired with an Italian Army brigadier general to ship—and maybe has shipped—weapons to the United States. These weapons I'm speaking of are not US or Italian–they are Russian-made AK-47s."

The general thought it important to immediately clarify the weapons' origin, as the United States and Italy were major producers of small arms, including those made by the Italian company Beretta for over four hundred years.

"How the AK-47s were acquired, we don't yet know. But we do have some idea of how they got from Naples to your state of Michigan."

The DCM, a seasoned diplomat, knew there was a time to speak and a time to listen, and this was a time for listening. But he did have one question for the general.

"Who is the US Army lieutenant colonel that you suspect?" asked the DCM.

"It's Lieutenant Colonel Beauregard Bragg," replied the general.

With a serious countenance, the DCM looked at the US Defense Attaché. He turned back to the Italian general.

"Please continue, general," replied the DCM.

"We believe there are few crime organizations in the world that could have pulled off–undetected by harbor masters or customs officials–the shipping of a crate of AK-47s by sea from south of Naples to northern Michigan. The Camorra and the 'Ndrangheta are our top suspected mafia organizations, but whatever help your FBI could provide us with figuring this out would be greatly appreciated."

"We are one hundred percent on board," interjected Special Agent O'Conner. "We have and will continue to work closely with the Carabinieri in the Naples and southern Italy areas, as well as on the island of Sicily, as to which organization it might be, if any."

O'Connor was delighted to receive this information directly from a senior Carabinieri officer. She knew the Combatting Terrorism Center (CTC) was trying to ascertain information about the AK-47s, and while not specific, the general just handed her some investigation leads on a silver platter.

"Thank you very much," replied the general.

"Now, for the more sensitive part," continued the general.

"By all means, let us know how we can help," said the DCM. "The part concerning our US Army lieutenant colonel has my full attention."

Meanwhile, the DCM was pondering how a bunch of AK-47s might have been shipped—and *why* they were shipped—to northern Michigan.

"The bottom line, as I believe Americans say, is that we have a confidential witness—whom we all in this room need to protect—who came forth after a hearing a conversation between our Italian Brigadier General, Constantino Cadorna, and your Army Lieutenant Colonel Beauregard Bragg. Bragg has been our US conduit to your embassy Office of Defense Cooperation and the US Defense Department. The witness provided enough details about an arms shipment to the United States that we believe the AK-47 shipment in question was arranged by Bragg and Cadorna. What's more concerning is that Bragg apparently paid Cadorna $20,000 for the shipment. However, at this point, we only have one witness's testimony, so it would be his word against that of the two senior officers in court. We will need more evidence to prosecute."

"Go on," replied the DCM.

"We have means for accessing Cadorna's bank transactions as well as some of his contacts. But what would reinforce our case is if you could provide us evidence from your side connecting Bragg with Cadorna."

"I see," said the DCM. He looked at O'Connor, the US legal and law enforcement representative.

"Your thoughts, Jean?"

"Sir, we can definitely help with trying to collect more evidence."

O'Connor did not think it appropriate to discuss how her office intended to collect more evidence, but she instantly thought of several

229

investigative techniques, as well as the legal authorities needed to investigate a US Army officer.

"I am not at liberty to state how that will be done," she continued, "nor will I try to predict how successful we will be, but I can assure you we will do our best to determine if Bragg has broken any US laws in his dealings with Brigadier General Cadorna. And if he has, we will let you know soonest."

"Thank you, Ms. O'Connor," replied the general. "And we will investigate further to see if he might have broken any Italian laws as well."

Both the DCM and Jean O'Connor nodded affirmatively. Both O'Connor and the DCM considered Bragg's diplomatic immunity.

As the general stood up to shake hands with the DCM and Legal Attaché, Sara Simonetti pondered what she'd just heard. She also pondered how much of it–or more precisely, which parts of it, if any–she could share with Jake. The answer was not immediately clear to her.

Immediately after the Carabinieri general and his small entourage left the meeting, Jean O'Connor began to formulate her plan. It included acquiring full legal authority to access Bragg's unclassified email, place acoustic and video surveillance in his office or on his belongings and establish human surveillance of his activities if required.

Beyond the alleged purchase of the AK-47s, she had a greater concern, though: *did Bragg give away or sell any classified US information, i.e., US secrets, to Cadorna or anyone else?*

CHAPTER 59.

NEED TO KNOW

THE INTELLIGENCE COMING FROM US EMBASSY ROME was alarming. After a small nuclear bomb had been inexplicably set off in northern Finland, killing only a couple of unfortunate elk, a few birds and a lot of fish while rocking the world, now this. A *suspected* nuclear weapon was allegedly being stored in Italy, not far from Rome. It was purportedly secured by the most famous Russian living outside of Russia. Anatoly Roman Volkov, aka the Wolf, whose yacht was seized by the Italian government some two years prior. The yacht's seizure had been splashed all over social media, major television and print news outlets, and countless tabloids. The alleged discovery–just weeks after the nuke had exploded in Finland–of a tactical nuclear weapon in his compound outside Rome created an entirely different problem set for US national security leaders.

The scenarios regarding the weapon's purpose, if indeed confirmed as a nuclear weapon, were virtually endless. The national–and international–security implications boggled the mind. Which foreign intelligence agencies could know about the suspected weapon? Who should know? Who had a *need* to know?

With the serious nature of a potential nuclear threat, even if on foreign soil, these questions were for the US Director of National Intelligence (DNI) to address. Ultimately, they were for Thomas Perry, President of the United States, to answer. The DNI, James Howcroft, was appointed to the most prominent intelligence role in the US government after the new US presidential administration had taken over in 2020. A retired Marine intelligence officer who was elected to Congress and had served on the United States House Permanent Select Committee on Intelligence (also known as the House Intelligence Committee) for three terms, DNI Howcroft, knew what recommendation he would make to the President.

The other people present in the West Wing Situation Room were the Vice-President, the Secretary of State, the Secretary of Defense, and the

Chairman of the Joint Chiefs of Staff (CJCS), the United States' top-ranking military officer.

"Mr. President, we must keep this intelligence 'US only' and very 'close hold' among us, for now," said Howcroft. "It's too sensitive to share with any of our Allies. Everything hinges on confirming that the purported weapon–that suitcase–is indeed a tactical nuke. And we must confirm it ourselves. There is too much at stake here to leave it to others to confirm. If this case of a suspected suitcase nuke located near Rome leaks out to the wrong people, it will be like a red flare–or in this case, a red missile–launched over the entire planet. After the nuke explosion in Finland, European countries are skittish. Among other effects, knowledge of a second nuke in Western Europe may crash the international stock markets and embolden our enemies."

President Perry nodded.

The Director of National Intelligence continued.

"Our intelligence sources in Italy tell us that the Wolf, this Anatoly Roman Volkov, has both mafia and Italian political connections. If the wrong people in the Italian government find out that we in the US are aware of that weapon's presence, the bad actors in the Italian government will surely inform the Wolf. And he'll waste no time in moving the supposed nuke to an undisclosed location. The mafia will help the Wolf do it ... and we will lose complete track of that weapon. We Americans–alone–must confirm that the object is indeed a weapon of mass destruction. Thereafter we can inform the Italians ... and those we choose to inform must be Italian government officials that we know are not compromised."

"How do we proceed?" asked the President.

"We have a small US military and embassy team in Rome working on this case. They are in daily contact with my office and with the Pentagon. This team is in communication with an American–a retired US soldier–inside the Wolf's organization. That team is working to infiltrate the Wolf's operational field location. They call the place the Farm. It's located about 15 miles east by southeast of Rome. The team's mission is to verify the weapon is indeed a tactical nuke."

"And if they confirm it *is* a nuclear weapon? Then what?" asked the President.

"Then we immediately go in behind the initial team with a stronger and more capable force to snatch that weapon and get it to a safe place, a place we control."

"What *kind* of stronger force and for what purpose?" asked the President.

The DNI nodded to the Secretary of Defense ... otherwise known in US government and military circles as the SECDEF (pronounced *seck-def*).

The SECDEF took the DNI's clue to answer the President's question.

"Our Task Force, sir," replied SECDEF. "Their purpose will be to provide on-the-ground firepower, applying the minimum force necessary, and only if needed. Their primary objective is to seize that weapon, get it out of there, and bring it back to the US for analysis and, in the end, disposal."

"How do we get the Task Force into Italy without raising eyebrows?" asked the Vice-President.

"Well, we certainly won't bring them in as a group...but we do intend on doing this *with* a *select few* Italian eyebrows aware, sir," replied the SECDEF. "In other words, with the knowledge of a select few Italian officials beforehand."

"How do you mean? Won't that potentially compromise our operational security? Please explain," asked the Secretary of State.

"We'll bring the TF members into the country using the Rome, Milan, Florence, and Venice commercial airports. They will travel in pairs. We will have military travel orders for them indicating they are going to Vicenza to participate in a military exercise with the 173d

Airborne Brigade Combat Team (ABCT). The 173d Airborne Brigade commonly holds international training exercises, so nobody should bat an eyelash at that cover story. Meanwhile, all of TF's weapons and gear will be flown into our US Air Force Base at Aviano, then flown by helicopter from Aviano to Vicenza.

"What about the *'with* Italian eyebrows' part you just mentioned?" asked the Vice-President. "Which 'select few' Italians are you referring to?"

"We have strong, trustworthy connections with a handful of senior Carabinieri officers," replied the SECDEF. The Carabinieri are Italy's most competent law enforcement organization. The Italian people respect them tremendously. Some senior Carabinieri officials do not trust their current Italian government leadership to do the right thing. If they can get that nuke safely off Italian soil, they will jump at the chance. They'll act now and ask forgiveness from their Italian government leaders later and resign if they must."

"Why would they do that?" asked the Secretary of State.

"Because they know some Italian government officials are in the pockets of the Wolf, the mafia, and even Russia. They would rather risk their careers than see the Wolf set that weapon off in Italy. God forbid somewhere like Rome."

"That sounds like a stretch...but I'm listening," said the Vice-President.

"At Vicenza, we will have our TF members link up with, train with, and rehearse with a handful of the Carabinieri Special Intervention Group (*Gruppo Intervento Speciale, GIS*) before the assault on the Farm. The GIS is Italy's crack counter-terrorism group, but they also perform other high-stakes missions. When we, shoulder to shoulder with the Carabinieri, are successful in taking this nuke out of play, we will make sure the Italians get all the credit."

"I like that," interjected the President. "I don't care who gets credit as long as we prohibit that weapon from killing innocents."

"How many TF operators are we talking about?" asked the Vice-President.

The SECDEF looked at the Chairman of the Joint Chiefs, a four-star Air Force officer.

The Chairman responded.

"About 20, maybe 25, but certainly no more than 30," responded the US Armed Forces' top uniformed officer. "But we will defer to the on-scene TF commander as to what that final number will be."

"So, a bit less than a platoon, then?" asked the talkative Vice-President again.

The VP, a former Army National Guard officer, prided himself as the only civilian in the room—except for the DNI—who knew the difference between a US Army squad, platoon, company, battalion, regiment, brigade, or division.

The Air Force general had been well-prepped by his Army military aide to anticipate this question.

"Yes, exactly, sir," responded the general. "No more than a platoon of operators."

"And if they find a real nuke in there, what will TF's mission be?" continued the VP with his line of questioning.

"To take possession of that nuke, sir. If they can do it without firing a shot, they will. If they must take down some guards, they'll do that, too. With our inside-the-Farm US operator, we will have the complete lay of the land before we go in. The operation should not create much of a local ruckus as the TF and Carabinieri will all be firing with silencers. But if the Pack guards end up doing a lot of shooting in return, then a few folks in the nearby countryside might get a wake-up call, but that is not our intent."

"What will we do with the nuke once we get possession of it?" asked the President.

"We will fly it to Aviano Air Base via a US Blackhawk helicopter," replied the SECDEF. "We will make sure we obtain flight clearances for three US Blackhawks beforehand. We will do so under the guise of a joint US Army-FBI-Carabinieri training exercise. The Carabinieri will help us get the flight clearances beforehand."

"And if they don't?" asked the President. "Seems like you are putting a lot of this on the Carabinieri."

"We are, sir. But we have had a great working relationship with them for decades. If, if they can't grant us flight clearances, we'll have a contingency plan to get the weapon and the Task Force to Aviano by ground. We'll have a ground transportation contingency in place no matter what, even if we get flight approval," replied the Air Force four-star general. "It's just good business to have a Plan B."

"OK, got it," replied President Perry. "Tell me what happens when the weapon and TF get to Aviano."

"The US Air Force will fly the Task Force along with that nuke out of Aviano back to Charleston, West Virginia. We'll bring 'em all home with a C-17 (an agile and powerful Air Force cargo plane), and we'll make sure they have a couple of F-16 fighters accompany them across Western Europe. Once the C-17 cargo plane and the F-16s get to the Atlantic, just west of Ireland, some F-22s from Langley Air Force Base, Virginia, will meet them and take over the escort operation across the Atlantic from there. The F-22s will bring the C-17 and its cargo back home to the US, to Charleston, West Virginia."

The Vice-President interrupted again.

"What the hell is at Charleston, West Virginia? Why Charleston?"

The SECDEF nodded to the CJCS to respond.

"It's a West Virginia National Guard Air Base. It's quiet there," responded the four-star Air Force officer.

"Hell, it's West Virginia, so it's quiet everywhere, isn't it?" replied the President, chuckling.

The entire room laughed, except the Vice-President.

"Please continue," said the President.

"We'll land the Task Force and the nuke at the Charleston National Guard Airbase at 3 a.m. All TF members and the nuke will be gone from the airfield by 3:15 a.m. The two-star general commanding West Virginia's National Guard and the local base commander, a colonel, will only know that there is an Army special operations team coming in at that hour. We won't tell them it's the Task Force, and frankly, they probably don't want to know. They will only be informed that it's a SOCOM (US Special Operations Command) exercise. And they won't know that the C-17's carry-on luggage includes a nuclear weapon."

"What happens to the nuke after they land?"

"It gets turned over to the National Nuclear Security Administration (NNSA) for final examination, dismantling, and burial in a deep underground bunker," replied the SECDEF. "We've been doing this stuff for decades with our old US nukes."

"One final question," again, from the Vice-President. "Is there any danger in carrying or transporting the nuke itself?"

The Chairman of the Joint Chiefs spoke.

"Almost zero. We will take all necessary precautions, such as covering the nuke in a lead blanket. The suitcase nuke, unarmed, will only emit trace amounts of gamma rays, not enough to do any lasting harm to those who are close to it. Unless the nuke has been armed, if we drop it from 500 feet or 5000 feet, it won't go off when it hits the ground," continued the Chairman.

"Seriously?" interrupted the VP.

"Seriously, sir," replied the Chairman. "The only way it will go off is if somebody knows the codes and has set the timer. Shock or trauma to the suitcase will not set it off. We suspect, from the description we got, that it's an old Soviet device. Only about one in 30 million people would know how to set that thing off. Many of the former Soviet nuclear weapons experts, a select bunch in any case, have either long since retired or are dead from alcohol poisoning."

The SECDEF smiled.

Having socially consumed his fair share of vodka with his Russian counterparts before Russia's first invasion of Ukraine in 2014, the CJCS Chairman knew what he was talking about.

The President looked around at each person in the room.

"Any issues with what was just briefed? If so, speak now or forever hold your peace."

Silence.

The President let about ten seconds go by before speaking again, just to be sure nobody had any issues.

"OK, ladies and gentlemen, I approve this plan of operation, as well as its execution."

He looked directly at the SECDEF and CJCS.

"Godspeed to you and our great military forces, gentlemen."

CHAPTER 60

SURVEILLANCE

US ARMY CID SPECIAL AGENT CHARLIE MITCHELL loved his job. The Black American and three-sport athlete from Magnolia, New Jersey, had graduated from Sterling High School. He'd considered West Point but decided he wanted to follow his first love, law enforcement. Mitchell went off to a community college in nearby Philadelphia. While spending two years there, he'd enrolled in a criminal justice program. But then came the epiphany: he wanted to serve his country and wanted to travel "to see America and the world." A friend of his had told Mitchell about the Army's Criminal Investigation Division (CID). Its mission was essentially to investigate felony-level crimes perpetrated within the US Army. For Charlie Mitchell, the rest was history.

Mitchell entered the US embassy's Office of Defense Cooperation (ODC) office spaces at 1 a.m. With him was Special Agent Martina Lopez, a bright and always-enthusiastic woman of 28 years from San Antonia, Texas. The pair had been given the cypher lock entry code by the US embassy's Chief of the ODC, Colonel David Chapman. The embassy's Marine Guards, who were responsible for the overall security of the embassy, had been alerted in advance of their late-night entry. The CID agents had received special military legal authorization to place Lieutenant Colonel Bragg's office under acoustic and video surveillance, as well as to monitor his unclassified email network.

"This should be straightforward," noted Special Agent Mitchell, the senior agent, to

Lopez.

Given that the largest concentration of US soldiers in Italy was located at Vicenza, in northern Italy, and about five and half hours by car from Rome, Mitchell never thought he'd be investigating a case in Rome, let alone at the US embassy.

Mitchell placed three listening devices in the office: one in the corner of a framed military print hanging on his wall, one in the bathroom adjacent to his desk, and one in the desktop phone's mouthpiece. That one was perhaps the most necessary since authorization to get his phone line externally tapped, outside of embassy grounds, would need to come from Italian government officials. The CID did not want to take too much time—nor expend too much cache—to get that done. The receiver and the embassy were on US property, so that made the CID's listening efforts easier.

Monitoring Bragg's official unclassified email accounts would also be easy. This could be done remotely from the US embassy's server. Bragg's dealings with Cadorna were being investigated as possible crimes, but US military intelligence analysts were also keenly interested in whether Bragg had sold, traded, or given away any US secrets to Cadorna. The analysts were given the authority to examine the CID's work once it was complete.

Within a few days of Bragg's office being acoustically bugged, a similar activity took place in the office spaces of Italian Brigadier General Constantino Cadorna. But the Carabinieri officials took the surveillance a step further than the Americans. They added visual surveillance. They wanted to ascertain that Bragg was the only guy with whom Cadorna was cutting deals. Visual surveillance would provide additional evidence if required.

CHAPTER 61

TRUFFLE HUNTERS

THE 68-YEAR-OLD MAN quizzically observed the *Roma* (Rome)-plated Fiat sedan. He couldn't understand why the car was parked there. It was 9 p.m. The sun had gone two hours earlier.

It's parked well off the road, he thought. *A car passing by at night on the paved road would never see the car parked back there. Are there lovers in there? Why is it here? I must know!*

He approached the car from behind. He shined the small flashlight hanging from this key ring into the car. The vehicle was empty.

His concerns turned into distress.

Has someone discovered my secret truffle hunting grounds?

Whenever it suited him to look for the world-famous delicacies growing in the area, the man had headed out from his farmhouse, mostly in the evening. He would only do so in the daytime when the weather was miserable, and nobody else was out. For the past years, he and his talented cocker spaniel (unlike the French, who used pigs for truffle hunting, the Italians employed dogs) had their best success finding the highly valued edible fungi near the Alban Hills, southeast of Rome. The man prided himself in having found "his" special area some twenty years prior. It was chock full of the more valuable black truffles (the white ones being worth one-half to one-tenth the value of the black ones).

For years the man's neighbors had been trying to figure out where the great truffle hunter was finding the highly valuable culinary delicacies. A few neighbors secretly watched his every move. Some tried to follow him. None were successful in locating his black truffle gold mine.

The man had been curious about the metal fence-enclosed compound built adjacent to his favorite hunting grounds. He was always angered when the guards gave him a hard time as he searched for truffles within eyesight of the compound's main guard post.

With some valued at over $3000 per pound, black truffles provided a substantial additional income for the man and wife. A former bricklayer, he was thankful his father had passed down the traditions—and more importantly—the secrets of where to find the aromatic and highly valued food complements. Growing attached to roots, typically about two to 12 inches below the topsoil, some truffles took 20 years or more to reach full maturity. A well-trained dog with a good nose could literally be worth its weight in gold in sniffing them out.

***

The dog pulled on his chain excitedly, alerting his owner. It was different from the excitement the dog showed when he homed in on a buried truffle. For fear of giving away his prized secrets, the man had trained the dog never to bark in the forest. But the dog would pull like the dickens on his master's leash whenever another animal or human was nearby.

The truffle hunter saw the two figures through the darkness just as they saw him.

"Who are you? What are you doing here?" asked the man in Roman-accented Italian.

Jake Fortina and Manny Alvarez stopped dead in their tracks. They thought they had parked far enough—a solid mile and a half—from the compound to not be discovered at night. They had taken the additional precaution of parking their vehicle forty yards off the hardball road, on a narrow and muddy two-track road, back in the thick pine trees.

Their reconnaissance of the Farm, completed at precisely the time when the Farm would eventually be breached by the Task Force, had been very successful. Fortina and Alvarez had moved with professional stealth and acquired all the information they needed about the compound to assist the Task Force's planning of their operation. It had helped that it was a dark night, with only marginal starlight and no moonlight peeking through the thick clouds overhead.

And for this contingency, thankfully, the two had their stories straight.

"Who are *you*?" replied Fortina, clutching the Beretta 9-millimeter pistol holstered in his leather shoulder holster.

Fortina could barely make out the image of the dog beside the man standing about twenty feet away.

"I asked you first," replied the old man. "*Where* do *you* come from?"

The man did not hear a foreign accent, but with dozens of dialects in the Italian language, the man knew the responder was not from the greater Rome area.

He sounds like he might have a Veneto accent, thought the man.

And the man was right. Fortina had picked up the accent during his first US Army assignment in Vicenza.

"We are chefs," replied Fortina. "We work for a Michelin-starred restaurant in Rome."

"Which one?" asked the man.

"I am not at liberty to tell you," Fortina replied, feigning a laugh. "Why do you care?"

The man became increasingly worried.

They are truffle hunters and have discovered my treasures, he assumed.

"Why don't you have a dog with you?" asked the man.

"Our dog has been lame for over a week," replied Fortina.

"I'm sorry to hear that," replied the elderly man.

Dammit, thought the man, *they have come out to follow me, to pinpoint my favorite truffle stashes.*

"It's OK," replied Fortina. "Our dog will be better soon. It's nothing serious. Late this afternoon and into tonight, we thought we'd have a look around for some special fungi," replied Fortina, not wanting to use the word truffle. "But we had zero success. I doubt we'll be back here anytime soon."

The man didn't know if Fortina was telling the truth, but he desperately wanted to believe that Fortina was. Perish the thought that someone was on to him and his black truffle treasure trove.

"I understand," replied the man. "I bid you *buona sera*, gentlemen," he added, still speaking in Italian.

"Buona sera," replied Jake.

After Fortina's salutation, the man and his dog disappeared into the night.

Their heart rates elevated, Fortina and Alvarez approached the parked car and got in it.

Once seated, Alvarez spoke first.

"Dang, sir, you did a nice job of pulling all that out of your fourth point of contact," said Alvarez. ("Fourth point of contact" is US Army paratrooper talk referring to one's derrière.)

"Sometimes, Manny," replied Fortina, "I'd rather be lucky than good."

CHAPTER 62

MORE GUNS

BEAUREGARD BRAGG WAS PLEASED to be sitting in Italian Brigadier General Constantino Cadorna's office again. Bragg had good news to announce.

"Constantino, I want you to know that those AK-47s arrived in Munising three weeks ago without a hitch. The Michigan militia boys love 'em. They've already unpacked the rifles and given them a go. As you know, it's extremely costly and time-consuming to purchase fully automatic AK-47s on the open market in the US, so your support is helping our mission tremendously."

"It was my pleasure to get them to you," responded Cadorna. "What else can I do for you?"

"I've gotta ask, Constantino: how can I get more guns?"

"How many more, and for what purpose?" replied Cadorna.

"I have other militia groups from other states under my command who would love to get their hands on more of those weapons. Given that fully automatic AK-47s are so hard to acquire legally on the open market, this would be an excellent way to supply my militia units in other states who are asking for them. The feds won't be able to track their sales or anything having to do with them if we can continue to receive them the way we just did. Your idea of making a trial run with just 30 weapons was brilliant. We need to continue to beef up our militia units with more capabilities in case this socialist stuff keeps building in America."

"And the number you'll need for the next shipment?" asked Cadorna.

"I'd like 500 this time. Will that work?"

"I can make it happen. Given the volume, I can offer you a ten percent reduction in price from the cost of the previous shipment. *Va bene?*"

Bragg ran some quick calculations in his head. He knew that the Four M militia units in Missouri and Montana were being increasingly financially supported by far-right extremist Americans who believed in their cause. They were willing to pay almost whatever Cadorna asked for the weapons.

"That sounds fair," replied Bragg. "But I'm also going to need *at least* ten times the amount of ammo from my last purchase. That would make it 50,000 rounds of 7.62 ammo…but can you do 100,000 rounds, maybe?"

Cadorna, knowing Bragg was pushing his luck, paused. He looked at Bragg with a look that implied Bragg was asking a lot. It would also give Cadorna the upper hand when negotiating the final price.

"That will be very difficult," replied Cadorna. "I'll see what I can do. But I'm sure we will work something out."

The two men eventually agreed on the deal's final terms, including how the much larger amount of money than in the first deal would be transferred to Cadorna.

The electronic surveillance bugs in Cadorna's office worked perfectly, clearly recording every word spoken between the senior military officers.

CHAPTER 63

TASK FORCE

THE FORCEFUL KNOCK STARTLED JEREMY BUCKHALTER. It was 5:30 a.m. Since Lee Roland had shot the lieutenant governor, missing his heart by two inches but severely wounding him and paralyzing his left arm, Buckhalter was always on edge. The fact that the Michigan lieutenant governor was alive, possibly able to describe or provide a clue as to what happened right before he was shot, deeply worried Buckhalter.

Had the lieutenant governor spotted Roland before he'd fired the shot?

As unlikely as it was, it became a paranoia that kept Burkhalter up at night.

"Roland should've killed that son of a bitch," Buckhalter had thought several times since the shooting.

There were three fully loaded automatic AK-47s in Buckhalter's bedroom: one on the floor on each side of his bed and one standing up in the corner near his nightstand.

Often imagining himself a militiaman of America's early colonies, *always ready for (British Army) attacks*, Buckhalter had told his fellow UP Boys, "Every good militiaman always keeps his weapon at the ready."

With the second knock on the door, Buckhalter, who had grabbed an AK off the floor from his side of the bed after the first knock, set the weapon to fully automatic. He could see three men through the screen and glass of his front door. There were a half-dozen more behind them, keeping a good standoff distance from the house, each with some cover from any potential shots coming from the house.

Buckhalter sprayed the front door with a burst of 7.62 mm bullets.

There is no way these sonsabitches are gonna git me for being an accessory to murder, thought Buckhalter.

Unknown to Buckhalter, that is not why the agents were paying him an early morning visit. Although FBI and Michigan State Police investigators had considered that the lieutenant governor's shooting might have occurred at the hands of a white supremacist, and they had reports of Buckhalter traveling in the lower peninsula around the time of the attempted assassination of the lieutenant governor, the evidence for bringing in Buckhalter on accessory to murder charges was circumspect at best. An arrest warrant would have been next to impossible to obtain. Instead, their early morning presence was focused on the AK-47s that had been traced back to Italy and some organized crime group. For that, they had received a warrant.

After the burst of bullets fired by Buckhalter, Joe Clairey's young assistant went down. He had been shot in the thigh and abdomen. Two Michigan State policemen quickly dragged the wounded FBI agent away from Buckhalter's door and behind the cover of a State Police "blue goose," the nickname given to the standard Michigan State Police sedan. Because of excellent prior planning, a medic was assigned to the Task Force. She immediately began to assess and treat the young agent's wounds.

Wasting no time from the rear of the house, two SWAT-trained state policemen simultaneously burst through the small home's two back bedroom windows. One broke through Buckhalter's bedroom window, while the other crashed through the window of an adjacent bedroom.

Having been told beforehand that it was imperative to arrest Buckhalter alive, Tommy Kamp, a local football star who had joined the Michigan State Police not long after getting his associate degree in law enforcement, fearlessly leapt through Buckhalter's bedroom window. Kamp's teammate went through the second bedroom window. The noise got Buckhalter's attention. Buckhalter thought he'd heard just one sound, and he believed it had come from the second bedroom, not his bedroom. The noise prompted him to slowly move from the living room to the hallway that led to both bedrooms.

As Buckhalter stood in the hall, he committed himself to moving toward the second bedroom. Kamp acted decisively. He quietly emerged from Buckhalter's bedroom and stepped behind Buckhalter. He got about ten feet behind Buckhalter, who was about to reach the second bedroom door opening. It was just the kind of bold and decisive action the team would need to avoid getting into a long-term negotiation situation.

"Drop your weapon now," said Kamp, aiming his Glock 17 Gen 5 9mm handgun at the center of Buckhalter's back.

Buckhalter froze. He considered trying to turn around and fire on Kamp.

"Lay your weapon down now, Buckhalter, or I'll put three nine-millimeter rounds up your ass before you can even *think* about turning around," said Kamp. "Don't make me do that."

That's not what Kamp was trained to say. But he knew it was language that Buckhalter understood.

Looking to his front left through the second bedroom door, Buckhalter could now observe the second state trooper aiming at Buckhalter's head.

"OK, OK, I'm gonna put it down," replied Buckhalter.

Buckhalter complied with Kamp's order, slowly placing the AK-47 on the hardwood floor below him.

Before mid-morning, five men, four in Michigan's upper peninsula, including the UP Boys commander, and one man in Michigan's lower peninsula, were apprehended by a combined FBI-Michigan State Police-ATF (Bureau of Alcohol, Tobacco, Firearms and Explosives) Task Force. Since the charges included illegal weapons possession and suspicion of weapons racketeering, the ATF was brought in. Buckhalter was the only one who had put up a fight. Local television news stations in Marquette, Munising, Traverse City, and Lansing reported the arrests on the 11 a.m. news.

Within three weeks of his arrest, Jeremy Burkhalter copped a plea deal, agreeing to testify against Lee Roland for the attempted assassination of Michigan's lieutenant governor. The deal was in exchange for reducing Buckhalter's eventual sentence for being an accessory to murder and for the possession of illegal firearms. Lee Roland went to prison for life.

CHAPTER 64

VICENZA, ITALY

ALMOST ALL THE US 173D AIRBORNE BRIGADE paratroopers had deployed away from Vicenza, Italy, to a major tactical exercise conducted at the expansive US Army Grafenwoehr Military Training area in eastern Bavaria, Germany. Under the guise of being "regular" Army Green Berets from Fort Campbell, Kentucky, it was an excellent time for the 18 Task Force members to arrive at the US Army's newest base in Italy, *Caserma Del Din*. Except for a dozen or so paratroopers left behind by the 173d Brigade's leadership due to medical injury or because they were transitioning back to the States, "the Unit" practically had the base to themselves. For TF's on-scene commander, that's exactly how he preferred it.

Joining the specially tailored Task Force were six members of the Carabinieri's elite *Gruppo di Intervento Speciale (GIS)* (Special Intervention Group). The six special operators were hand-picked for the upcoming mission by the Group's commander.

Three people from Rome joined the Group, too: Lieutenant Colonel Jake Fortina and Sergeant First Class Manuel Alvarez', both from the US embassy in Rome, and Carabinieri Lieutenant Colonel Sara Simonetti-Fortina. Fortina and Alvarez would have operational roles with the team, while Simonetti-Fortina would serve as a liaison and facilitator for the six Carabinieri GIS members joining the Task Force crew.

For a place to physically rehearse their operation, the 173d Brigade Commander and Command Sergeant Major had made a large hangar available to the combined US-Italian task force. A simple plywood and plasterboard mockup, resembling a cheap Hollywood movie set, was constructed inside the hanger. The mockup replicated the Farm's handful of key buildings. The spacing between the buildings did not perfectly replicate the Farm's dimensions, but it was close enough, enabling the entire force to better envision and understand what they were getting into. Google Maps also added to their understanding of their target area.

The hangar also contained a local FedEx van procured by the Italian contingent. The van would be used to rehearse the movements the team would need to go through to make sure their arrival and departure sequences outside and inside the Farm worked perfectly.

At the first morning's meeting of the Task Force, Fortina, Alvarez, and Simonetti-Fortina each had key speaking roles. Jake and Sara agreed beforehand that they did not want the TF team members to know they were married, thinking it might become a distraction. At least one member of the GIS members had heard that Simonetti was married to an American, but Simonetti had gotten to him early, getting him—and the GIS's leader—to swear to keep that information secret.

During the entire period of working with the Task Force, Sara wore her old "Simonetti" Carabinieri nametag. She was addressed as "Lieutenant Colonel Simonetti" or "*Tenente Colonello* Simonetti" by the Italian members of the Task Force.

It was Fortina's job to brief the Task Force about the mission's key individual enablers, Blake Conners and "LeBeau the Frenchman." Both were inside the compound. He also relayed what Conners had told him about the alleged nuclear weapon's disposition inside the compound. For overall situational awareness, Fortina noted that a Crimea-born Ukrainian, who was not enamored to be working with the Pack, was also inside the compound.

"How the Crimean will respond, however, is not clear," said Fortina.

It was Simonetti-Fortina's role to talk—in near-perfect English—about the Italian airspace flight clearances granted to the three US Blackhawks. They would land and take off about seven miles from the Farm.

"Any closer, and depending on the weather and atmospheric conditions, and we might risk Pack members hearing our rotor blades," she said.

She also provided some of the Italian political-military background surrounding the operation, as well as some things the Task Force should know, such as driving on Italian roads in the event Plan B, the ground transportation option, was needed. She concluded her remarks by acknowledging local emergency medical support in the event any US-Italy team members might be wounded to the point of needing trauma-level medical care.

"The local Carabinieri will have two emergency hospital rooms on standby in the event major medical emergencies occur," she said. "If it's anything minor, however, to retain operational security, we recommend getting injured team members on the Blackhawks for the flight back to Aviano and treating them enroute."

For his part, Sergeant First Class Alvarez talked about the Air Force component of the operation, including the linkup with a C-17 airplane at Aviano air base and the immediate return of the nuclear weapon and Task Force members back to the United States.

Later in the morning, it was the Task Force Commander's turn—as well as that of his senior noncommissioned officer, an Army sergeant major—to talk about the core operational aspects of the operation.

"Our primary objective is to secure that nuke and get it out intact," said the senior Army lieutenant colonel and on-scene commander.

"Our secondary objectives are to evacuate Blake Conners and the Frenchman safely," said the commander. "There is a Crimean guy in there, too, who might be friendly to our efforts, but we don't know how he'll react if we get compromised."

He followed those comments with the key operational movements of the operation.

"Lieutenant Colonel Fortina, riding shotgun, and Sergeant Alvarez, the driver, will arrive at the Farm's gate at 2130 hours (9:30 p.m.). The gate guard is on our team. A Frenchman, he's served with France's top counterterrorism intervention force, so this operation is not his first rodeo. When the van pulls up to the Farm's guard shack, the Frenchman will address Fortina in French. Fortina will respond in French and English. That will be their mutual confirmation that the operation is a GO. FedEx trucks in Italy are authorized to deliver up to 2300 hours (11 p.m.), so a truck arriving at 2130 hours should not cause alarm or suspicion. The Frenchman, a guy named LeBeau ...."

Upon hearing *LeBeau*, one of the TF operators got a big smirk on his face.

It was rare for the Commander to stop during an operations briefing, but the Task Force was like family. The Commander had to ask.

"What are you smiling about?" he asked Sergeant First Class Driggers, a former Army Ranger from Seattle, Washington.

"It's that name," replied Driggers. A couple of other TF operators chuckled.

The Commander, the oldest special operator in the room, knew that Driggers was referring to the character from the old American television TV series Hogan's Heroes.

"Well, that means his name should be easy to remember, right?"

Driggers nodded affirmatively, still smiling. The Commander knew that a little levity among the TF warriors was a good thing from time to time, particularly when preparing the team for high-stakes US national security missions.

"OK, as I was saying," continued the Commander. "After LeBeau and Fortina exchange words, LeBeau will emphatically point to the Operations Center. That's for show, in the event a Pack member happens to be watching from afar. Both the Operations Center and the storage shed with the weapon are in sight of the entrance gate."

"After LeBeau points to the Center, Alvarez will begin driving there. But halfway there, he will veer off to the right and head straight for the shed. Blake Conners will have eliminated the guard by then. When the van pulls up to the shed, Conners will have entered and opened the safe. Fortina will exit the van first. Fortina will enter the shed and employ the Geiger counter. Fortina will have one minute to take a Geiger counter reading. Conners will be positioned at the shed's door. If the Geiger counter records a positive reading, Fortina will say "Go" to Conners, who will relay the command to the van. At that point, the two GIS members will exit the back of the van, enter the building, and secure the nuke."

The Commander paused for five seconds, then continued.

"I understand the suitcase nuke can be carried by one man."

The Commander looked at the GIS team lead, whom the Commander had already met.

"So, Giovanni, I would advise you to pick beforehand which of your men will get the honors. If they both end up carrying it, that's fine too."

"*Sì, signore,*" replied the Carabinieri major.

The TF Commander looked at Sara Simonetti for confirmation.

"That means 'yes,'" said Simonetti, leaving out the "signore" (sir) part.

The TF Commander smiled. Many of the rest of the gathering chuckled.

"I thought so," he responded.

"Once our two Italian teammates exit the van, our four TF members will be right behind them, forming a 360-degree security perimeter around the van," he continued. "Coming back out of the shed, the first to enter the van will be our Italian teammates with the nuke, followed by Fortina and Conners to the back of the van. That will leave the van's passenger seat open. Our four TF operators will be the last to enter the back of the van. Once they have shut the back door, Alvarez will drive to the gate, where our buddy LeBeau will jump in the shotgun seat, and we will continue the mission to the airfield."

The Commander looked at several people in the group.

"Any questions?"

"Yes," replied a TF operator, "what if Fortina gets a negative reading from that suitcase?"

"We don't expect that to happen, but if it does, we will leave it," replied the Commander. "We flew across the Atlantic to retrieve a nuclear weapon. If we verify that thing is not a nuke, then we're leaving it because neither I—nor anybody else—knows what the hell is inside that suitcase."

Several US and Italian operators nodded affirmatively.

"Over to you," said the Commander, looking at the team's senior sergeant.

The sergeant major nodded affirmatively to the Commander.

"Before the FedEx van arrives at the gate, a separate FedEx van with our support element—ten Unit operators and two from the GIS—will stop a half-mile from the Farm," began the Army senior sergeant. "There is a small dirt road there which turns off the main paved road. The support team will offload there. They will then move under cover of darkness to the compound and take up security positions in the forest on both sides of the compound's entrance. If needed, they will intervene with the minimum force necessary. Be advised that there is a cyclone fence around the compound, so direct your fire accordingly. The same FedEx truck that dropped the support team a half mile from the compound will pick them up at the rally point four hundred meters from the gate of the compound. Once the support team is recovered, they will be driven to the Blackhawk site for extraction."

"The first two Blackhawks, piloted by our Army brethren from Vicenza," continued the sergeant major, "will fly our US team and that nuke to Aviano Airbase. The third Blackhawk will serve as a backup. A fourth Carabinieri helicopter will pick up our six amigos from the GIS. The US birds will fly to Aviano, and the Italian bird will fly to Viterbo."

"That many moving parts seems like it might draw some local attention," said a senior TF operator.

"You're right. It is a lot of moving parts," replied the sergeant major. "But the Italian Carabinieri have registered this operation as a joint US-Italy special operations exercise."

The sergeant major looked at Simonetti for confirmation.

She nodded her head.

"That's our cover story. And we have a big farmer's field that will easily hold all four birds at the LZ (landing zone). The locals will be expecting some military activity in the area. The farmer and his neighbors have been advised that there will be some commotion between 2100 hours (9:00 p.m.) and midnight, but we will be clear of that field by 2200 hours (10 p.m.) at the latest."

"Those are the major moving parts. Any further questions?"

No response came back.

For the next three days, like a US football team practicing plays for a major championship, only with far higher stakes, the combined US-Italy special operations task force spent 10 hours per day rehearsing the operation over a dozen times. After each rehearsal, they conducted open and honest after-action reviews, ensuring that everybody knew the overall mission, their individual roles in it, the timing of the events, the risks, the possible contingencies, and anything that needed to be accounted for, cleared up, or improved upon beforehand to ensure mission success.

CHAPTER 65

ALWAYS A MASTERMIND

Joe Clairey sat in his FBI office in Marquette, Michigan. It was a beautiful morning, with a blue-bell sky outside. Clairey was excited about calling his old friend, Lauren Sanders. Sanders, who had previously served as the FBI's legal attaché to France, had been promoted to the US government's senior executive ranks as the FBI's senior special agent in the National Counterterrorism Center. The Center was located just outside Washington D.C., in McLean, Virginia. While Clairey knew Sanders would learn of the news through official channels before her long workday ended, Clairey wanted to be the first to deliver the news to his friend.

"Lauren," began Clairey, "we believe we have cracked the code on the Michigan Lieutenant Governor shooting."

Holding the desktop phone's receiver in her right hand, Lauren Sanders raised her eyes off her desk and looked out her window toward the partly cloudy skyline.

"I'm listening," she said.

"You remember those arrests we made of the Michigan UP Boys militia members, the ones who were in illegal possession of AK-47s?"

"I do indeed," replied Sanders.

"Well, we just got a confession. One of the so-called sergeants of the UP Boys, Jeremy Buckhalter, copped a plea deal. Suspecting white supremacist involvement, one of our special agents just happened to ask Buckhalter if he knew anything about the Michigan Lieutenant Governor shooting. In the presence of his lawyer, Buckhalter said he *might*. His lawyer stopped the interrogation right there and then later offered a plea deal to the prosecutor and the judge. In exchange for Buckhalter giving a full testimony–which he gave about a guy named Lee Roland, whom Buckhalter claims did the shooting–Buckhalter's weapons charges will be reduced, and Buckhalter's charges as an accessory to murder would also be reduced."

"That news that we have had a breakthrough in that case has made my day," replied Sanders.

While Sanders knew the case still had a way to go before justice would be served, Sanders let out a sigh of relief. She sat back in her chair.

"But there's more," said Clairey.

"Fire away, Joe," said Sanders, her spirits uplifted.

"The UP Boys' commander cracked, too. He gave testimony–and some evidence–linking the UP Boys to a larger interstate-militia operation called Four M."

"What was that? Did you say Four M?" asked Sanders.

"I did," replied Clairey. "Ring a bell?"

"It does," replied Sanders. "After an arrest of a guy in Missouri, that term was found on his cellphone, but local agents haven't quite figured out its significance."

"Well, apparently, it's significant, *very* significant, Lauren. It refers to a coalition that has joined together militia units of four states: Michigan, Missouri, Mississippi, and Montana. We don't know who the mastermind is yet if there is one, but we're getting close."

"Oh, there will be a mastermind, alright," replied Sanders. "There always is, isn't there, Joe?"

Clairey laughed.

"I guess you're right," he replied. "Every single time."

Both smiled before saying their goodbyes over the phone. A good day had just become a great day for the two FBI special agents.

CHAPTER 66

READY

MARCO RISI KNEW HE WAS READY. The 29-year-old *maresciallo* (warrant officer) from Italy's crack *Gruppo Intervento Speciale* (GIS) had prepared for this his entire life. An exceptional triathlete and rock climber from Trento, Italy, Risi joined the Carabinieri when he was 21. After a 2-year stint as an *alpino*, an Italian mountain soldier, he was accepted for service with the Carabinieri. From the beginning, Risi's sights had been set on joining the all-star GIS Carabinieri team that stood among Italy's finest, if not the finest, special operating forces.

On this day, Risi could not believe how fate had smiled upon him. It was his job, once the American Lieutenant Colonel Jake Fortina confirmed the weapon was nuclear, to seize the suitcase weapon and bring it back to the FedEx van. It would then be driven to the waiting helicopters seven miles away.

With Risi in the FedEx van was his 30-year-old GIS teammate, Federico Bonato III. Bonato's father had been a general who had once commanded all of Italy's *Alpini* (alpine mountain) troops. Young Federico, however, born in Turin, decided to take a different route. At the age of 19, he went straight to the Carabinieri. Unlike Risi, Bonato had not sought to join the GIS from the beginning. But his martial skills–shooting, land navigation, adaptability, quick mind and body, never-say-die attitude, and moral and physical courage–could not be denied. More than one of his supervisors had recommended Bonato to the GIS. He finally realized that GIS was his destiny.

Today, it was Bonato's mission to serve as a backup to Risi. If Risi got hurt, it was Bonato's mission to grab the nuclear suitcase and get it to the van.

Riding in the back of the van with the two Italians were four Task Force members. Their job was straight-up security: protect the two Italians, who were focused on retrieving the suitcase weapon, and protect the driver, Manuel Alvarez, and the man riding shotgun, Jake Fortina.

As the van approached the Farm's guard post, the TF support team, per the plan, was already in position. The support team surrounded about two-thirds of the Farm. The team had excellent fields of fire. The Farm was secured by a cyclone fence with barbwire at the top. Stepanov had considered reinforcing the fence, but he finally figured doing too much to it would also attract too much unwanted attention from either the occasional nearby hunter or mushroom seeker.

Inside the Operations Center, two men were on duty. In the event the Center had to be fully activated, they comprised the skeleton nighttime crew, which Stepanov had insisted upon. Occasionally, overnight communications traffic would come into the Ops Center from Pack members working in Russia or from one of the contacts in the Coalition, the global fascist leader cabal that the Wolf and Stepanov had established.

Located about 80 yards away from the guard post, there were five Pack members in the old farmhouse. In the event of intruders trying to gain access to the compound, they were meant to be the reaction force. But tonight, like on most nights, they were each four shots of vodka into the evening while playing a rousing poker game. The vodka drinking used to bother Conners. During the periods that Pack members were on call for the reaction force, Conners wanted the drinking stopped. Conners thought it was unprofessional and could negatively affect duty performance. Ever the Russian, Stepanov overruled Conners. But tonight, the thought of reaction force members getting partially impaired by excessive alcohol consumption made Conners smile.

The Wolf and Stepanov never stayed at the compound. On this evening, they were both in the Wolf's penthouse apartment near the Spanish steps, in Rome, about fifteen miles away.

***

Manny Alvarez eased up to the guard post and stopped the van. The guard, already standing outside the post before the van stopped, came up to Alvarez's driver-side window. The guard leaned sideways and looked past Alvarez into the cab. That same instant Jake Fortina leaned forward in his seat, allowing the guard and Fortina to make eye contact.

"*Bonsoir, monsieur,*" said the Frenchman, speaking past Alvarez to the man in the shotgun seat.

"Good evening, *mon ami*," replied Fortina.

Their verbal exchange confirmed that the mission was a "GO." LeBeau greeted the van exactly as he should have. And Fortina, too, answered him exactly as expected.

Having seen the van slowly approach the gate, Blake Conners made his move. He quietly moved from his position at the back of the storage shed containing the weapon. He positioned himself behind the back of the Pack member guarding its door. The Pack member was doing exactly what Conners had expected him to be doing: he was focused on the van now at the gate. The guard was not concerned. The guard had been pre-informed by Conners that the operations center would be receiving a FedEx delivery—two new desktop computer systems—at around 9:00 to 9:30 p.m.

Conners approached the guard from behind. In one swift move, Conners put a suffocating choke hold on the guard. After a slight delay, the guard dropped his weapon and tried to stop Conners' choking efforts. Conner increased the pressure on the guard's larynx, almost crushing it. The guard blacked out and went limp. Not wanting to kill the guard, Conners relieved the pressure and shot him in the neck with a powerful dose of Propofol. The guard would be out for eight hours.

Conners dragged the guard into the shed and then re-emerged. As he did, Alvarez pulled the van up to the shed. Fortina got out of the van and casually walked up to Conners. Conners opened the shed's door for Fortina.

"It's ready for inspection, sir," said Conners.

Fortina nodded.

Fortina entered the shed and approached the large, open metal container. He switched on the Geiger counter. At first, he held the Geiger counter about two feet above the suitcase. The counter's needle moved slightly, reflecting a positive reading. Fortina placed the counter on the suitcase itself, and the needle jumped markedly.

"Well, look what we found," said Fortina.

He looked at Conners.

"You were right. It's the real deal. Go!"

Conners relayed the "Go" signal to Alvarez, still seated in the van's driver's seat, and Alvarez passed the "Go" signal to the six men in the back of the van. Four TF Operators jumped out the back and formed a 360-degree perimeter around the truck. The two Italians jumped out right behind them. The Italians went into the shed. They both lifted the nuke suitcase out of the metal container. But once they both realized it did not weigh more than 20 pounds, Marco Risi carried it out of the shed as Conners held the door. Risi took the suitcase to the back of the van.

All team members, including Conners and Fortina, efficiently re-entered the van behind Risi and shut the van's back doors. The van's presence at the shed took no more than ninety seconds.

Alvarez drove the van straight for the guard shack, about 70 yards away.

Alvarez heard a distant shot fired, then another. It was coming from the Operations Center. One of the fired rounds hit the top back corner of the van. At least one person inside the ops center saw the van unexpectedly stop at the shed.

From the Farm's front entrance guard post, LeBeau returned fire at the ops center shooter. More shots were fired from the Operations Center, only this time, they were being fired at LeBeau instead of the van. That is exactly what LeBeau wanted: to distract the shooter from firing on the passenger-filled van.

TF support team members began firing from the tree line outside of the compound, slightly wounding the Pack member who had been firing on the van from the Operations Center. That seemed to quiet the shooter down, at least for now.

Alvarez finally got the van to the guard shack.

Meanwhile, the half-drunk reaction force, which had heard shots fired, got up from their card game, stumbled, and ran through the house to grab their rifles from the weapons rack.

Alvarez eased the van up to the guard shack. He could see LeBeau had been hit in his right thigh and left arm. Holding his rifle in his right hand, he told Alvarez to "go, and go now. I will cover you!"

Alvarez turned in his seat and looked at Fortina, who was in the back of the van. The plan had been for LeBeau to jump in the shotgun seat and return to the helicopters with the Team.

"What do you want to do, boss?" asked Alvarez.

Already moving to get to the right-side passenger door, "Stop the van!" Fortina shouted.

Fortina opened the shotgun passenger door and let himself out of the van. Fortina crouched low and got to LeBeau. LeBeau was sitting up outside the guard shack, with the shack between him and the shooter.

"*Vive la Normandie*," whispered LeBeau, remembering the Americans' (and Allies') liberation of Normandy in June 1944. "Leave me here … and continue the mission."

"Bull*shit*!" said Fortina. "*You* are the one who is going to live long, Frenchie! You are coming with us!"

Fortina grabbed LeBeau under his right armpit and dragged him to the back of the van. Alvarez shouted something to the back passengers, and the van's doors quickly opened. Two TF operators grabbed LeBeau and Fortina and pulled them into the van.

Two more shots rang out from the Operations Center.

This time, they were not from the Pack member shooting at the guard post. They were from the Crimean. But the shots were not directed at the van.

Two TF operators positioned in the wood line had observed the shooting. One had his rifle scope on the Crimean, while the second was scanning the area with his naked eye. What he observed surprised him.

Did that Pack dude just kill his buddy? thought the Task Force operator.

The TF operator's partner had had his scope on the Crimean and was just about to kill him when he observed the answer.

"That Pack guy just shot his buddy, dropped his weapon, and is sprinting toward the van. I don't know that the hell he's up to, but he just saved a lot of people in that van from getting hurt."

The TF operator's partner now had a bead on the Crimean and was thinking about dropping him in his tracks. But then his partner remembered their training and multiple mission rehearsals.

"Wait!" he said to his Task Force partner, "That must be the Crimean, the guy Fortina said he was not sure how he would react. Looks like he's coming over to our side!"

In the next instant, as the van began to pull away, shots rang out from the five alcohol-impaired yahoos—three Russians, a Belorussian, and a Bulgarian—who were emerging from the farmhouse. They were shooting at the Crimean.

Alvarez, not aware that the Crimean was trying to reach the van from the back, kept his foot on the gas pedal and headed for the rendezvous point at the helicopter landing zone.

Rounds being fired by the Pack reaction force through the semi-darkness were flying all around the Crimean. But it was not the Crimean's day to die.

Firing from the wood line, just outside the cyclone metal fence on the opposite side from the guard post where the two TF members had spotted the Crimean, three other TF members opened fire. Their accurate and deadly fire killed the five drunken members of the so-called reaction force within seconds.

The Crimean ran about thirty yards past the guard post to the outside of the compound and onto the hardball road. He prayed that the van's driver, even though Alvarez was now about 120 yards down the darkened road, might see the Crimean in his rearview mirror. If he was lucky, the van would turn around and come back for him. The Crimean, his hopes completely dashed, finally realized it was pure folly to keep running in the darkness. He stopped. Bent over at the waist, he gasped for air and vomited.

The two TF Operators who had observed the Crimean's 100-yard dash carefully–and with all due stealth–moved efficiently through the trees toward the Crimean. When they got about 20 yards from him in the darkness, the Crimean was still standing in the middle of the road, bent over at the waist, breathing hard, and still looking toward where the van's red lights had faded into oblivion. It was the hardest he had run since he'd played midfield as a 17-year-old soccer player some 16 years earlier.

One of the TF operators, standing just inside the tree line at the edge of the road, spoke in a barely audible voice.

"Are you the Crimean?" he asked.

The Crimean heard the voice. He stood up straight, and one could almost see his ears perk up like a deer does when it senses danger nearby. At first, the Crimean thought the question was from a ghost or an angel. The Crimean slowly turned to his right.

He squinted his eyes. Inside the tree line, he could see two dark figures, one appearing to have a rifle pointed directly at him and the other with his weapon pointed at the ground.

The one with his weapon pointed down spoke again, only this time a bit louder.

"Are you the Crimean, the one we were told about?"

The Crimean didn't know if his answer would get him killed or allow him to live. But at this point, not knowing if the Packs' reaction force was dead or alive, he knew he couldn't go back into that compound.

"Yes, I am from Crimea," he said. "And yes, I am finished working with those crazy assholes."

"Good. We are Americans," answered the TF operator. "And we are going to get you safely out of here. Are you carrying any weapons?"

"No," answered the Crimean. "And I will strip down to my underwear to prove it if I need to."

"That won't be necessary," said the TF operator. "But I am gonna check you out, just to be sure. Take five steps toward me."

The Crimean did as he was told, counting out five deliberate steps. The TF operator stepped toward the Crimean and frisked him while the operator's buddy kept his weapon aimed at the Crimean's head.

"He's clean," he told his partner, who was still holding a bead on the Crimean's head.

"Come with us," said the operator to the Crimean.

Again, the Crimean did as he was told.

Per the plan, the support team members quickly exfiltrated through the forest to the waiting FedEx vans and were driven to the helicopter landing zone.

Once back at the helicopter rendezvous point, the Crimean was flown, along with the Italian Carabinieri team members, as well as Sara Simonetti-Fortina, to Viterbo.

The Crimean would later trade information against the Wolf, Stepanov, the torturer Nikolai, and the Pack for significantly reduced time in an Italian jail.

Safely on a Blackhawk helicopter with the US contingent, LeBeau was flown back to the US Air Force health clinic in Aviano before being flown to a US hospital in Germany for further treatment. He healed up well, all things considered. LeBeau later married a gorgeous Italian woman, and the couple had two children.

The TF team's mission continued all the way back to West Virginia.

CHAPTER 67

THE ARREST

THE US C-17 CARRYING THE TASK FORCE MEMBERS, Blake Conners, and the nuclear suitcase was 200 miles off the western coast of Ireland and over the Atlantic Ocean when the 14 members of Italy's *Gruppo Intervento Speciale* (GIS) pulled up curbside two blocks from the Wolf's apartment. As an additional operation security precaution, they did not want to pull up on the street right below his apartment. They knew it was better to bring more operators than needed when arresting a high-profile individual like the Wolf, who had his own private security. On the streets surrounding the Wolf's apartment, additional Carabinieri police officers were posted to block all exit roads, just in case the Wolf tried to make a break for it by car or some other conveyance.

Surprisingly—and wisely—the Pack member seated outside the entrance door to the Wolf's $12 million dollar penthouse apartment, just two blocks from the Spanish steps on the *via Condotti*—did not make a fuss when approached by the lead GIS operator at 5:30 a.m. There were five more GIS members, all with their faces masked, standing behind the lead GIS operator.

The Wolf's luxurious apartment had been under Carabinieri surveillance for almost two years. After they seized his yacht, a few months after Russia's invasion of Ukraine, the Italian government authorities placed the Wolf on house arrest. Within the previous six months, however, due to the Wolf's political allies in the Italian government, the Carabinieri were directed to abolish that restriction. They did, however, place travel restrictions on him requiring him to notify the police whenever he left Rome's city limits. In the Italian government, the Wolf had paid too many people off for the government to be more restrictive than that.

But on this morning, the Wolf's political allies were not aware of his pending arrest. The Carabinieri, under the top cover of only a handful of senior government officials, including the Deputy Prime Minister, had decided to act. What the GIS, along with its American allies—the Task

Force—had discovered the night before provided more than ample evidence that the Wolf was in way over his head and had broken plenty of Italian laws, without even including the nuclear suitcase in those charges.

The Wolf's arrest was uneventful. The Wolf and Stepanov figured the police had fresh evidence incriminating them both, but they had no idea what had gone down at the Farm some seven hours earlier. After all, how could they? All the guards left at the Farm were dead, except the guard at the shed where the nuclear weapon had been stored.

Within an hour of the shootout at the Farm, the dead bodies were quietly removed by a special Carabinieri intelligence task force, and the guard found in the shed had been taken to a secure hospital to be monitored until he regained consciousness.

The Wolf was not going back to Russia, nor was Stepanov.

CHAPTER 68

PRESIDENT TO PRIME MINISTER

ITALIAN PRIME MINISTER SILVIA MOSCONONI was anxious about the phone call. She was told in advance that US President Thomas Perry was going to offer his thanks for the excellent cooperation between a US military special force (there would be no mention of the Task Force), the US embassy, and Italy's Carabinieri forces, particularly its highly professional Special Intervention Group (GIS). But Moscononi was still a bit unsettled that her Deputy Prime minister informed her about the raid after the fact, after the raid and the arrests of the Wolf and Stepanov. It had only been four hours since the Wolf and Stepanov were arrested.

Her senior military aide took the call on the bright red phone and passed the receiver directly to the Prime Minister.

"Thank you for taking my call, Madame Minister," began Perry.

With each subsequent sentence, Perry paused for the online interpreter to relay the message to the Prime Minister in Italian.

"I want to thank you for the spectacular service of your special Carabinieri forces in accomplishing, I'm sure you'll agree, a most important mission, a mission that likely saved thousands of Italian lives, and possibly even American and other Allied lives."

Prime Minister Moscononi responded with a simple if awkward sounding "Si."

"We couldn't have done it without your government's cooperation," continued Perry. "And I promise you, we will provide any intelligence we have concerning that weapon, Volkov's so-called Pack, and any other intelligence that we collected that is of national security value to Italy, *va bene?*" added the President.

"Va bene," replied Moscononi.

Finally deciding to take the high road, the Italian prime minister continued.

"Thank you for helping us rid our country of this terribly menacing weapon. We will remain vigilant as to other similar weapons in our country," she said. "We are very proud of our Carabinieri, and you should be proud of your military forces, too." She added, "And we are honored to continue to host America's military forces in Italy."

"Thank you, Silvia," replied Perry. "We very much appreciate our partnership with you."

"As do we with you, Thomas," replied the Italian PM.

After wishing each other and their citizens well, the call ended.

CHAPTER 69

CONSPIRACY

THE AFTER-ACTION FOLLOW-UP with the Pentagon and senior members of the US intelligence community had been intense. Three weeks after the successful operation on the Farm, Jake Fortina was hoping for a routine day. As Jake parked and exited his "Rome special" personal vehicle–a Lancia with a few dings on its fenders and about 120,000 miles on the odometer–in the embassy parking lot, he was happy to be headed to his office. Along the way, he observed an out-of-place grey van with an official US Naval Forces license plate.

In the Office of Defense Cooperation (ODC) office spaces, not far from Fortina's office, US Criminal Investigation Division (CID) Special-Agent-In-Charge, Charlie Mitchell, was awaiting Beauregard Bragg's arrival at work. With Mitchell was Martina Lopez, a junior CID agent. Two Marines, part of the embassy's embedded security force, accompanied the military law enforcement duo to provide security backup.

The embassy grounds, from a US government and US military perspective, were the best–if not the only–place to conduct the arrest. Outside of the embassy, a legal arrest by US authorities, even of a US citizen, was almost impossible. Such an arrest would have brought Italian law enforcement jurisdictions into play, making the arrest far more complicated, if not illegal, under Italian law.

The two CID agents were standing by in Colonel Chapman's office when they heard the footsteps leading to Lieutenant Colonel Bragg's office. Once Special Agent Mitchell heard Bragg unlock his office door and walk into his office, it was on. The two CID agents, followed by the two Marines, made their move.

Knocking on the frame of the open office door and walking in first, Special Agent Mitchell walked up to Bragg's desk. Bragg had just sat down behind it.

"Lieutenant Colonel Beauregard Bragg," began Mitchell, "I am US Army CID Special Charles Mitchell. With me is Special Agent Martina Lopez."

Mitchell, wearing civilian clothes with a jacket that said "CID" above his left breast pocket, showed Bragg his CID badge and military ID card. Lopez followed suit.

Bragg quickly glanced at the items. He nodded affirmatively.

"What do you want?" asked Bragg in a surly tone.

Mitchell addressed Bragg with the first of several charges.

"Lieutenant Colonel Beauregard Bragg, under the US Uniformed Code of Military Justice (UCMJ), chapter 881, article 81, you are hereby being charged with conspiracy."

Mitchell continued with several other charges. Once complete with all charges–at least those established to that point in time–he continued, following Article 31 of the UCMJ. The UCMJ's Article 31 is comparable to US Miranda Rights. Article 31 covers service members' rights against self-incrimination, as well as against the use of coercion.

"You have the right to remain silent. You do not have to make a statement. Any statement you do make can or will be used against you. You have the right to speak to an attorney whether or not you committed a crime. You have the right to have an attorney by your side when you talk to any investigator or anyone in your chain of command."

The headache from Bragg's hangover got worse. And he wasn't about to stand up for the morning visitors to his office.

Special Agent Lopez, about seven inches shorter than Bragg, walked around to the side of Bragg's desk and looked down at him.

"Please stand up, sir," she said firmly.

Still seated, Bragg defiantly shook his head and looked down at his desktop. He looked up at the two white Marines as if they were somehow going to help save him from these non-white interlopers. The Marines stepped toward the still-seated Army officer. Both Marines, physically suggesting they were about to use force, leaned toward a surprised Bragg.

The senior Marine, a sergeant, responded.

"Sir, you need to stand up ... *now*."

Finally facing reality, Bragg slowly stood.

Lopez went behind Bragg and placed him in handcuffs.

On the embassy grounds two floors below, the armored van from the US Naval Base at Naples stood by, the engine running. Two US Army military police soldiers stood outside the van, and a US Navy petty officer third class was seated behind the steering wheel. As Bragg was taken down the back stairs, the out-of-place Navy van, at least for the US embassy, was beginning to attract some diplomatic eyeballs from the back windows of the embassy's main building.

Fortina looked through his office window and down at the van. He observed a Black special agent, Charlie Mitchell, leading Bragg by one arm, along with a Hispanic special agent, Martina Lopez, on the other arm. They were walking Bragg to the van. Bragg had his head down, looking defeated.

Fortina recalled the epithets with which Bragg had referred to Americans of Black, African, and Latino heritage. Fortina smiled.

"That is *some* poetic justice right there," he said out loud.

Alvarez, next door to Fortina's open office door, heard the comment and walked into the open office.

"What was that about, sir?"

"I don't exactly know the entire story behind what's going on down there," replied Fortina, still looking through the window. "But all I can say is that it's a good day for our Army."

Bragg was driven two hours south to the US naval base near Naples. From there, he would be flown to the U.S. Army Regional Correction Facility-Europe at Sembach, Germany. Sembach was a US Air Force base until 1995 when the US Army took it over. For decades after World War II, the US Army's major detention facility on European soil had been in Mannheim, Germany. At least, it *used to be* in Mannheim until Mannheim's mayor told the then US Army Europe (USAREUR) commander that he was not a big fan of American soldiers being stationed in his town. After the collapse of the Soviet Union in late 1991, the USAREUR commander made sure the first US Army troops to leave Europe did so from Mannheim, taking well over a thousand jobs for local Germans with them. Thereafter, the US military detention center moved to Sembach.

Since then, and for the past dozen years or so, U.S. service members who were accused or convicted of crimes in Europe, Africa, and the Middle East were brought to the jail that many local Germans and or Americans living in Germany didn't know existed.

From Sembach, Bragg would be driven by ground transportation to nearby Ramstein US Air Base, and from Ramstein, he would be flown by military aircraft to the United States for trial.

In one sense, Bragg was fortunate. As a military officer assigned to a US embassy, he held a US diplomatic passport. Under international law, that black passport afforded him some protection from prosecution by the Italian government. That is not to say Bragg's prosecution and fate would have been better or worse with the Italians. It just meant that Bragg would not have to go through two different prosecutions.

The United States Penitentiary at Fort Leavenworth, Kansas—colloquially known as "Leavenworth" or "the long course" by US Army soldiers everywhere—would eventually become Bragg's new home.

At Leavenworth, Beauregard Bragg's drinking problem stopped. As to the hate in his heart, God only knows what happened to that.

CHAPTER 70

THE DEAL: THREE MONTHS AFTER THE RAID AT THE FARM

BLAKE CONNERS COULDN'T BELIEVE he was back at Fort Liberty, North Carolina. A former US Army 82d Airborne Division paratrooper, decades prior, when it was called Fort Bragg, he thought he'd forever put the place in his rearview mirror. Now he was in Fort Liberty's brig, awaiting further disposition as the "big brass" of the US Department of Defense and US law enforcement figured out what to do with him.

In Italy, he had been the operations officer for a private special operations group directed by the Wolf. The Italian government wanted him extradited to Italy for questioning. Conners had been implicated in some crimes conducted by the Pack. Increasingly, after the discovery and seizure of the old Russian suitcase nuke from the Pack, the Italians, the Finns, and many others began to speculate if there was not indeed a connection between the nuke that went off in Finland and the one that held by the Wolf and his band of merry men.

The Americans, for their part, saw retired Army Sergeant First Class Blake Conners as a wayward retired soldier who had mostly redeemed himself. He had turned himself into the US Embassy and then risked his life to save American sailors and perhaps even civilian Italians from the destructive detonation of a nuclear weapon. To the Americans, his was not only a case of "no harm, no foul" but someone whose actions, in the end, were laudable if not heroic.

After speaking with his defense attorney, Conners knew what his course of action would be.

"I'll tell the Americans and the Italians *everything* I know about the great painting heist that took place in the *San Luigi dei Francesi* church. Everything."

Within three months of making the statement, negotiations with the Italian government were complete. For detailed information about the great painting heist, the Italian government would drop the request to have Conners extradited to Italy for trial. US civilian and military legal authorities agreed that Conners would be released from the Fort Liberty brig with one year of probation. After that, his record would be clean.

Within another year after the Italian government negotiations were complete, two of the three original Caravaggio paintings had been recovered by the Italian government.

And as for Blake Conners, while the Task Force on-scene-commander from the Farm operation wanted to give Conners a unit coin or a certificate of appreciation, but, for operational security (OPSEC) reasons, "the Unit" had no such thing. A simple handshake and "thank you" from the Commander, with five other special operators present, all masked up for OPSEC (operational security) purposes, would have to do.

Blake Conners never made the Task Force.

But a thank you from their commander is priceless, thought the US Army veteran.

CHAPTER 71.

"GET OFF THE X!" SIX MONTHS AFTER THE RAID.

JAKE AND SARA WERE THANKFUL to have been invited to the special mass inside Saint Peter's Basilica.

"How thoughtful it was of the Ambassador to invite us," said Sara to Jake.

"The Ambassador" Sara was referring to was not the US Ambassador to Italy, but rather, the US Ambassador to the Holy See (more commonly understood as the Vatican).

Periodically, the Pope would celebrate mass publicly and occasionally privately. Sara and Jake, both Catholic, were delighted to be going to the public mid-week mass.

Sara thought back to when she'd attended a private mass the Pope had held for the Carabinieri forces. On that day, the Pope thanked the Carabinieri for their service at the Vatican. Since 1506 the Swiss Guards have been the main guarantors of the Vatican's security, but in recent decades their security mission has been heavily augmented by the Carabinieri. The last time the Pope addressed the Carabinieri was in October 2020.

"Your esteemed work around Vatican City enables the peaceful running of events that, throughout the year, attract pilgrims and tourists from all over the world," said the Pope, adding that the Carabinieri's service was "an activity that requires, on the one hand, the need to enforce dispositions, and on the other, patience and openness to the needs of others." The Pope also highlighted the Carabinieri officers' sense of sacrifice and duty.

For attendance at public masses, the Vatican always kept a couple of rows reserved for Ambassadors, their families, and friends, as well as senior Italian government officials. For the Vatican, a sovereign state of just .19 square miles, the territorially smallest country in the world, it was good diplomacy.

For a Catholic to attend mass inside the cavernous, exquisitely marbled, and magnificent Basilica, where the apostle Peter's remains are said to be buried under its main altar, was something extraordinarily spiritual and moving.

As they sat down in their second-row seats near the center aisle, Jake felt the presence of the Holy Spirit. Jake knew that you didn't have to be in church to feel the spiritual presence of the Almighty. But on this blue bell morning, and inside this spectacular edifice that Michelangelo designed and took 150 years to build, Jake sensed a powerful Spiritual presence.

Looking down at the mass's printed program, Jake felt the cell phone buzz in his pants pocket. Thinking he should switch off the phone completely, he punched his security code on the phone's screen. He noticed a text message from Sergeant Manny Alvarez, who was on duty in the US embassy.

"Get off the X!" the message read.

As US soldiers sent overseas to US embassies and remote locations, it was the first action they were trained to take when they found themselves in imminent or immediate danger.

"Look for nearby carbs now!"

"They will move you to safety!!" said the next message. "Pls ack this msg!" (Please acknowledge this message.)

Jake read the messages twice. As he finished reading them, he typed in "Roger" and immediately felt a tap on his shoulder. A Carabinieri officer simultaneously looked Sara in the eye. Another Carabinieri officer stood behind the one who had just alerted Jake.

"Come with us, now," whispered the officer who had tapped Jake.

Jake and Sara quietly and deliberately got up from their seats and began walking with the two men.

"What's going on?" asked Jake, walking quickly as the lead officer was one step ahead of Jake while the other trailed Sara and Jake.

"We have information that your lives are in imminent danger. The threat might already be inside the Basilica."

While Jake and Sara immediately wanted to know more about the threat, they also understood their best course of action was to walk quickly and follow the instructions of the two officers.

In the back of the Basilica, two assassins were surprised to see Jake and Sara get up and get moving, with two Carabinieri flanking them. The assassins had planned to wait for the two to emerge from the church service and then, among the many tourists and churchgoers, stab them in their carotid arteries with sharp plastic composite knives that had evaded the Basilica's magnetometers.

The mafia capo who directed the hit declared, "Your mission is to kill them. But if you just seriously wound them, it will send a message."

The Carabinieri guard who was following the trio sensed the two assassins moving up through the large crowd of tourists behind them. With urgency in his voice, he told his police partner to "pick up the pace, *amico.*"

The lead Carabinier policeman switched from a fast walk to a slight jog.

At that point, the two assassins backed off, realizing their pace—and knives—were no match for the armed Carabinieri officers.

The lead Carabinieri officer stopped at a massively thick, 250-year-old wooden and steel door. It was embedded in an even thicker massive stone wall.

A Vatican Swiss guard nodded affirmatively to the lead Carabinieri officer.

"It's open," confirmed the Swiss guard. "Just pull."

The door's weight surprised the Carabinieri office, and he needed a slight assist from the Swiss Guard to open it.

Once through the door, the Swiss guard locked the door behind the foursome.

"We are safer now," said the Carabinieri officer, "but we must keep moving."

"Safer? *Where* are we going?" asked Jake.

"We are headed for the *Passetto di Borgo*," replied the officer.

"What's *that*?" asked Jake.

For once, Jake was clueless about something concerning Italian history.

Sara answered. "It's the secret, 900-yard-long passageway that several popes used to escape the Vatican. Whenever they were under imminent threat, this was their safe way out. It leads to Castel Sant'Angelo," said Sara, referring to Saint Angelo Castle, an iconic Roman landmark near the Tiber River.

"This passageway is almost 1000 years old," added one of the Carabinieri officers.

"Well, heck," replied Fortina. "I hope the Pope has paid the maintenance bills on it. If it worked for the popes, I guess it will work for us."

Jake winked at Sara, and Sara smiled at Jake.

Acknowledgements

The author acknowledges and is grateful for manuscript reviews by Major General (Italian Carabinieri, Ret) Sebastiano Comitini; Lauren Anderson, (FBI, Ret); John J. Le Beau (CIA, Ret); and Colonel (US Army, Ret) Alex "Alpo" Portelli.

The author is also deeply grateful for the exceptional editing collaboration and insights provided by Rachael Rhine Milliard.

About the Author

RALPH R. "RICK" STEINKE is the author of *Next Mission: US Defense Attaché to France*, a memoir selected as a finalist for the Indie Excellence Awards and honorable mention for the Readers' Favorites Book Awards. He is also the author of *Major Jake Fortina and the Tier One Threat*, shortlisted by the Chanticleer Books Awards in the Global Thriller category for 2022.

Steinke has spent a lifetime in US national security roles, including twenty-eight years in the US Army and fourteen in the Department of Defense. His official duties have taken him from the U.S. Military Academy at West Point to over thirty countries on the Eurasian landmass, including Afghanistan and Ukraine.

He holds master's degrees in West European studies and diplomacy from Indiana and Norwich Universities, respectively, as well as post-graduation certificates in national and international security affairs from Harvard and Stanford Universities. His personal passions include faith, family, fly-fishing, and travel.